He peered down at her menacingly.

"Don't try to run when you get to Andros," he cautioned. "The island is the largest tract of unexplored land in the entire Western Hemisphere. If you run away on Andros, no one's ever going to find you, at least not alive. It's just three million acres of forest, and people get lost out there all the time."

Anna looked out the window, deliberately ignoring him, and thinking there was no way he or anyone else could stop her from running if she wanted to. . . .

# bad girls

A NOVEL

## alex mcaulay

Pocket Books

New York   London   Toronto   Sydney

 MTV BOOKS

POCKET BOOKS, a division of Simon & Schuster, Inc.
1230 Avenue of the Americas, New York, NY 10020

ISBN-13: 978-0-7434-9733-6
ISBN-10:     0-7434-9733-3

First MTV Books/Pocket Books trade paperback printing June 2005

10   9   8   7

For information regarding special discounts for bulk purchases,
please contact Simon & Schuster Special Sales at 1-800-456-6798
or business@simonandschuster.com

*For Lisa*

## Chapter One

# Betrayed

The girl with the dirty blonde hair ran down the hillside and began to pick her way rapidly through the trees. Her arms were scratched and torn from their branches, and her damp hair lay plastered across her forehead. She was desperate to get away, but had no idea where she was headed.

The trees parted in front of her to reveal a small pond of brackish water, and she moved to the left, trying to skirt it without being seen. She heard a noise and froze, her breath loud in her ears. Slowly she sank to her knees, keeping as still and silent as possible. Had they found her already?

The noise came again. At first she thought it was the cry of some exotic bird, but it resolved into the sound of a person whistling. Her body stiffened and she pressed herself flat in the shadows between two large rocks at the water's edge.

Maybe they won't see me, she thought. But, oh God, what if they do?

The whistling was audible but distant, somewhere on the other side of the pond. She realized the rocks wouldn't provide enough cover, so she began inching backward, low to the ground.

The whistling ceased.

"Anna?" she heard a voice call out, and her heart pounded in fear. "I know you're out here somewhere." She heard the crackling sound of breaking twigs, the man getting closer. Her muscles coiled to spring into action. She would run again if she had to, she knew that much.

"Pretty stupid," the voice said. She hated the sound of it, like he was mocking her. "You could get hurt out here, easy." He paused. "Christ, it's hot." She heard deliberate footsteps approaching. Her heart was now beating so fast she thought it would leap out of her chest, and she blinked away a drop of sweat.

You can't see me, she thought, willing herself to blend in with the landscape. I'm invisible.

"Anna?" He was much closer now.

Please don't fucking see me, she prayed. Please let him walk right past me.

"Over there! By the rocks!" the man suddenly yelled, triumphant. "There she is!"

Anna exploded upward, limbs flailing for traction on the mud, and she spun like a cornered animal toward him. It was the small man, the one she'd dubbed the Boxer because of his crooked nose. He was just ten yards away, head down, racing toward her.

Anna plunged back into the trees, driven by pure desperation to remain free. She fought off branches with her hands as she forced her body forward. She could hear the Boxer close behind, cursing as the branches snapped back in his face. Her long sprinter's legs pushed her through the underbrush and for a blissful moment she was pulling ahead, until something collided with her so violently it blotted out the light and rattled her jaw. She fell hard onto the muddy ground.

Anna struggled for air as she felt strong arms grasp her around the chest, yanking her upward. She jerked her head back and twisted her body, trying to squirm out of the man's grasp. He smelled gross, like stale sweat and gasoline. It wasn't the Boxer, but the other man, the big one with a fat neck as wide as his shaved head. At least six three and two hundred and fifty pounds.

His breath was hot, and his arms felt like steel bands. Anna wriggled in anger and pain, and his arms pressed harder against her breasts.

"Fantastic!" the Boxer was raving to the big man. He clambered over a rock behind them, out of breath. "You shoulda been a linebacker! You knocked her back to her senses maybe. Boy, she can run."

The big man grunted in response.

Anna tasted iron. She ran her tongue around her mouth and realized she'd bitten her lip in the struggle. Her sides throbbed where the big man still clutched her firmly. She hated the feel of his chest rubbing against her back.

The Boxer materialized in front of them. "You all right?" he asked her.

Anna scowled, the fury radiating out like steam. She was so pissed off, she couldn't even think of what to say.

The Boxer just laughed. "She's giving us the silent treatment." Anna started to feel lightheaded, like she was going to faint, because the big man's arms were constricting her. The Boxer noticed and frowned at his companion. "Hey man, loosen that grip. We don't want to kill her, right?"

"It's loose enough," he replied, but Anna felt his arms slacken and she was able to breathe more freely again.

The Boxer surveyed their surroundings. "We're going to have to drag her up the ravine, and then all the way back to the van. I think I'm too tired." He scratched the crest of his thinning brown hair. He was wiry, with a tanned, angular face, and if it weren't for his mangled nose and receding hairline he might have been handsome. "Anna, if we let you go, will you behave? No more running? We can't spend the whole day chasing after you. There's nowhere to go anyway. It's just marsh and forest all the way down to Miami."

Anna met his blue eyes. "I won't run," she said hoarsely.

He grinned. "Good deal. It's a helluva lot easier if you walk than if we have to carry you."

The big man let her go and stepped away. "Don't do anything stupid," he whispered, "or else you might get your arm broken."

The Boxer frowned and pretended not to hear. Anna wasn't sure which man she hated more. "The road's back this way."

With the two men behind her, Anna began walking through the forest, back to the van and captivity. Hot tears of rage welled up in her eyes. She was so dumb to have tried running. What the fuck had she been thinking? Now she just wanted to curl into a ball and sob, but she wasn't going to let the bastards make her cry. As she stumbled through the forest, she promised herself when it was all over she'd make them pay for what they'd done to her. She'd make everyone pay, if she ever got the chance.

Back in the gray Chevy van, the heat was intense. The Boxer locked her in the back, and she slumped on the narrow metal bench, which was rusted and uncomfortable. She was trapped just like an animal again and the thought made her sick.

The engine started and the van pulled onto the highway. There were no windows except for two circular portholes on the back doors, and they were painted over, making it impossible to see out. The windows were also covered with a wire mesh, which had sliced her hands when she'd tried to break the glass. She'd also tried to kick in the metal partition between the space she was trapped in and the driver's cabin, without any success. Whenever she pressed her ear up to it, she could hear the Boxer and the big man talking, but was unable to decipher their words.

Anna sat back against the vibrating hull of the van. It was noisy and dark inside, hot and airless, and it smelled like old gym socks. She wondered how many girls they'd taken before her. Except for her escape attempt, which had lasted all of three hours hiding in the forest, she'd been in the van since six in the morning and guessed it was now late afternoon. The men had let her out only twice, both times to squat at the edge of the highway and pee. They didn't even care how embarrassing it was for her. Instead they'd laughed and called her a little princess. It was on the second occasion she'd made a break for it, sprinting down the embankment and into the thick forest. She'd known it was futile, but she'd tried anyway, because there was no sense going down without a fight.

Anna was now more tired than she ever remembered being, and she was starving, too. They'd only given her a box of survival biscuits all day and a plastic gallon jug of water. She felt dirty, and disconnected from her body, like it was no longer her own.

When the men stopped at a gas station, Anna heard them open their doors and get out. She leapt up and pounded on the wall. "Help!" she screamed, thinking someone might hear her. "Get me out of here!"

Someone tapped back on one of the painted windows, but it was just the Boxer. She could hear him chuckling and her skin crawled. "Keep it up, baby," he yelled. "No one's gonna rescue your sorry ass."

She pounded again in frustration and heard more laughter. She sat back down on the bench. In anger she kicked at the water bottle and sent it clattering against the side of the van. It rolled back to her feet and she suppressed the urge to cry again. The engine eventually started up and they resumed their journey.

Anna rubbed her eyes and thought about what a nightmare scene it had been when the two men came for her in those dark early hours of the morning.

If only I hadn't come home at all last night, she thought dismally. Then none of this would have happened. But she'd climbed through her bedroom window around three in the morning, after her boyfriend Ryan had dropped her off. They'd been at a party and Ryan had scored some weed for them. She'd been so quiet sneaking back in, totally satisfied her parents had no idea what she'd been doing. She remembered the feeling of sliding between the cool sheets, stretching out on her soft bed, her hair still smelling comfortingly of smoke. She still felt pretty stoned, and she was so tired she fell asleep right away.

The next thing she knew, the lights in her room were blazing, and a voice she didn't recognize was screaming at her. She sat up in bed, terrified, wondering what was going on, and saw a strange man standing over her.

This was the Boxer. The second man, the big one, was blocking the door.

"What the fuck!" she screamed, feeling like her veins had been pumped full of ice water. "Mom! Dad!" She scrabbled against the wall, trying to get to the window, but like a bad dream, everything was in slow motion and she got too scared to move.

"Get out of bed," the stranger commanded. "And knock off that yelling. Your parents aren't going to help you now."

"Dad!" she tried to scream again, but her larynx was constricting in fear and the words came out too softly. All kinds of awful scenarios were racing through her mind. Who were these men and what did they want with her? Was her house being robbed? Was she going to be abducted or something? That had always been a secret fear of hers.

"I said, get up! Maybe you need some help?" The Boxer reached over and grabbed hold of her left arm and yanked her right out of bed. She sprawled on the floor in her light blue sleep shirt and panties.

"What do you want?" she managed, trying to cover herself up. She could hear the fear in her trembling voice.

"Put these on," the man told her as he tossed her a pair of jeans, the same ones she'd been wearing just a few hours before. The big man at the door didn't move. He just watched as Anna stood up and struggled to get dressed.

"What's happening? What are you doing here? Are you taking me somewhere? I need to get my parents." She realized she was babbling, but she couldn't stop herself. She felt like she was going to hyperventilate and have a panic attack, not that she'd ever actually had one before.

The Boxer didn't respond, and the big man in the doorway was silent, too, just a shadowy, scary blob.

"Put some shoes on. Comfortable ones," the Boxer instructed. "Do it now, or I'll force you."

Anna obeyed his commands. Her mind was churning as she slipped on her favorite pair of pink Adidas sneakers. She felt like she was still in a dream, and she wondered if the two men were even real.

"Walk to the door. I'll be right behind you."

Anna did as she was told, in a state of utter shock. Her arm hurt from where the Boxer had pulled her out of bed, but that was nothing compared to her fear. The big man stood in front of her so she was effectively sandwiched between the two strangers as they maneuvered her out of the room.

"What's going on?" Anna asked, trying to find her voice again. "Where are my parents? Are they okay? Have you hurt them?"

"So now you're worried about your parents," the Boxer said. "Typical." His voice was dead and flat, like a serial killer's. "Let's move it."

Anna walked with the two men through her parents' sprawling suburban mansion, past the cavernous dining room with its vaulted ceiling, then the living room and its expanse of white leather couches. All the lights were turned on, which was weird, and the house was eerily silent, like an empty cathedral on a weekday afternoon. The procession approached the foyer and the oak-paneled front doors of the house. Anna thought when she got outside she'd just start running. If she could get to a neighbor's house and bang on their door, then she might escape her fate.

The big man opened the doors and the Boxer pushed Anna onto the porch. It was there she finally realized what was going on, and her heart felt as heavy as stone.

Her parents were waiting for her outside, fully dressed. Her mom looked like she'd been crying because her eyes were swollen and red, and had that certain puffy look that couldn't be disguised. Her dad's face was blank and expressionless, as it so often was. He stood ramrod straight, like he was still a general in the army. Anna's father had been in the military for twenty years, until he retired and his second career began—writing a series of best-selling religious books that prophesied the end of the world, and the punishment of all sinners. He looked at the Boxer and nodded.

So he's finally done it, Anna thought grimly, he's turned me over. He'd been threatening to send her to a wilderness survival camp for the last few months, and it looked like the day had finally come. Her heart was in her stomach. She hadn't thought her dad possessed the courage. Anna felt the betrayal just as surely as if a knife had stabbed her in the back.

"How the fuck could you do this to me?" she asked him. She knew it was his decision because her mom would never send her away, no matter how badly she behaved. Anna and her mom actually got along decently, especially when her mom stayed out of her way.

"I warned you, Anna." Her father's voice was cold and hard, like he thought he was giving a sermon. "Don't say you weren't warned. We gave you every chance to turn your life around, but you refused to learn from your mistakes, didn't you? You continued to sin even when you knew the penalty."

"But Dad," she urged, at a loss for words. Her mouth was very dry. If there was any chance she could talk her way out of the situation, she didn't want to blow it. She'd managed to get out of scrapes before, but to be honest, none this serious. "Dad, you don't have to do this. It's not going to help anything if you send me away. I know I've been screwing up lately, but I can change. You just need to give me the opportunity to prove it. I'll show you I can do better if you just give me a chance!"

Her words had little impact, and she knew it. "You've run out of chances, Anna. In fact, you ran out of them a while ago. I'm your father and it's my responsibility to step in and do something so you don't end up ruining your life. I'm doing this out of love, not hatred or anger."

"Please!" Anna exclaimed. That word seemed so small, so insignificant. Too small to have any effect. The reality of her predicament was beginning to sink in, and she felt sick to her stomach.

She turned to her mom, whose shellacked hair was immaculate even at that hour. She always hated how her mom looked more like a fifties housewife than like any of her friends' moms. "Don't I deserve a second chance? I'll be good, promise. Please don't let him do this to me."

"It's not just my decision," Anna's father said. It was typical that he didn't even let her mom respond for herself. Anna knew her dad believed women were emotional and incompetent, and neither his years in the military nor his obsession with the Bible had helped change his way of thinking. "We made this decision together, as one."

"But it's not fair!" Anna exclaimed, her voice cracking with anger. She felt rage welling inside her and fought hard to control it, because she knew it would just fuel their misconceptions of her. "You don't understand anything about my life! You've never listened to me or trusted me once, not in sixteen years! You're such a fucking asshole! I hate you—"

As soon as the words left her mouth, she knew she'd made a big mistake. Her therapist had warned her about letting her dad make her angry, but obviously she hadn't learned much from therapy. She was about to speak even more of her mind, but a hand suddenly clasped the back of her neck, fingers pressing so painfully into the skin that she gagged. It was the Boxer, who'd crept up behind her.

"You can't talk to your parents that way anymore." He sounded remarkably calm. "We won't allow it, even if they will, understand? You don't rule this household. You need to show some respect."

The big man moved toward her menacingly, like he might want to put his hands on her, too.

"Now apologize for cursing," the Boxer instructed.

"No," Anna declared, writhing in his grasp. "I won't! Who are you to tell me what to do? You don't own me."

His fingers constricted and she found herself being forced to the ground, face down, until her lips almost touched the stained wood of the porch. "That's the wrong answer," the Boxer said. "Let's try it again. Repeat after me: I'm sorry for being such an ungrateful, spoiled little brat." He tightened his grip. "Say it, Anna. I won't let you go until you do."

Anna repeated the Boxer's words haltingly, as if she had a mouth full of marbles. Slowly he released her and she got to her knees, her face burning red with anger and shame.

"See, that was easy," the Boxer said. The big man had stepped back and was leaning against the wall of the house, watching. He looked like he was enjoying himself, and Anna wanted to slap the hell out of him.

"You said you wouldn't hurt her," she heard her mother say to the men, out of nowhere.

"Don't worry, it's nothing," the Boxer explained, as if Anna wasn't even there. "It doesn't really hurt. It's a technique we use for restraint when the girls get too rowdy. Like in judo, or wrestling."

Anna eyed her parents warily. "So where exactly are you sending me?"

Her father met her gaze and held it. "It's a twelve-week wilderness program on Andros Island, off the coast of Florida." She could tell from his voice he'd been wanting to do this for a long time. "It's called Camp Archstone. It's for adolescent girls in crisis, troubled girls like yourself. You're going to learn discipline and respect, and how to act like a young lady, instead of a sex-crazed maniac."

Twelve weeks, Anna thought. Shit! It was worse than she imagined, much worse. Surely there was some way out of it. "Reform school," she muttered bitterly. "What the fuck am I going to learn there?"

"It's not reform school," her father corrected. "It's wilderness camp."

"What about high school? It's the middle of the spring semester. The tenth grade formal is in two weeks. What about my friends? I have a life!"

"It won't be a vacation out there," her father continued, as if he hadn't heard a word she said. "It'll be hard work, both physical and mental. Behavior modification classes and athletic challenges, as well. I've been in close contact with the administrators and they're eager to help. I have faith in you, Anna, and despite our differences, I know somewhere deep inside you is the little girl I remember and love. I want that little girl back, and so does your mother."

"You won't get away with this," Anna threatened, thinking about how deluded her dad was. "I'll come back worse than before."

"No, you won't. Besides, you couldn't shame our family more than you've already done. You'll be different after Camp Arohotono, I know it."

Anna looked around coldly at the assembled people. She didn't think her parents were acting out of love at all. She thought they just wanted to get rid of their problem child. "I need to call Ryan," she said.

Anna's father flinched at the mention of her boyfriend's name. "Don't even think about it. That little bastard has caused enough problems for you already. If he calls here, your mother will inform him of our decision. We've already told the school, and they support us one hundred percent. You've skipped nine days just in the last month, so they know you need help. When you come back from Archstone, they'll let you re-enroll. You'll be a semester behind, but you can make it up with hard work and summer school."

"But Ryan's my boyfriend," Anna pleaded. She was thinking that what they were doing was illegal, or against her civil rights, and she could get Ryan to call the police. "I have to say good-bye to him."

"Ryan Holloway is part of your past, not your future. And you'll talk to him over my dead body."

Anna scowled at her dad. He hated Ryan because he still thought Ryan was the one who got her pregnant. A little more than three months ago, the worst thing ever had happened, and Anna had needed to get an abortion, an event which enraged her dad and initiated the threats of reform school. Since then, things had steadily gone downhill.

"Please don't do this," Anna begged, trying one last time to sway his mind. "I'll do anything you want. I don't deserve to be sent away like this. I'm not a bad person."

"Anna, I told you. After what happened with Ryan, I warned you if you ran around with boys again, you wouldn't get another chance. I forbade you to see Ryan, yet you were out with him tonight, and three nights ago, as well. Your mother and I aren't stupid, although I know you think we are. We know what's going on, and we can't go through the pain again. Your sin has made us sinners, too. Think about us for a change, instead of yourself and your friends. And we know you've been drinking and smoking. I'm sure you're doing drugs, too, so don't deny it. You're ruining our family."

What about me! Anna wanted to scream. What did her dad know about the pain she'd gone through? Everyone said the abortion was for the best, but she was the one who'd suffered the loss. And if her dad were a true Christian, why had he sent her to get an abortion in the first place? What a hypocrite.

It was to save face, she knew, because she'd had the abortion in secret. As a prominent Christian author, it would have been hard, if not impossible, for her dad to conceal the origins of a baby born to his teen daughter out of wedlock. The scandal would have destroyed his career. Religious zealots comprised most of his readership, and they were a pretty unforgiving bunch.

"We better push off," the Boxer said. He seemed bored by all the drama. "It's a really long drive."

"What about my things, my clothes?"

"They'll be here when you get back. Your father's already given us your passport and the papers to get you to the island. Camp Archstone will provide everything else during your stay."

"But I need to get my cellphone and my laptop."

He laughed. "No chance. From now on, you'll be living the simple life. Now come on, the van's waiting." He pointed to the windowless gray Chevy Astrovan Anna would come to know so well, and she felt a surge of dread. The Boxer must have noticed because he said, "We can do this the hard way or the easy way. The easy way hurts less."

"It's for the best," Anna's mom called out timidly, as though trying to reassure herself rather than Anna. Anna realized there was nowhere for her to go but into the van. She stared at her father one last time.

"I'm going to hate you forever, Dad." She spoke the words with pure vitriol, although inside her, the feelings were much more complex. Looking at his face with hatred, when she'd once loved him so much, made her feel like her heart was ripping in two.

"Twelve weeks from now you'll be thanking me," her dad replied. "In fact, this may turn out to be the best experience of your life. May God be with you, and give you guidance. You'll be in our prayers, Anna. And remember that we did this because we love you. . . ."

Her reverie about the events of the morning was broken as she felt the van hit a patch of rough road. She shut her eyes. Despite herself, the noise and the heat were lulling her to sleep. Several times she slipped into troubled dreams and awakened with a start when the van slowed.

After many hours, the van finally came to a stop and Anna's head snapped up. She heard the Boxer and the big man talking in the front, then the door opening on the driver's side. She listened to footsteps approach the back door of the van. If the Boxer weren't so strong, she'd try to kick him in the face when he opened the door and run past him to freedom. But she was afraid of what he might do to her. Her chest still ached from where the other man had grabbed her.

The back door opened and glaring sunlight spilled into the interior. Anna blinked.

"You can get out now."

She stood up, massaging her stiff, aching legs and hobbled to the doorway. The Boxer held out a hand to help her from the van, but she didn't take it. "Where are we?" she asked, feeling very fragile.

"Dade County regional airport, right at the tip of Florida."

Anna looked around. It was even hotter than it had been at home in Georgia. A row of small jets and prop planes sparkled on the tarmac under the bright sun.

"You can only get to Andros by air or by boat," the Boxer continued. "You can't drive to the island, so we'll be leaving you here." He pointed at one of the planes. "See that plane? Our job is done when you get on board." He coughed and spat on the ground. "You've got a big surprise waiting for you if you think today was hard." He smiled. What an asshole, Anna thought. "Boy, I wish I could see you three months from now. You'll be a whole different person by then. I've seen it happen with my own two eyes, and I know it's gonna happen to you."

Anna didn't want to be a different person. "Whatever," she muttered.

"Yeah, keep up that attitude. The harder you go in, the softer you'll come out."

Anna didn't say anything in response, because she couldn't think of a decent retort. She knew the Boxer was just taunting her, and it made her angry. Hunger and fear gnawed at her belly. She wished she could get to a phone and call Ryan because he'd know what to do, but everything was happening too fast.

She weighed her options, realizing she was fucked. She couldn't make a break for it now because the big man was watching her from the van. He'd just drive after her if she tried to start running. She was stuck, powerless, and she was filled with rage at her dad for sending her to Archstone and at her mom for being too weak to stop him. She was also angry at herself. She'd suspected her parents would ultimately try something drastic and she hadn't done anything about it. She knew she hadn't been thinking too clearly lately.

"When am I going to get some food?" she asked the Boxer. "You've been starving me all day, and I'm thirsty, and I feel like I'm going to throw up. I can't take any more of this shit."

He shook his head sadly. "The shit hasn't even begun. And believe me, you're not gonna starve if you miss a couple meals. Besides, they'll feed you on the island. It might not be the best food you've ever tasted, but you'd be surprised what people eat when they're hungry enough."

Anna knew that being denied food was a deliberate psychological ploy. It was meant to break down her defenses and make her easier to control when she arrived at the camp. Her dad often played similar mind games, and she usually responded by getting so mad that she tired herself out. Her dad brought out the worst in her. In fact, she'd talked to her therapist a lot about her relationship with him. She pictured Dr. Cochran now, a flabby old woman with thinning gray hair who wore a silver cross around her neck, and always advised her to spend more time doing homework. She wondered bleakly if Dr. Cochran had helped advise her parents in their decision to send her to Archstone.

"Hey look, your ride's here," the Boxer said. He squinted into the distance, and Anna followed his gaze. A man was approaching them from across the tarmac. The Boxer waved. "I've got your cargo!" he yelled. "You better watch out for this one. She almost got away on the trip down."

"Losing your touch?" the pilot asked when he reached them.

"I sure hope not." The Boxer shook the man's hand.

Anna stood there angrily with her thumbs in the pockets of her jeans. She wondered if there were a lot of people like the Boxer, bounty hunters basically, who rounded up wayward girls and shuffled them off to camp like prisoners of war. No doubt none of these people cared that it was her life being ruined. They were just doing their jobs.

"The weather's good. We should get there in under an hour, then back in time for dinner. A late dinner." The pilot spoke directly to the Boxer, over Anna's head. When his eyes grazed hers, they were filled with disdain, like she was nothing but trash.

"Yeah, I'm sorry about that," the Boxer was saying. "She slipped out, what can I say? Shit happens. Thanks for making the extra trip."

The pilot shrugged. "No big deal. I get overtime."

"Oh, I almost forgot. Her old man wanted me to call when we got her to the airport, just to tell him she's on her way."

The pilot grinned, showing teeth yellowed from tobacco. "She's on her way all right."

The Boxer took out his cellphone and dialed. After a moment he asked, "Mr. Wheeler?" There was a brief pause. "Yes, sir. We got her down here safe and sound." Another pause. "I know, I know. We had some trouble on the way, but everything's fine now. She's safe and unhurt. She tried to run, like some of them do. No, no. Not at all." The Boxer held out the phone to Anna. "Your father wants to talk to you."

Anna shook her head, looking down at the tarmac, face like stone. Fuck him, she thought. He hadn't wanted to hear what she had to say back home, so why should it be any different now?

"She won't talk," the Boxer said into the phone, "but I can make her if you want." A brief silence. "Okay, sure, no. We'll just put her on the plane then." He hung up and slipped the phone back in his pocket, smirking. "Let's move."

With the Boxer close behind, Anna followed the pilot to the small twin-propeller airplane that would be taking her to Andros Island. The pilot climbed up on a wing and unlocked the hatch, pulling down a flight of metal steps. Anna felt like some poor, dumb animal being led to its slaughter, but she didn't know how to escape. The Boxer followed her up and into the narrow confines of the plane to make sure she was securely strapped into her seat.

He stood in the aisle and peered down at her menacingly. "Don't try to run when you get to Andros," he cautioned. "The island is the largest tract of unexplored land in the entire Western Hemisphere. If you run away on Andros, no one's ever going to find you, at least not alive. It's just three million acres of forest, and people get lost out there all the time."

Anna looked out the window, deliberately ignoring him, and thinking there was no way he or anyone else could stop her from running if she wanted to.

The Boxer sighed and shook his head. "Your attitude stinks, but fortunately you're not my problem anymore. Camp Archstone will beat the fight right out of you in no time." Then sarcastically he added, "Best of luck," before turning away and walking down the aisle without even a backward glance. He disembarked, and Anna could see him heading across the tarmac to the van. She watched him climb inside and envied his freedom.

The pilot started the propellers and the plane began to

taxi out of the lot and down a narrow runway. She wondered if the plane were safe, and if there should be a copilot. Anna shut her eyes. It would serve my dad right if I died in a crash, she thought. She hated tiny planes like this one, and it made her think about what had happened to Aaliyah. One second you're alive, and then the next, nothing. It felt spooky to be alone in the passenger cabin, and the noise of the propellers was deafening. The plane shuddered as it lifted up into the air and Anna felt a sensation of pressure in her ears. Her stomach turned over because there was no food in it. When she looked out the window, she saw the ground receding beneath her at a sharp angle.

Soon the plane was flying low above the ocean, the deep green water punctuated by whitecaps gleaming in the setting sun, and an occasional sailboat. The water stretched for miles in every direction without any sign of land. Although the flight would only take an hour, it seemed nearly endless to Anna. She was too nervous to be bored. Her thoughts alternated between hatred of her dad and concern about the future. She wondered how she'd make it through the next three months, and what the other girls would be like. Probably mean bitches who beat up their grandmas, she thought. Maybe they'd beat her up, too. Anna sometimes didn't get on too well with other girls, and she'd never felt confident at negotiating the shifting allegiances of her female friends. She worried that on the island she wouldn't be able to hold her own against a vicious bunch of troubled girls.

She also thought about everything she'd miss from home, Ryan being first on the list. Then there was hanging out with her friends, shopping at the mall, going to parties, and watching *The O.C.,* not to mention all the movies she wanted to see. Even simple pleasures like grabbing an ice-cream cone from Ben & Jerry's were gone.

Looking at the clouds and the ocean through the window made her wish she'd been allowed to bring her camera. It was sitting in its brown case under her bed at home, where it would remain gathering dust for the next three months. Taking photos was one thing she was good at. She thought about Mr. Spate, her photography teacher at school, and wondered what he was doing. Mr. Spate was a complicated issue because indirectly he was the cause of her being sent away. She decided not to obsess about him anymore, as she'd done for the past few months, because it was just too painful.

The plane dipped and Anna's stomach rose into her chest. She thought she might throw up, but then the plane leveled off. In the distance she could finally see land, a mass on the horizon that made her shoulders tense up. It looked dark and ominous. The plane banked left, heading toward the center of the island.

So this must be Andros, she thought, trying to suppress her fear. The pilot flew even lower as they got closer, and she began to see small boats in the water. Unlike the gleaming yachts off the coast of Florida, these vessels were old and ramshackle. She could see people on the decks, dark-skinned islanders small as ants, traveling the water with nets.

She heard static, and the pilot spoke on the radio to the control tower. Out the window the water gave way to land and Anna felt a growing sense of despair. The plane flew over miles of dense forest with no signs of civilization. It looked worse than the islands on *Survivor* and *Lost,* and that was pretty fucking bad. Occasionally there was a clearing with a few shacks on it, but for the most part the island seemed completely uninhabited, just like the Boxer had said.

The plane began its final descent and Anna tensed in her seat, making sure the seat belt was fastened. She couldn't stand landings. When she'd flown with her parents to San Diego three summers ago, she'd started freaking out and her mother held her hand until they were on the ground. That trip seemed a whole lifetime away, and Anna was sad that so much had changed since then. She wasn't sure how everything had gotten so out of control and gone so horribly wrong.

When the plane touched ground, Anna opened her eyes and saw trees rushing by on either side of the runway. She realized she was holding her breath and exhaled in a big burst of air. The plane slowed and eventually came to a shuddering, rattling stop. Looking out the window, Anna saw several low, red-brick buildings, and three rusted planes in various states of disrepair. She realized that this was the airport. There was a black pickup truck parked on the gravel near a building, with a man leaning back on the hood.

The pilot opened the door to the cockpit, barely acknowledging her presence. She wondered what he'd do if she attacked him and tried to hijack the plane. She seriously considered this plan for a moment, but then discarded the idea as impractical. She didn't want to get hurt, and thought there'd probably be better opportunities for escape later on. She unbuckled her seat belt and stood up slowly as the pilot opened the hatch and lowered the steps to the ground. He glanced over at her.

"Ladies first," he said mockingly.

Anna walked down the aisle and then down the stairs that led to the runway. The first thing that hit her was the unbelievable heat. The air was so hot and humid, it seemed to have a living presence, and she felt like she was in the heart of some tropical jungle nation, a thousand miles from America instead of a couple hundred.

"So what happens to me now?" she asked, confused and exhausted.

The pilot pointed. The man who'd been leaning on the hood of the pickup was walking toward them. "You came late so you missed the bus," the pilot explained. "Everyone else is already there, hours ago. Henry's gonna take you to Archstone in his truck."

Great, Anna thought. More driving. That was just what she needed. She stood there awkwardly, angry and afraid.

"Anna Wheeler?" the man asked when he reached them. He was old, Anna thought, maybe sixty-something. His hair was gray and he had a salt-and-pepper beard.

"Yeah," Anna said rudely. "Who are you?" It had been the longest day of her life and she didn't feel like being nice. If everyone thought she was a crazy bitch, then she might as well act like one.

"How are you holding up?" The old man smiled at her and stuck out his hand.

She wanted to slap it away, but instead she just didn't bother to shake it. The man let it drop to his side.

"I'm doing lousy," Anna told him. "I'm pissed off and I'm tired." She swatted away a mosquito.

"Well, are you hungry, too?"

"Yeah." She couldn't deny that, as much as she wanted to.

"Then you better eat something. I've got a couple PBJ sandwiches in the truck, and I've got an apple in there, too, if you're interested. And if you're thirsty there's a can of Coke, though it's probably not cold anymore."

Anna's mouth watered, but she was still glad she'd refused to shake the man's hand, even though he'd offered her food. It was out of principle, because the way she saw it, anyone involved with Camp Archstone was an enemy of hers.

"My name's Henry O'Connor," the old man said. "I'm going to drive you out to the camp."

Anna nodded. Despite herself, she was thinking about how good those sandwiches would taste.

"We can chat in the car, okay?" He guided Anna across the tarmac and toward his pickup truck. He opened the passenger door, and Anna slid into the comfortably worn seat as he walked around to the driver's side. He started the truck up and began driving.

The road was bumpy and the old truck trundled along slowly. Anna devoured the sandwiches as they drove in silence, thinking it was the best food she'd ever tasted. It was rapidly getting darker, but Anna could make out trees lining the sides of the dirt road, thick walls of vegetation. In some places dark vines hung overhead like electrical cables. At one point she saw burned-out cars, and figures in huts made from scrap wood along the edge of the forest. She felt a chill despite the heat, and hoped she was safe in the truck with the old man.

Somehow he noticed, because he said, "There's lots of poverty on Andros." Then he added, "Hey, you mind if I smoke?"

She shook her head. She considered asking him for a cigarette, but decided not to. She didn't want to owe this man anything, although now that she'd eaten, she actually craved a smoke. She figured he'd probably refuse to give her one if she asked anyway.

Henry fished in his jacket pocket, extracted a pack of Marlboros, and lit one up. The truck passed another shantytown, the huts lit up with tiny lights, and in a second it was gone. It was pretty clear to Anna the island was no tropical paradise.

"Are you feeling any better after that food?"

"Yeah," Anna replied, trying to make her voice sound cold and detached, older. She was determined to say as little as possible.

"Well, that's good." The old man took a long drag on his cigarette. "I'm the last kind voice you're going to hear for a while. You probably won't pay me much mind, but maybe you could hear me out anyway as we drive. Even if you just do it to humor me."

Anna was too tired to do anything else so she nodded like a punch-drunk fighter. "Sure."

"I used to be a military man, just like your dad. That's right, I know all about you, Anna. The camp has a file on every incoming cadet. I spent thirty years in the army, but I'm retired now and live on the island, mainly for the bonefishing. I've got a house outside Nicholl's Town. That's the largest settlement on Andros, a whole six hundred people." The smell of smoke was filling the hot confines of the car, and Anna found it soothing. Her arms and legs felt heavy as lead after the stress of the day.

"I'd do anything for my kids," Henry continued. "And my grandkids." He looked over at Anna. "Anything to stop them from messing up their lives, even if that decision was painful for me, understand?"

Anna nodded. It sounded suspiciously like what her dad had said before the Boxer and his companion hauled her away.

"Family is what counts at the end of the day. Your parents must love you very much, or they wouldn't have sent you here. You probably think it's the worst thing that's ever happened to you, I'm sure. But if you keep your head on straight you'll get through these twelve weeks and learn something about yourself in the process." He patted her on the leg in a way that was no doubt meant to be paternal, but it made her flinch. "I know it's hard, Anna. I know you've been through hell today."

"Do you?" she muttered.

"Of course. You got ripped out of your house, sent here to a place without friends, where you don't know a soul. That's got to be pretty rough."

Even though she understood she was being patronized, she suddenly felt like crying. The feeling was unexpected, because she felt more angry than sad, but it was there nonetheless.

Maybe it's because I'm so tired, she thought. It was pretty dumb to let the old man's platitudes affect her, but they did, like one of those cheesy movies on Lifetime or Oxygen that her mom watched. She wished he wasn't trying to be so nice to her because it just made everything worse. She bit her tongue, hoping the clarity of pain would wash away her unwanted emotions, but it just made her tongue hurt. How strange that the old man's kindness brought tears as readily as the torture of the van.

"If you look at Camp Archstone as a learning experience, then you'll do fine," Henry told her. "Kids get stuck in their ways even more than us old folks do. Change is hard, but sometimes it's necessary. The woman who runs this place, Miss Richards, knows what she's doing. She started Camp Archstone in eighty-six, after her daughter had a few troubles of her own. She's turned some lives around, I'll tell you that for free. I work for the camp as a volunteer, though I usually don't do the driving. I wouldn't work for a place I didn't believe in."

Anna got her emotions under control, and blinked. "Well, what if I think you're full of shit?" she asked. "What if I don't like the idea of getting sent to a wilderness camp in the middle of nowhere? What if I hate my parents and all their religious bullshit? What then?" She sighed angrily and pressed herself into the seat, trying to make herself small. The old man probably had no idea what really went on at Archstone.

Anna, on the other hand, knew all about wilderness programs. The first time her dad had threatened her with one, right after the abortion, she'd Googled them and IM'd all her friends to see if they knew anything about them. It turned out places like Archstone represented everything she hated and everything her father held dear: conformity, military values, and the so-called great outdoors. She and her father were polar opposites when it came to those topics. She remembered it hadn't been that way when she was young, that she and her dad had once been good friends, as hard as that was to believe. But as soon as she turned thirteen, and developed a mind and a will of her own, things had started to change. Suddenly her grades were never high enough, she was being lazy with her chores, and she was always in trouble for breaking curfew.

Worst of all, her father went insane whenever any boys phoned the house asking for her, even if they were just friends. He'd begun calling her into his study to read her passages from the Bible like they did in Sunday school. He'd even assigned her readings from one of his own Christian books, but she'd never done any of it. It wasn't that she had no faith, it was just that her dad's obsession was too overwhelming. He acted like he owned God, and there was no place for Anna when it came to religion, unless she were willing to do everything his way.

Then there was the pregnancy, of course. She understood why her dad had flipped out about that one, but maybe if he'd been a better father it never would have happened. Her dad just wasn't the kind of person who was emotionally available to her on any level. Often he wasn't even literally available, because he was too busy writing and promoting his books. Her mother was also part of the problem. Anna could never talk to her mom about personal stuff because her mom just went straight to her dad with it. That's how he found out about her pregnancy in the first place.

Her mom was scared of her father, Anna knew that much, so maybe that was why her mom could never keep a secret. Anna often speculated that the only reason her parents stayed together was because her mom was too frightened to stand up to her dad. He treated everyone he met like they were in the military and he was their commanding officer. Unfortunately, since his books had become so successful, his attitude had only worsened.

Henry finished his cigarette and stubbed it out in the ashtray. Anna noticed he didn't seem as friendly to her after she'd sworn at him, and she felt pleased that she'd gotten to him. They drove in silence for a long stretch.

"Well, here we are," he said finally. "This is it. Camp Archstone."

Anna sat upright in her seat. She'd spent the whole day cramped in vehicles and was eager to get outside, but her heart skipped a beat when she saw the place that was going to be her home for the next three months.

Jesus, she thought, it really is a prison, like a fucking Alcatraz. Although it was nearly dark, she could make out tall gates with barbed wire strung across the top, and two tall structures that looked like guard towers with spotlights on them. There was a buzzing sound and the gates opened outward automatically. Henry pulled the car through and the gates swung shut behind them with an ominous clanking sound. When a man in uniform appeared at the driver's side window, Henry rolled it down.

"I got the girl here," he said, and the guard waved them over to a parking space next to a military-style barracks. To Anna the entire place looked like a military base in miniature. The buildings were ugly and squat, some built from faded gray brick, and the whole enclosure was encircled in a wide perimeter by a high chain-link fence. An American flag, of all things, stood proudly in the center of a patch of green grass, illuminated by a yellow spotlight that cut through the darkness.

The passenger door to the pickup truck flew open and the guard shoved a bright light into Anna's face.

"Anna Wheeler!" he barked in military cadence. "Is that you?"

"Yes." She looked straight ahead, blinking because the light hurt. I will not be scared, she told herself, willing her legs not to shake. I will not let this asshole intimidate me, and I definitely won't show any signs of fear.

"Yes what?"

"Yes, sir!" she called out. So it was beginning. She could play this game as well as anyone after living under her dad's rigid set of rules.

"That's right. You will address me as 'sir' from now on, and don't you forget it or I'll be forced to remind you. Now disembark from that vehicle at once and stand at attention."

Anna swung her legs around and stepped out in the sweltering Bahamian night, the air so thick it felt like she was in a swimming pool.

The man standing in front of her had a bristling crew cut and a protruding chin. He was gangly and ugly, with a small mouth and big nose set between narrow eyes.

"Do you know what standing at attention means?" he yelled.

"Yes, sir."

"I don't think you do! Pull those shoulders back and stick out your chest." He walked around her, inspecting her posture as she fumed inwardly. "Anna Wheeler, my name is Counselor Adler. For the next twelve weeks you belong to me. You do nothing unless I say so. I control your every action and your every thought, understand? You failed to show respect for your parents back home, so now it's my duty to teach it to you. You've lost your rights as an individual because you weren't mature enough to handle them." He recited the words like a robot, as though he'd said them a million times before. "At Camp Archstone you'll learn responsibility, discipline, and self-respect. You will be remade into a self-sufficient young lady who can bring pride to her family, instead of sorrow and shame. Do I make myself clear, Cadet Wheeler?"

"Yes, sir," Anna parroted back. Her head ached. Cadet. How ludicrous. She wondered how she'd bear three months of this torment without losing her mind. There had to be a way out.

"Follow me, Cadet Wheeler. You will be assigned a uniform and a duffel bag. These are the only possessions you'll be allowed during your stay here at the camp. Afterward, I'll show you to your sleeping quarters. Bedtime here is early—nine o'clock on the nose, because you'll be getting up at five A.M. Your fellow class of cadets are already in their bunks, because they arrived here on time. None of them tried to run away on I-95 like a lunatic."

Shit, Anna thought. He obviously knew all about her escape attempt. This was bad news because now she'd probably be marked as a troublemaker and singled out for extra abuse. She'd have to watch her step and bide her time, until she could figure out a way to escape again.

"Come this way," Adler instructed. She obeyed, following him toward a long, wooden building, all vertical slats and peeling white paint, like an old barn. She looked back to see Henry pulling his pickup truck out of the lot and toward the gate. At least he'd tried to be nice to her, even if it was all just an act, and she felt vaguely sorry to see him go.

Adler opened the door of the building and they stepped into a room with stacks of clothes folded on shelves against the walls, and rows of metal lockers beneath them.

"What's your shoe size?" he asked, as she stood in the doorway nervously.

"Seven."

Adler rummaged in a crate below one of the shelves and pulled out a pair of scuffed black boots with thick soles. They looked like something an old man would wear.

"What size pants?"

Anna shifted from foot to foot. "Five."

"Don't mumble. Five, you said?"

"Yeah."

Adler's face contorted and he spun toward her, just as she realized she'd forgotten to add the "sir." "Goddamn it, yes *what?*" he yelled, the words echoing off the walls.

"Yes, sir," she said hastily. She was very aware she was alone with this man, in a foreign country, in his domain.

He stared at her with a look of total disgust. "Forget again and you'll get two demerits. Get six and then you'll be disciplined. Physically." He walked over to the shelf and picked out a uniform for her, muttering angry epithets to himself.

Anna was horrified to see the uniform consisted of a tank top, pants, and a jacket, all in bright, ugly orange. I'll look just like a convict, she thought. Like one of those work-release prisoners picking up trash at the side of the road. She sometimes saw them outside Atlanta and they always gave her the creeps. Now she was one of them.

"These are your clothes for the next twelve weeks," Adler declared as he thrust them at her chest. She took them from him, holding them in both hands. "Your old clothes and shoes will remain here in a locker until you're discharged. Everything in your pockets will be placed in a plastic bag and held until then, as well. From now on, you'll get fresh underwear and socks daily in your barracks, and clean uniforms once every three days. Just so you know, the camp works on a system of tiers, and laundry is done by level-two cadets. You missed Miss Richards's orientation today, but to make things clear, you are a level one. The lowest level. The higher the tier, the more responsibilities you have, but also the more freedom, like phone privileges and television time. You also get to wake up later. Most cadets work their way up to level three before they graduate. You get to advance a level every four weeks, unless you receive more than fifteen demerits in that time period, understood?"

The numbers made Anna's head spin. She didn't even want to understand their ridiculous, convoluted system, but she answered, "Yes, sir," anyway.

"Good," Adler said. "Now strip down to your panties and put on your uniform."

Anna hesitated. "What?" She didn't want to challenge him, but she felt very uncomfortable. There was no changing room in sight, and she wasn't about to do a striptease in front of this guy. Surely there was some sexual harassment law he was breaking.

"Do it!" Adler snapped, his face rigid. "I'm not interested in how you look, missy. I've seen enough tits and bare asses to last a lifetime. I just need to check and see if you're concealing anything. Alcohol, cigarettes, and illegal drugs are all contraband, as are any weapons. No jewelry or makeup, either. Acquisition or possession of any of these items during your stay at Archstone will result in multiple demerits. Now get those clothes off, ASAP."

Anna reluctantly placed her new outfit and boots on the table. She sat on a folding metal chair and slowly took off her sneakers. Then she stood and peeled off her shirt under Adler's unflinching male gaze. Without her shoes on, the guard seemed even taller.

It's just like being at the doctor, she told herself, but she didn't believe it. It was a violation, and she felt self-conscious and exposed. Anna put her old shirt on the table and picked up her new orange tank top. She put it on. The fabric felt coarse and the top was a size too large, but she didn't think complaining would get her very far.

"Pants," Adler said. "Come on. Hurry up."

Anna undid her belt and let her jeans drop to the floor. She slid into her new pants and zipped them up. Like the shirt, they felt baggy and scratchy. She sat on the chair and put on the boots, which fit a little better than the rest of the outfit, but were still uncomfortable. They smelled bad, too, like someone else had worn them recently. She picked up the orange jacket. With each item she put on, she felt increasingly dehumanized. She wondered if they'd just assign her a number, and not even call her by name anymore.

"Stand up," Adler said. "Let me have a look at you." She stood. He moved over to her and adjusted her collar, deliberately invading her personal space. "Much better. I like you in orange." He stepped back and faced her. "Your days here on the island will be spent in constant activity and service. You'll be attending classes five days a week, and completing individual and group projects. You are now on Camp Archstone time, which means you won't have any time to cause trouble. You'll learn the meaning and value of hard work, even if we have to shove it down your throat." He smiled grimly. "Because you were three hours late today, that means you owe me those three hours. You'll pay for them in hard labor, because no one leaves the camp without doing her fair share."

Anna felt a headache growing above her eyes with every command that he uttered. She hated the way he stood, his shoulders back and chest pumped out like her dad, like a parody of a man. Who was this prick to tell her what to do? She'd love the chance to tell him what she thought of him, but she was smart enough to keep quiet. She knew she needed to rest and conserve her strength until she could figure out a loophole in the system. There was no way she was spending a week at Camp Archstone, let alone three whole months.

"Tomorrow is the first full day of activities," Adler continued. "You'll be meeting the other girls in your class and starting the program. You'll be briefed about the island and the camp with everyone else after breakfast." Adler picked up Anna's old clothes and put them in a locker with her shoes while she stood there woodenly. "I'll take you to the barracks now."

She followed him out of the building and back into the night. It was hot and the noise of the crickets and the other insects swelled in the darkness. They walked down a dirt path to a long, flat-roofed brick structure with no windows. Adler opened the front door and Anna went inside. It was dark in the barracks, and she saw a bald, muscular man sitting at a table, reading a paperback by the light of a small desk lamp. She guessed he was another guard, or rather a counselor, as they called themselves in a lame attempt to disguise their true role. Anna thought most of them were probably just creeps who got off on telling girls what to do. And who knew? Maybe some of them liked being around girls her age, out in the wilderness where they could do whatever they wanted to them.

Small lights rimmed the edges of the room, like in a movie theater. Anna saw rows of bunk beds extending back into the barracks, and noticed swaddled forms in them, lumps under the blankets. She felt nervous and regretted her escape attempt earlier. The other girls had all seen one another and met, if just for a few hours. Now she'd be the newcomer in the environment, and if Camp Archstone were anything like high school, new kids didn't get treated too well. Even though she was only a little bit late, girls teamed up fast, and all kinds of cliques had probably already formed.

"This is Counselor Ellis," Adler said to her, motioning to the man at the desk. "You'll be under twenty-four-hour surveillance here, so there's no point trying to run."

Counselor Ellis looked up at Anna with distrustful eyes. "You're the last one here. The bunks are arranged alphabetically, and there are twenty-eight girls in your class, so you're at the end, in bunk fourteen B. That's the bottom one. Put your boots at the foot of the bed, and roll your socks inside them. You'll find an empty duffel bag underneath the bunk. Put your pants and jacket inside it. You sleep in your underwear and tank top here, so get used to it. There's no sleeping in the nude. The bathroom's at the front, right behind me. You'll need to ask permission to use it during the night, and if you're in there for more than five minutes, I'm coming after you."

Anna stood for a moment, unsure of what to do. It was like she'd stepped out of her own reality and into a prison movie. What the hell did my dad get me into, she wondered.

"You heard the man," Adler said. "Fourteen B. C'mon."

Anna walked down the center aisle, past the numbered bunks and their restless occupants. It was only 9:30. Sometimes she hadn't even eaten dinner by that time, so going to sleep so early seemed insane. Obviously a lot of the other girls felt the same way, because she was aware of eyes staring at her from the darkness. She ignored them and looked straight ahead. At the end of the room, she saw a bunk with NO. 14 painted on the floor in front of it in reflective white paint, so she sat down on the bottom half. She noticed there was someone asleep on the top, but didn't get a good look at her. As Anna took off her boots, she heard Adler and Ellis talking in low voices, and wondered if it was about her.

When her boots and pants were put away, she pulled back the covers, just a white sheet and a thin brown blanket. Her whole body sighed with relief as she relaxed onto the bed. The mattress was hard and lumpy, and the pillow felt like a block of concrete under her neck, but she didn't care. She pulled the sheet up and stared at the underside of the top bunk.

She could hear the sounds of the other girls tossing in their beds and the occasional whisper. From outside came the drone of the crickets and what sounded like the buzzing of a cicada. The girl above her rolled over suddenly, and the whole metal frame of the bunk bed creaked. Anna turned on her side and curled up, watching the lighted area by the doorway. She saw Adler leave and Ellis return to his book.

Could this really be her life? Torn from everything and everyone she loved and locked up on some desolate island, like no one wanted her? She wondered what her dad was doing. Probably having a celebration, overjoyed she was no longer around. Anna had no doubt her father's conscience was completely clear and he saw no clash between his religious beliefs and how he'd treated his own daughter.

And what about Ryan, Anna wondered. It made her sick to think he might not know where she was. They'd had plans to meet tonight, too, at their friend Kevin's place. She was sure he had no idea what had happened to her yet. Could she even trust her parents to tell him the truth about where they'd sent her? Knowing them, they'd probably lie to Ryan and tell him anything to get him to go away.

She also thought about Mr. Spate. He was sound asleep, she was sure, in his tidy little apartment back in Atlanta. He's the one who should be here, Anna reflected. The seducer, not the seduced . . .

Eventually her thoughts gave way to the demands of her body and she fell into an uneasy sleep.

## Chapter Two

# Camp Archstone

Anna opened her eyes to fluorescent lights illuminating everything with a harsh, white glow. The bunk was shaking as a heavy blonde girl descended the ladder at Anna's feet. She stopped at the bottom, stared at Anna, and blinked. Her features were pretty, but her face was bloated and her eyes were narrowed against the light.

"Where did you come from?" the girl asked, in a cross between a hiss and a whisper. Then, before Anna could respond, she added. "We heard about you. You tried to escape."

Anna couldn't tell if the girl approved or not. Before she could find out, a hand tapped the girl on the shoulder. The girl seemed to shrink in size and hastily got out of the way. An older woman appeared, short and thin, with a weathered face and her hair cut into a gray bob. She was even older than Henry, and wrinkles cascaded from the corners of her eyes.

"Get out of bed," she told Anna. "It's time to wake up." Her voice was firm but not unkind. Anna pushed the blanket back and stood, her feet cold on the cement floor. Other girls rushed around behind the woman, making their beds, changing their clothes in a whirl of energy. Anna was surprised to see them acting this way, as though it were a race. These were not the bad girls she'd expected.

"My name is Cecilia Richards," the woman told her. "You may address me as 'ma'am' or 'Miss Richards.' I'm the founder and director of Camp Archstone. I met the other cadets in your class last night upon their arrival, but I wanted to meet you, too. I was, of course, informed about the incident that occurred on your journey here. I trust nothing like that will happen again?"

Anna nodded. "It won't," she lied.

"Good. You realize how little tolerance we have for those who break the rules."

Anna looked down at the concrete floor. It was scuffed and marked by the black soles of hundreds of boots. She wondered how many girls had come to this hellhole before her.

"In any case, I'm sorry you got delayed. You missed meeting the others, and you missed my opening lecture. Do you understand how things work around here?"

"Not really."

"You girls constitute a class, or a session, as we also call it here. For the next three months you will be working with these girls, side by side, and bonding with them under my guidance and the guidance of the counselors. Did Counselor Adler explain how the different levels work?"

"He tried."

"Well, some of you will progress faster than others, but assuming you behave, every month you'll progress to a higher level, until graduation. There are two other sessions here at the moment—a class that's been here one month and another that's been here for two—but in general, you will not be mingling with them. When you switch levels you switch barracks." She looked around the room. "Most of the girls here are brand new in your class, except for a couple who were held back because of the way they acted."

Anna instantly wanted to know who those girls were, but of course Miss Richards wasn't saying.

"I know you feel angry and alone right now," she continued, "but if you put those feeling aside, you'll prosper here at Archstone and graduate with level-three status." Miss Richards pointed to a laundry cart in the middle of the aisle. "Put your underwear and tank top in there. Those get washed daily. Pants and jackets get washed every three days." A pudgy girl with a scowl was putting fresh laundry on a table. "She's a level-two cadet," Miss Richards explained, noticing Anna's gaze. "That means she's behaved, and has been here for a month."

"Can I ask you a question?" Anna asked suddenly, hoping the old woman would be more amenable than Adler.

"Yes."

"When do I get to use the phone?"

"Only level-three cadets get phone privileges, Cadet Wheeler, so you'll have to wait a while until you can earn those. Until then you can write letters. We have paper and envelopes in the office."

If she understood correctly, that meant it would be two months, at best, before she could make a call. Two months! Shit, Anna thought. Even mass murderers and rapists were allowed to make phone calls. This place was *worse* than prison.

"From now on you'll have twenty minutes to get ready each morning, like the other cadets," Miss Richards said. "You will shower, change, and make your bed in that time. That's why they're rushing. This was all explained to them yesterday, you see. If you're late, then you don't get any food for the day. Each morning you'll be lining up for the refectory at five-twenty sharp. Breakfast is served at five-thirty for level-one cadets."

Anna wondered who the fuck even wanted breakfast at 5:30 in the morning. She usually didn't eat breakfast at all.

Anna noticed some of the girls were already lining up at the door, and she was struck by their near total silence. What had been done to them to make them so passive? The camp obviously sucked, but so far she hadn't seen any torture implements or anything.

"Today is an important day," Miss Richards continued. "You'll be learning more about the camp and doing some team activities and exercises. Archstone will test your endurance and encourage character building. You may want to give up along the way, but giving up is not an option. You and your fellow cadets will be briefed in greater detail about the day after breakfast, by me and Counselor Adler."

"Yes, ma'am," Anna said. She suspected that like the food deprivation she'd experienced on the way down from Atlanta, the exercises and activities were merely designed

43

to make her too worn-out to cause trouble. From what she'd learned on line, the main point of wilderness camps was that they made life so totally awful, the threat of ever returning to one straightened any wayward teen out for good.

"Now hurry up and shower. We'll wait for you. Ten minutes, Cadet Wheeler."

The showers were in a large room at the front of the barracks, just off the bathroom. They were lined with green tiles, and while there were stalls with dividers between them, there were no doors or curtains. The room smelled like chlorine and liquid soap, and there was mildew on the tiles. Anna showered and toweled off quickly, unused to being awake so early in the morning and hating every minute of it. She slipped on her uniform and pulled back her wet hair in a ponytail. When she left the bathroom she moved quickly to her bunk and laced up her boots. No one else was wearing their jacket, so she left hers off. The other girls were standing in a silent line against the wall with Miss Richards. They all stared at Anna, so she glared back.

She was actually glad to see they weren't the hardened juvenile delinquents she'd feared. Except for a few who sported heavy tattoos, they looked surprisingly normal, like the kids in her high school class. Most of them were white, and Anna thought most of them looked as pissed off and bitchy as she felt.

Anna joined the line right at the back. Miss Richards called roll and then led the girls out of the barracks and into the light of day. The sun was just rising and it gave the sky a curious pink glow. It was already hot and muggy, and Anna felt sticky in her clothes. She could see the camp was much larger than she first thought. Within the fenced perimeter were at least ten buildings, and three large fields, with a few mahogany trees scattered between them. The pink glow coming through their branches made the trees look like the mushroom clouds of nuclear explosions.

Another great shot lost forever, Anna thought. At that moment she missed her camera more than anything or anyone else back home. When she had her camera, she always felt more comfortable, and more self-confident, too. None of her friends really understood it, and she knew some of them thought her photography was dumb, but it meant something to her. The irony was that Andros would have been the perfect place to take photos, were it not for the fact that she was a prisoner.

Deprived of the one thing that might have made the island bearable, Anna scoped out her surroundings, idly looking for a means of escape. Her prospects didn't look too promising, mainly because of all the fences and barbed wire. Even if she escaped the confines of the camp, there wasn't anywhere to go except into the dense, uninviting forest. Anna hoped she'd have better luck later, if they ever went hiking outside the camp. Maybe then she could slip away and find a town.

Anna and the line of girls followed Miss Richards, snaking down a gravel path until they got to the refectory. Thankfully, like the barracks, the building was air-conditioned. In silence, Anna lined up for her breakfast, which consisted of plain, lumpy oatmeal and a melon plate, with orange juice and a carton of milk to drink. She noticed the utensils were all made of plastic, probably to prevent any stabbings. There were seven other girls at her table, including her bunkmate, and they ate mechanically. Anna saw some eyes flicker in her direction, inquisitive more than hostile. There was little opportunity for Anna to talk to anyone, because Miss Richards appeared at the front of the room. "Cadets, may I have your attention." She was standing next to a bulletin board with a large map of the island stuck to it with multicolored thumbtacks.

"Today is your first morning on the island," she proclaimed, "and there are many issues to discuss. Last night before curfew, most of you got to see Camp Archstone, but you didn't learn about the island itself." She pulled out one of those pens that turned into a pointer and tapped the center of the map. To Anna it looked ugly and misshapen, like a massive upside-down shoe. The island appeared to be mostly green forest, crisscrossed by rivers and waterways. It's just a big, stinking chunk of land in the middle of nowhere, with nothing on it, she thought.

Miss Richards moved the pointer upward to a red thumbtack near the top of the island. "There are only two large towns on Andros, and this is one of them. Nicholl's Town." Then she moved the pointer about halfway down the island to a white thumbtack near the right-hand edge. "And this is the second one. It's called Andros Town. Other than that, and a number of small settlements on the eastern coast, the rest of the island is forest and mangrove swamp." With a flourish of her pointer, she touched a pink thumbtack placed lower, and a little bit inland, from Andros Town. "This is Camp Archstone, where we are now."

Anna paid attention, filing the information about where the towns were away for future use. It might help her escape if she was ever given a chance.

Miss Richards ran her pointer down the right-hand side of the island. "All along here is the barrier reef, the world's third largest, and it runs for about a hundred and fifty miles. Scientists from all over the world come here to study it and the marine life that inhabits the reef. As you spend time here on the island, you'll be learning more about it and its ecosystems. In fact, on the weekends, we'll be taking you on wilderness excursions and hikes both into the interior of the island and to the coast. Nature, as you'll discover, is the ultimate teacher. Your first such trip will be tomorrow, assuming all of you behave today."

There were many more thumbtacks on the map, but Miss Richards didn't offer to explain them. None of the girls asked any questions, and Anna assumed they probably weren't allowed to. She definitely didn't want to bring any attention to herself by raising her hand. She picked at the remains of her breakfast, feeling full, even though she hadn't eaten much.

Miss Richards continued speaking. "For today, you will all be confined to the boundaries of the camp. Your classes and activities will take place here, where you can be closely monitored by the counselors. Each morning, Monday through Friday, we will meet like this and I'll review the day's activities with you. For today, Friday, April fourteenth, there's a lot on your plate. At oh-seven hundred hours you will convene outside and begin the physical training element of your program. At oh-nine hundred you'll get a fifteen-minute break and then head inside for your first class. After that will be an early lunch at eleven hundred, followed by more outside activities and individual counseling sessions with one of our staff psychologists."

Perfect, Anna thought. Sounds like a day from hell. She'd thought high school was bad enough, but here she wouldn't be able to skip classes, or even chat with her friends in the back.

"At fifteen hundred will be an outdoor game, followed by dinner at seventeen hundred. After dinner will be Bible hour and then resting time before bed."

Anna wanted to roll her eyes at the mention of Bible hour, and she obviously wasn't the only one who felt that way. There was a groan, fairly loud, from one of the girls at the table next to her. Miss Richards stopped talking right away and silence filled the room. Anna turned her head, looking for the perpetrator.

"The next time I hear any sound of complaint, all of you will be disciplined. And I'll reduce your food allowance for the day by half. The choice is yours. A lot of you could stand to lose some weight anyway."

What a bitch, Anna thought.

"Have I made myself clear, cadets?" Miss Richards asked sternly.

"Yes, ma'am," the girls muttered.

Miss Richards glanced at her watch. "From now until oh-seven hundred hours I've scheduled contemplation time, because for most of you, it's your first day here. The time will provide a chance for rest and silent meditation in preparation for the day. I believe all of you have the potential to become strong, intelligent women, but you need to start demonstrating it, and I'm going to help you learn how. That is all for now, cadets."

Obviously the briefing was over, and as Miss Richards left, Anna heard a girl nearby whisper, "This fucking sucks." Anna's bunkmate giggled and then tried to pretend she was coughing.

When Anna and the other girls returned to the barracks, a counselor she hadn't seen before sat at the desk in front. The girls trooped back to their bunks, tired and homesick. Resting on the mattress, Anna discovered that "contemplation time" was just a fancy term for doing nothing, other than just sitting there, though she was glad for the rest. Anna sensed that a dab of self-help psychobabble was an integral part of Archstone's philosophy, no doubt present only to temper the military-style torture. She didn't buy that somehow the combination of nature, other screwed-up chicks, and Miss Richards's teachings would magically transform her into the perfect daughter her dad wanted. She felt like she could see through the agenda at Camp Archstone pretty clearly, and that alone made it doubtful the camp would have any effect.

Copies of a book had been provided by the staff, placed carefully on each of their beds while they ate. The book was called *Self-Growth, Self-Knowledge,* and the author was one Cecilia Richards. Anna leafed through the book, grimly amused at the ridiculously obvious chapter titles. "Saying No to Alcohol and Drugs" was one such example, and "Abstinence: The Only Way to Be Sure" was another. There were some cheesy illustrations, too, of teenage girls shooting up smack and in various states of despair. It reminded her of the books from health class, and Anna doubted they'd work on a twelve-year-old, let alone on her.

*"Pssst,"* Anna heard, and she looked around. A dark-haired girl in the lower bunk across from her was staring. Anna had noticed the girl before. She had short, black hair and a pretty, if somewhat square-shaped, face. There were five blue stars tattooed in a circle on her right forearm and a grinning black skull on the left. "What's your name again?"

"She's Anna," a voice whispered from above before Anna even had a chance to reply. It was her fat, blonde bunkmate.

"Shut up, Kelli," the tattooed girl cautioned. "I'm talking to her, not you."

"You shut up."

"Hi," Anna said warily to the girl with the tattoos, ignoring Kelli.

"This place is a fucking dump, right?" the girl volunteered. "Are you ready to go crazy yet? I'm Erica, by the way."

"Anna tried to escape," the voice from above whispered.

"I know. Julie heard Miss Richards talking about it last night and told Beth, who told me." Erica stared at Anna. "You're famous. No one else had the guts to try that, at least that I know of."

Anna felt strangely flattered. She didn't want to admit it was fear more than courage that had motivated her to run. She'd definitely never thought of herself as especially brave.

"This place sucks ass," Erica continued. "When I got here yesterday I couldn't believe it. The food sucks and you never get any time alone. Yesterday they gave us a half-hour tour of the place. They actually have a metal box here outside, like a torture box, where they lock you up whenever they want. And they have eight padded cells with just slits in the door, no windows. When they gave us the tour there was a girl in one of them, crying and talking crazy. She'd been in there for a week!"

Starvation, torture, isolation. Anna thought at least it explained why the girls were so well behaved. Had her dad known the camp would be like this? Probably so, she thought, and it made her furious.

"And there are no boys here, either," Kelli said from above. "That's the worst. Just think about that. No boys for three months."

"Go away," Erica whispered back, sounding annoyed. "No one wants to talk to you."

Undeterred, Kelli's pudgy face appeared over the edge of the bunk, looking down at Anna. "Erica doesn't like boys," she said. "Did you know that about her? She said yesterday, at orientation. Erica's a lez-bee-an."

"Shut up, Kelli. So what if I'm gay? At least I'm not a fat, disgusting porker like you. Can't you go stick your head in a trash can or something?"

"Lesbo."

Erica propped herself on an elbow and glared up at Kelli. "Do you want to start something with me?" she hissed. "You look like Miss Piggy with zits, bitch, so who are you to talk? You better watch out, or you might get punched in the fucking nose. I'm not afraid to hit you." Kelli's face disappeared pretty quickly, and Erica turned back to Anna. "Like I was saying before the interruption, it's exactly like a maximum-security prison here. They lock us up and torture us while they talk about respect and loving our families. Real phony apple-pie bullshit. This place just makes me hate my family more, actually, and it makes me hate our whole fucking fascist country. Where are you from anyway?"

"Atlanta."

"Good. At least that's a city. Small-town girls are the worst. Kelli's from a small town, can't you tell? I'm from Chicago. What did you do to get sent here?"

Anna didn't want to say. It seemed like giving too much away. "Nothing. My dad's crazy. He's really religious and thought I was too wild."

"I don't have a dad, it's just me and my mom. She's a famous lawyer. Catalina Ventress. You ever heard of her?"

Anna shook her head. "No."

"She's defended serial killers and that lady who shot her own kids. She's on Court TV all the time. Anyway, I got out of control, she said, so she sent me here. Now tell me, you must have done something."

"Not really. I mean, nothing too bad."

"I'll tell you what I did." Erica sounded kind of pleased with herself, Anna thought, like she was bragging. "I skipped school until I got expelled, but then I hid it from my mom. One afternoon she came home early from work and found me in bed with a girlfriend, who happened to be black. That drove her right over the edge because my mom's racist and only dates white guys. She already knew I was a dyke. Then we got in a fight, our biggest one ever, and I just snapped. The next morning I put some bleach in her coffee, on purpose, but it didn't kill her, it just made her really sick and she had to go to the hospital." Erica laughed. "It was a bad scene. You sure you won't tell me what you did?"

Anna felt totally horrified by Erica's litany of events. The girl had actually tried to kill her own mom? Jesus.

Suddenly the girl on the top part of Erica's bunk, who Anna thought had been napping, sat up and peered down over the edge. She was thin and unattractive, and looked about ten years old, although Anna knew she had to be older. Her face was sharp, dark, and pinched, with a look that was like a ferret's.

"You want to know what I think about Anna?" the girl asked softly. She was wearing an expression of great concentration that wrinkled up her forehead. "I think she got in trouble with a boy."

Anna was surprised and felt her face getting hot. How the fuck could this girl know that about her? They'd never even met.

"Really, why?" Erica asked, sounding interested.

"The powers of deduction," the small girl continued. "She's cute. Nice hair, nice body. Big blue eyes. Kind of like Hilary Duff, but not as pretty. Boys go for her, I'm sure." The girl spoke in a detached way, as though she were making scientific observations. "She seems a little shy, too, not mean and crazy like you, Erica. No offense." Again Anna was struck by the clinical tone. She supposed she should be offended the girl was discussing her like that, right in front of her face, but she just felt embarrassed. "She did try running away, though," the girl added, "so maybe appearances can be deceiving."

Anna didn't know what to say.

"I'm Stacey," the girl introduced herself. "Stacey Vargas." If anyone looked more out of place at Archstone than Anna, it was her. With her thin face and wiry hair, she looked like the kind of mousy girl who might grow up to be a school librarian, at best. Anna wondered what Stacey could possibly have done to get sent to a place like Archstone.

"So am I right about the boys?"

"Maybe," Anna replied. She wasn't going to admit anything to these girls. "Why are you here?"

"I volunteered."

Anna looked at her blankly. Obviously that was bullshit. "No, really."

"It's the truth. My mom and I sat down and talked about it. We decided it was the best thing for me, because I never fit in at school. That's how I got in trouble at first, always talking back to the teachers. It got so bad none of them could stand to have me in their class. It was mostly their fault for being so stupid. I made three teachers cry last year, and one of them was a guy, if you can believe it."

"Well, you're pretty dumb to volunteer to come here," Erica offered. "Couldn't you have just switched schools?"

"Maybe. But you see, then I got caught stealing five thousand dollars' worth of computer software and equipment from Best Buy. I'd done it over a six-month period, which made it worse, according to the judge. So it was either here or the local juvenile detention center. My mom and I thought this would be better. Besides, this is only three months and juvie would have been for eight. It wasn't much of a choice."

Erica laughed. "Nice."

Just then Kelli's round face appeared over the edge of the bed again, and she whispered. "Shut up! Counselor Brody's coming!"

"Fat-ass," Erica muttered back at her. Then to Anna she said, "Kelli's just scared they'll take her food privileges away."

But within seconds Erica and Stacey had rolled flat on their bunks, so Anna followed their lead and watched Counselor Brody come down the aisle toward them. He looked much younger than Adler, maybe early twenties, and he lacked a stiff, military bearing. His brown uniform was rumpled and he hadn't shaved in a couple days. He was thin and looked a little nervous, maybe unsure of himself, which seemed weird to Anna. She realized he was checking the bunks to make sure all the girls were there.

"Hi, Brody," Erica murmured when the counselor reached them.

Anna thought for sure he'd start yelling at her, but he just stopped at the foot of the bunk and stared. Anna didn't understand what was happening until she glanced over and was shocked to see the girl fondling her breasts under her orange tank top.

"Stop doing that," Brody said, but Anna noticed he didn't stop staring, and his eyes remained fixed on her chest.

"You can come get this anytime you want," Erica purred. "Do you know that?"

"You want me to tell Miss Richards on you?" Brody asked. Anna felt unease permeating the air. Brody and Erica were talking pretty softly, but she could tell the other girls were straining to listen. "Miss Richards doesn't tolerate little tramps."

"Do you?" Erica asked.

"Do I what?"

"Tolerate little tramps, like me." Anna thought she heard Kelli stifling a nervous giggle. From the corner of her eye she could see Erica's hand going lower, moving down to her crotch. Anna was grossed out, but also fascinated. Most girls she knew weren't quite as sexually brazen, at least not in front of a stranger. "I bet you get lonely at night. I bet it gets frustrating seeing all us wild girls, day after day, not being able to touch us. . . ." Her words trailed off.

"Oh, I can do better than you," Brody finally managed. But Erica had a comeback for everything.

"On a fucking island?" she laughed, or pretended to. "Please."

Brody scratched his nose. "You're not that attractive, Cadet Ventress. You look like a boy with that hair and all those tattoos."

"Some guys like that. Maybe you're one of them?"

Brody glanced up at Stacey then and saw her watching him. "What are you looking at, cadet?"

"You," she replied unflinchingly. "Where are you from, Brody?"

"Why?"

"Just curious. I'd guess West Virginia, probably. You sound like a hayseed with that accent of yours. Did you even graduate from high school?"

"Brody doesn't want us to know anything about him," Erica teased, before he could think up a response. "Isn't that right? We're not supposed to know any personal details about our counselors. Miss Richards said so last night. It's a rule. So can you get fired for answering our questions, Brody?"

"No. But I can make you lose your lunch privileges for a week."

"Harsh. And the meals here are just so tasty."

Brody sighed. "You keep up this attitude and I'll tell Miss Richards for sure."

"Stuff it up your ass, Brody," Erica told him. She was laughing for real now, Anna noticed. He had no power over her because he was weak and because Erica could tell he was attracted to her.

"Keep this shit up, and you *will* get in trouble."

"See how this conversation has degenerated," Stacey interjected. "Threats and bad language on both sides. You're not very good at your job, Counselor Brody. You might want to consider a new line of work."

He glared at Stacey. "I'm watching you, too, smart-mouth." His eyes flitted over to Kelli and then to Anna. "Why can't you be quiet like these two?"

"Well, Kelli's retarded and the new girl is shy, so that's why they don't talk much," Erica explained.

"Maybe you could learn a lesson from them," Brody said, "and save all your energy for today's activities. You're going to need it."

"I'm saving my energy all right," Erica said, smiling. "My sexual energy."

Brody looked tired and confused. "You've only got a few minutes of contemplation time left, cadets." He started back up the aisle to the sound of muted laughter.

"Yes, sir," Erica called out mockingly. When he was out of earshot she whispered to Anna, "Men are so stupid, and Brody's the dumbest. That's why I'm into girls."

"Yeah," Anna replied, thinking of Ryan and Mr. Spate. Then she added, "I mean, I like guys." She felt a sudden need to affirm her heterosexuality. In high school the worst thing you could be called was a homo or a lesbo. "I have a boyfriend, actually."

Or had one, Anna thought. Was Ryan the kind of guy who'd wait around for her? She realized she didn't even know. They'd only been going out for a few months, and he seemed cool, but it was hard to be sure. She'd always thought he was cute, since ninth grade, but had never really talked to him until one night when they hooked up after a party. After that they'd hung out a lot, often drunk or stoned. She tried not to picture him making out with some other girl, but it was definitely possible he'd dump her when he realized she'd be gone for so long.

"Hey, I've had boyfriends, too," Erica said. "It's no big deal. I bet I could get Brody if I really tried. Hey Stacey, you and Anna want to make a bet with me? I bet I could get him to fuck me, or at least let me blow him. Then I could tell Miss Richards and he'd probably get fired. Just give me a couple days and I can do it."

"If he didn't go for it, or Miss Richards didn't believe you, then you'd get in a lot of trouble," Stacey pointed out. "Remember the box."

"And the restraints and handcuffs. Hey, maybe I'd even like it."

"They have handcuffs and restraints here?" Anna asked.

"Oh yeah. They've got all kinds of stuff. They mean business. They're not afraid to use force with us, or so they say."

"They probably don't use those techniques very often," Stacey said. "The threat of punishment is usually much more effective than actual punishment. See how well it's worked on most of the girls here, ourselves included."

"Maybe." Erica yawned. "This fucking place needs a revolution."

"We're not going to revolt," Stacey said. "I'd like to think we would, but we won't. We're just one class of hundreds that have passed through here."

As if to prove her wrong, just as she said those words, a chubby girl with braces and dark, frizzy hair leapt off a top bunk near the center of the room and started screaming at the girl on the bottom. The girl on the bottom was just lying there with a wide smile on her face. Anna had noticed her earlier in line because she was much prettier than most of the girls, with long legs and thick, blonde hair. She had one of those beautifully cruel faces, with high cheekbones and thick lips that Anna often admired on models in *Cosmo,* or in the pages of the Abercrombie catalogue. Even the way she was lying on the bed looked like a pose. The girl's pouty mouth was twisted into an arrogant sneer.

"It's not true!" the chubby girl with the frizzy hair screamed at her. "You stupid bitch! You cunt! Stop saying those things about me!"

"Girls!" Brody yelled, heading toward the fray.

"Take it back, Kara!" the chubby girl screamed, her voice filled with hurt and disbelief. Her bunkmate continued to stare at her smugly. Whatever she'd said must have been pretty bad, Anna thought. How had the blonde girl gotten under her skin so much in less than a day? Maybe they were the two girls who'd been here longer than that. Brody ran up behind the girl who was yelling and she spun around.

"I hate this place!" she screamed in his face. All the girls were watching. "I want to go home! I'm going to slit my wrists if I can't get out of here! Here, cut me! Cut me!" She threw her arms at Brody and he grabbed her and wrestled her down to the floor. The room was suddenly filled with scream-ing girls, shouting, "Go for it!" and "Fuck you!" A pillow sailed through the air and bounced off the back of Brody's head. It was followed by a shoe, and then another one.

Anna was shocked at how quickly things got out of con-trol, and she felt a secret thrill as she saw the chubby girl on the ground flailing at Brody with her fists. More objects flew through the air like hailstones. The girl who'd apparently started the argument reclined blissfully on her lower bunk, watching the scene unfold with an expression approaching pure delight. She caught Anna staring and smiled, so Anna looked away. Some of the girls were running around, trying to open the front doors, while others ran to the windows.

Brody was bellowing into a radio he carried on his belt. "Help! Help!" he was yelling. More girls leapt from their bunks like demons and began kicking both him and the chubby girl as they rolled on the cement floor. It was almost as if every-one had just been patiently waiting for the opportunity to go insane. Anna tried to stay calm and think. Maybe there was a way to use the violence as a distraction to get out, or get to a phone.

"Kill him!" one girl screamed. "He deserves to die!"

Anna stood up, horrified, but she also wanted a better view of the action. Brody was getting his ass kicked pretty hard. For a second she thought worse things might follow, like someone gouging out his eyes, but Counselor Adler burst through the door, dark eyes blazing, and barged through the girls, pulling them off the fallen counselor. Anna saw that he wasn't playing around. He was vicious, grabbing girls by their hair, throwing them back against the rails of the bunks with force. Brody staggered up, clutching his side. His radio looked shattered and he had a swollen eye.

Adler picked up the girl with the frizzy hair and shook her like she was a rag doll, crying and thrashing about in his arms. Brody recovered his senses and grabbed her from behind. Together Adler and Brody hustled her out the door. The room was still in chaos, with all the girls screaming and cursing, although the explosion of physical violence seemed over. Erica emitted a war whoop. A second later Adler emerged again, furious.

"Stop it!" he barked, loudly enough to cut through the noise. The room fell silent. Adler was a scary presence, not like Brody. He looked like he could really hurt you and not give a damn. Anna could hear the frizzy-haired girl screaming from outside and wondered what was going to happen to her. "Stand at attention!" The girls stood sullenly in front of their bunks. Anna realized she'd been clenching her fists so hard her fingernails had left little semicircles on her palms.

"Get down on the floor, cadets!" Adler yelled. "If you're going to act like animals, then you're going to get treated like them. Fifty push-ups, and then fifty sit-ups. Then repeat the whole goddamn thing. I'll make your stomachs bleed like you got an ulcer. This isn't a three-ring circus or a zoo, and it's not your mommy and daddy's house, either. Two demerits for each of you. Natalia and Dana, you get four. I saw you kicking. Both of you should know better, as you've been here a month already. Beth is going to the box, in case you were wondering about her. She'll be sweating it out in there for the next twenty-four hours. The rest of you are damn lucky it's your first day." He was greeted by silence. "Move!" he commanded. The girls got down on the concrete floor and he prowled the aisle, counting out numbers.

At least now Anna knew which two girls had got held back from becoming level-two cadets. As she began to do push-ups, Anna watched Adler walk over to Kara, the girl who'd started the fight. Unlike most of the girls, she was having no trouble doing her push-ups, and wasn't even using her knees like everyone else.

Adler stared down at her long and hard. "Cadet Parker, did you start this?" Anna heard him say.

"No, sir," she answered, sucking on her lower lip. "Of course not. Why would you think that?" Her voice was low and raspy, seductive and sticky sweet. Anna bet wherever Kara came from, she was the most popular girl in school. She just had to be. Kara even looked good in the orange outfits that made all the other girls look like pumpkins. What the hell was she doing at Camp Archstone?

"I'm keeping my eye on you," Adler told her. "You're on my shit list from now on. If you screw up again today, I'll make the next three months of your life a living hell. Every class has one queen bitch, and I make it a personal mission to crush her spirit and break her will. Are you going to be that girl, Cadet Parker? Give me fifty extra push-ups when you're done with your set."

He continued down the aisle. "All of you are scum. If you weren't, you wouldn't be here. It's my task to transform you into something better than that, and it's a job I take very seriously. I will not fail, which means that you won't be allowed to fail, either. Discipline is the key, cadets. If anything like this happens again, you can kiss good-bye to lunch and dinner, and say hello to running laps all day in the heat."

When all the girls had completed their exercises, or pretended to, he stood at the front of the room. Anna's stomach ached and her arms were trembling from the effort. Fuck, I'm out of shape, she thought. She found Adler's scowl unsettling, but consoled herself with the knowledge that in the real world he must be a complete loser, because who'd want to work at a wilderness camp? He probably couldn't get into the army, so he had to play pretend with a bunch of teenage girls.

"All right, cadets. Put on your boots and form two lines. Last names A through M on the left, and N through Z on the right." The girls obeyed, lining up silently.

Anna scanned her fellow inmates. They ranged in age from Stacey all the way to Kara, who looked about seventeen. To her, most of them seemed to fit into recognizable types. There were some big girls who looked like bullies, a couple Goth chicks, and a few skinny, mean girls with crazy eyes that indicated they just loved causing trouble. Very few of the girls were hot, with the notable exception of Kara. Just your regular, average, run-of-the-mill reform school girls, Anna mused. She couldn't put names to most of the faces yet, other than the girls she'd already talked to, but she assumed she'd get to know them a whole lot better unless she found a way to escape.

In the meantime, Anna wanted to figure out these girls. Figure out who to stay away from and who was safe. She didn't plan on making friends here, but she didn't want enemies, either. She'd learned the hard way that you couldn't turn your back on some girls, and you certainly couldn't trust them to be straightforward. Guys thought girls were sugar and spice, but being a girl herself, Anna knew the truth—that girls could be much nastier and far more vicious to each other than boys. A lot of times, girls only acted nice on the surface, when bubbling underneath was hatred and anger.

"Forward march!" Adler commanded. He pushed open the doors to the barracks and the girls followed him out into the yard, where Miss Richards and the two other counselors were waiting. Anna stood behind Kelli, right at the end of her line. Erica and Stacey were in the same line ahead of her, as was Kara, way up at the front.

"Halt!" Adler ordered.

The line stopped moving. The heat was as intense as ever, oppressive and unforgiving, and she felt nauseous from the sun. She looked down at the dirt and saw a tiny green lizard scurrying past her on its way to freedom.

"Listen up!" Adler yelled. "Group one goes over there with Brody and McGathy. Group two stays here with me and Miss Richards. Move it!"

When the lines had arranged themselves, with group one heading off about a hundred feet away, Adler began calling roll rapidly.

"Emily Nichols?" he yelled brusquely.

"Here, sir," a voice responded, its owner obscured by the bodies of the other girls. From her position at the end of the line, it was hard for Anna to see the faces of her companions. She also didn't want to attract unwanted attention from Adler by staring too much.

"Alice Norwood?" he continued.

"Here, sir," Alice replied sullenly. Anna caught a glimpse of a squat, plain girl of about fourteen, with a low forehead and unruly brown hair. Anna had noticed her before, in the cafeteria. The girl was kind of dumb and brutish looking, and always wore a mean smirk on her face. Anna thought she looked like someone it was best to avoid.

"Kara Parker?"

"Here, sir," Kara replied, her voice slightly mocking. Adler either didn't notice her tone or chose to ignore it.

"Maria Ruiz?"

There was no response to this name, but Anna saw a dark-haired Latino girl, darker than Stacey, raise her arm. Strangely, it didn't seem to make Adler angry that the girl refused to speak, and he just continued down the list. Anna was really surprised he hadn't started yelling at the girl. Instead, he called the names of two more girls, Laura Seaton and Amelia Stevens, but Anna couldn't get a good look at either of them.

"Lindsay Taylor?" he continued.

"Here, sir," answered a thin, Gothic-looking girl with short, blue hair. Her voice trembled when she spoke, like she was very frightened or nervous.

"Michelle Thompson?"

"It's Shelly, I told you," a voice complained earnestly. "Not Michelle." Anna leaned sideways and saw the girl. She was a redhead, lanky and pale, her skin so white it glowed in the sunlight. Anna was surprised she'd spoken back to Adler.

He glared at her. "You're Michelle from now on. Got that?" He held her gaze until she looked away.

"Yes, sir," the girl muttered finally, sounding pissed off, but knowing there was nothing she could do.

"Jennifer Tully?" Adler continued, still annoyed.

"Here, sir," mumbled a fat girl with greasy black hair. She was tall and heavy, built like a boy, with wide shoulders.

"Stacey Vargas?"

"Here, sir," Stacey replied loudly. Adler then called Erica and Kelli's names before concluding with Anna's. Everyone was present except for Beth, the girl who'd been sent to the box. Anna noticed that Adler hadn't called her name, as if she'd never even existed and had been written out of history. In this heat, Anna could only imagine that sitting in a metal box outside would be unbearable. In fact, she wondered how long a person could even survive that kind of torture. She vowed that no matter what happened, she wouldn't let them put her in the box.

"Okay, so this is group two," Adler said to the thirteen girls standing before him. "Miss Richards and I are your team leaders. I'm disgusted by what just happened in the barracks." He paused like a general surveying his troops, finding them sorely lacking.

Miss Richards stepped in. She looked even older under the harsh glare of the sun, the wrinkles chiseled into her face. Anna thought she'd either been a chain smoker or spent most of her life outdoors. "I was very disappointed to hear that contemplation time turned into a brawl. That kind of behavior will not be tolerated at Archstone. Beth is in confinement right now, but it could be any one of you next. If you don't like the idea of spending twenty-four hours in a windowless heat box, with no food or light, or companionship, then shape up." She cleared her throat. "I want you to use your time here to think about the things you did that brought you to Archstone. If you feel anger and frustration at us or your parents, consider how your own actions are responsible for your present situation. This program isn't designed to hurt you, but to help you grow, despite what you probably believe.

"Society will deny you a voice if you don't play by the rules of civilized conduct, and without a voice, you're powerless. Believe me when I tell you that. I'm a woman, and I know. Physical fitness and self-discipline are the first steps to harnessing the power of your minds. This camp will be your introduction to a new way of thinking, behaving, and living." She strafed the girls with her bloodshot eyes.

"Daily physical exercise will become part of your routine from now on. It might be hard at first, but you'll soon get used to it, whether you want to or not. You can't have a strong mind without a strong body. The two go hand in hand. A healthy lifestyle of exercise and good nutrition, without any drugs, alcohol, or tobacco, will be a key part of your transformation. Every weekday morning we'll meet outside like this at oh-seven hundred hours until oh-nine hundred, and you'll receive physical training through a variety of different activities."

So it would be like one long gym class every morning, in intolerable heat, Anna thought. Usually she wasn't even awake at 7:00 A.M.

Miss Richards kept talking, but Anna wasn't listening anymore. She sighed. The day was going to be a total nightmare.

## Chapter Three

## Girls at Play

Finally, Miss Richards instructed the group of thirteen girls on how to line up for their exercises. They formed two long horizontal lines, with the first seven girls in the front and the other six, including Anna, in the back, spaced far enough apart so Miss Richards and Adler could see everyone.

"We're going to do some simple exercises to get the blood flowing," Miss Richards declared. In the distance, Anna could see a group of girls, level-two or three cadets, heading out the camp gates into the forest. "We'll start with jumping jacks," Miss Richards continued, "like you're all probably used to from high school gym class, if you bothered to attend, that is." She gestured to Adler to begin.

"How many do we have to do?" Alice suddenly called out from the front row. Anna thought it was pretty stupid of her to ask the question, because obviously they were stuck doing however many jumping jacks Miss Richards and Adler wanted them to do. She figured Alice had to be as dumb as she looked not to realize that. Why piss off the counselors for no reason?

Miss Richards glared at Alice angrily. "Excuse me, cadet, but did I say that you could speak?"

Alice shrugged her shoulders and kicked at the dirt.

"Answer me, Cadet Norwood."

"No," she muttered. "But it's so fucking hot, and this is a fucking—" Before she could even finish her sentence, Adler's face was in hers and he was screaming, in full drill-sergeant mode. Anna couldn't even catch all his words at first. It was more like a torrent of rage.

"Don't you ever swear at me or Miss Richards again, little missy! This isn't your hometown high school! We're not your friends! That kind of language is allowed to come out of my mouth only, not yours, unless you want to pay the price." He was so mad, his spit was spraying Alice's face. "And to think you interrupted everything to ask your stupid question. You want an answer? I'll give you an answer, Cadet Norwood. You have to do twice as many jumping jacks as everyone else here, how do you like that?" He paused for breath. "No wait, don't answer, because I don't want to hear another word come out of your hole."

Alice looked a little surprised, but not as startled as Anna felt. Maybe Alice was used to getting yelled at like that. Anna then heard a weird, sniffling noise and looked around. Adler heard it, too, and got distracted. He realized what it was at the same time Anna did, and he stepped back to get a good look.

"Oh my God!" he exclaimed dramatically, in mock surprise. "I can't believe what I'm hearing!" He zeroed in on the source of the noise, a girl in the front row to Anna's left. She was one of the younger ones, short with blonde hair, and Anna thought her name was Laura. "Cadet Seaton, are you crying?"

"No, sir," she snuffled, trying to hold back her tears. She rubbed the corners of her eyes with a fist.

"Don't lie to me! You're crying. I can see that, and so can the rest of your peers. Don't you have any sense of dignity, Cadet Seaton? Why are you crying in front of everyone, like a weak-minded sissy? Answer me, because I genuinely want to know."

"I don't know," she managed to choke out, then added, "sir."

Anna and all the other girls were staring at her. Anna could understand why the girl was upset, but Anna hoped she'd stop crying or else Adler would just keep abusing her.

"I wasn't even yelling at you," Adler continued. "I was yelling at Cadet Norwood. She's not crying, is she? She might be rude and she might be stupid, but at least she's not crying. Now give me one good reason why you're crying like that or everyone here will get to do double exercises."

Laura tried to find words, but they weren't coming.

"What's wrong, cadet? Do you miss your mommy? The same mommy you probably treated like dog crap back home? Or maybe you miss your daddy. Are you homesick already, is that it?"

"It's the heat," she finally managed. "And I'm tired, sir. And I don't feel well."

"Your answers suck, Cadet Seaton. I don't buy them for a

second." Anna felt bad for the girl, but there was nothing she could do about it. Adler sighed and addressed the whole group. "Okay, cadets, because of Cadet Seaton, all of you get to do double jumping jacks and stand out here in the sun twice as long."

There were some murmurs and groans, but Anna could tell everyone knew to keep quiet. Adler was such a prick, she thought, even though she knew he was just trying to break them down. Miss Richards seemed to condone his behavior, because she stood there silently, scrutinizing them.

They began their jumping jacks at Adler's command. Pretty soon Anna was drenched in sweat, and her thighs were chafing from where her pants rubbed her. She kept having to swat mosquitoes and gnats away from her. She was also dying of thirst.

"Keep it up, cadets! No slacking!" Adler called out from time to time, as he counted off the jumping jacks. "If it weren't for Cadet Seaton, and hell, Cadet Norwood, too, you all would be done now," he yelled gleefully at one point. "If you feel like shit, you have them to thank."

So much for unity and bonding, Anna thought. It sounded more like Adler was trying to make them hate one another. The sun beat down relentlessly on the top of her head, giving her a headache. At least I'll come out of Camp Archstone with a decent tan, she thought bleakly. Her arms and legs were completely exhausted, and she was even struggling to breathe.

Finally the torture came to an end, after three hundred jumping jacks, and the girls were allowed to collapse to the ground for a few minutes and get water in plastic cups from a large container on the grass. The girls were too tired to talk. Anna just wanted to crawl back into the air-conditioned barracks and rest, but unfortunately the day was just beginning. After she and the others had recovered enough to be functional again, Adler had them on their feet. Miss Richards explained that next they'd be taking a jog, in a single-file line around the camp, to get a better feel for the layout of Archstone.

"You'll be living here for the next three months, so you'd better get used to it," Adler added. Anna perked up, because the jog meant a chance to scope out a possible escape route, and to find out where they kept the phones. Not that she was planning on doing anything crazy so soon, but she could start gathering knowledge about the camp's weak spots. She was determined to beat the system, even if she didn't know how yet.

They lined up again, with Miss Richards way at the front and Adler right behind her at the end. She wished she could be more in the middle of the line, because she felt uncomfortable under his gaze. She tried to pretend he wasn't there, but it was hard because often he'd yell commands so loudly it made her flinch in surprise.

The girls jogged slowly around the edge of the camp, just inside the chain-link fence, on a well-worn dirt path. Anna could see other groups of girls that looked like hers. Some were doing exercises, while others were moving crates and doing chores. The camp was like a miniature city, or beehive, in which everyone had their place.

As they jogged, Anna checked out the different buildings. She'd missed the tour last night, but it was pretty easy to figure out what most of the buildings were. She recognized the refectory in the center, and their dormitory near the back of the compound. There were two other structures that looked similar and she assumed they were dorms for the level-two and three cadets. The buildings that housed the classrooms were easy to pick out, too. They were three stories tall, made of red brick with large windows, and she could see girls inside at desks as she ran past. Only a few of the buildings remained mysteries. One of them looked almost like a chapel, with a low roof and a tree-lined walkway to the front door, and another was large and dark with no windows. Maybe this was the punishment building, the place with the padded cells, Anna thought.

There was no sign of the box that Beth was supposedly roasting inside, but it made sense that they kept that out of sight somewhere. Anna could hear Adler's breathing close behind her and it encouraged her to keep up her pace. Kelli was having some trouble in front of her. The girl's breath came in ragged gasps and the back of her neck was bright red. Anna wondered what would happen if Kelli got heat-stroke. Had they even been given enough water to prevent it? Anna felt like she'd lost a gallon of water just from her sweat.

"Keep moving!" Adler's voice blared when the line started to slow. "We got three whole laps to go, did I mention that?" Anna didn't know how far it was around the camp, but it felt like at least a mile. It wouldn't have been as painful except for the heat and humidity, and the insects. Her arms were already itching from mosquito bites. She looked at the heads bobbing in front of her and wondered if the other girls felt as bad as she did.

By the time Anna and the girls had completed their run, most of them could barely move, and stood swaying in the hot air. Adler and Miss Richards herded them to a shaded area near one of the red brick buildings and let them rest for a while in the prickly grass. Anna saw it was teeming with small ants, but she didn't care. A bird call that sounded like the squawk of a parrot came from the forest somewhere and she looked in its direction.

She saw the other half of her cabinmates approaching, looking as tired and bedraggled as she felt. Anna's group hadn't passed them on the way around the camp, so presumably they'd been given some other awful activity to do. Counselors Brody and McGathy led them to the grassy area, where they collapsed alongside Anna and the others. She noticed Brody was sporting a very prominent puffy eye.

"I'm glad all of you survived," Adler said sarcastically. He wasn't tired or out of breath at all, but then again, he did this for a living. "As you remember from your tour yesterday, this is the building where your classes will be held. Your first class is due to start in fifteen minutes."

Anna wanted to know what the class would be about, but she figured she'd get yelled at if she asked.

"I'm thirstier than a motherfucker," she heard one girl whisper to another.

After a few minutes of rest and hydration, the three counselors and Miss Richards led Anna and the others into the red brick building. They walked down a wide hallway until they were led into one of the rooms. It was a pretty typical classroom, Anna thought. It had six rows of chairs, five to a row, and desks bolted down to the floor, as well as a big green chalkboard on the front wall. The only difference between it and any of her classrooms back home was that there were bars on the windows, and Brody and McGathy stood guard in the back of the room, right behind her. Like everything else at Camp Archstone, the rows were arranged by last name, which meant she was at the back of the room, next to Kelli.

Adler didn't come inside, and Anna felt relieved. He was the only one of the guards who actually scared her a little. Miss Richards walked to the front of the room and stood at a lectern.

"Okay, cadets," she said, "listen up. From now on, you'll be coming to this building and attending classes five days a week. Usually we won't be meeting in a group this large. You'll be separated into two smaller groups of nine and one of ten, depending on your abilities."

Abilities? What did she mean by that? Anna's question was quickly answered as Miss Richards continued speaking.

"Here at Archstone the classes will be tailored to your individual needs and capabilities. Today you'll be completing a series of questions, so we can get to understand you better and know which group to place you in."

"Shit, we have to take a test today?" Erica mumbled. "That sucks."

"Quiet!" hissed Counselor McGathy from behind.

Anna figured that Miss Richards was talking about either an IQ test or a psychological profile. She'd taken both kinds of tests before, one in high school and one at her therapist's office, but she didn't know how she'd done on them. From what she remembered they were long, and pretty boring. Still, sitting in the classroom was a thousand times better than running around outside in the heat. Through the windows she could see girls doing exercises while another group rested under a tree.

"I urge you to focus on the test and give it your full attention," Miss Richards said. "If you fail to take it seriously, you'll be disciplined and given demerits." She paused. "You should also be aware that your parents will receive updates on your progress twice a week. It's sometimes necessary to keep a cadet here for longer than three months, if they're not satisfied with your progress. . . ."

It took a second for the implied threat to sink in, and then the room went very quiet. Oh no, Anna thought. That meant she could be stuck here forever! She couldn't believe it.

She decided it was just one more reason why she had to escape, because no matter what she did, her dad might want to keep her at Archstone for longer. He certainly had enough money to pay for it. Anna could tell Kelli was shocked, too, from the stunned expression on her face, and she imagined all the girls were thinking the same thing.

"Well," Miss Richards continued, "it only occasionally happens, but it's something to keep in mind, isn't it? The test you'll be taking today will last for two hours. The first half will be multiple choice, and the second will involve you writing an essay. Don't worry if you can't write well. Your essay will be read for content only, not spelling or grammar."

Anna slumped back in her seat. She was still in shock that she could be kept here more than three months. Did that mean somewhere there were girls who'd been on the island for six months? A year? What was the time limit on something like that?

"If you need to use the bathroom during the test, just raise your hand and one of us will assist you." Miss Richards then handed stacks of papers to the girls at the front of each row and instructed them to pass the pages back to the others, along with tiny number-two pencils. Anna got hers last.

"You can get started right away," Miss Richards told the class. "Fill in the circles for your answers on the bubble sheet. And remember, only give one answer for each question."

With an inward sigh, Anna flipped through the pages. It was just like the PSAT, but with different questions. She began answering them right away, suppressing the urge to tear the whole thing up and yell "Fuck you!" at Miss Richards.

The questions were pretty silly: *When was the last time you considered using physical violence to solve a problem?* she read silently. *A) Today. B) Sometime this week. C) In the past month. D) In the past six months. E) Never.* She scratched in the bubble for "never." How would they know whether she was lying or not? Besides, there was a big difference between considering violence and actually doing it.

The questions continued in a similar vein:

*When was the last time you used alcohol?*

*If you use alcohol, on average, how many drinks per day do you consume?*

*When was the last time you used nonprescription drugs, such as marijuana, cocaine, amphetamines, or others?*

*How many cigarettes do you smoke per day?*

Some of them got even more personal:

*Are you sexually active?*

It was just a yes or no question, and Anna filled in the bubble for "yes," figuring there was no point lying about that one.

*Have you ever been treated for a sexually transmitted disease?* No.

*Choose the number closest to the number of sexual partners you've had.* Four.

Some of the questions just got bizarre, like, "Do you lie?"

How could anyone answer no to that, Anna thought. Was there seriously anyone alive who'd never told a lie? Anyone dumb enough to answer no would prove themselves a liar, which she supposed was the point of the question.

*Which of the following would make the best role model?* she read, shaking her head at how stupid it all was. *A) Your parents. B) A teacher. C) A priest. D) A movie star. E) Your best friend.* What was that one even testing?

For some of the questions, Anna told the truth, but for others she didn't. She thought it would help her odds at escaping if they had a totally screwed-up read on her personality.

The questions started to repeat a lot as she continued, and the same questions were asked again in slightly different ways. She remembered this tactic from earlier tests she'd taken. Obviously, it was to try and trip her up in any lies. She focused and made sure to be consistent with all her answers.

Then she hit a question that made her stop, like she'd been hit in the gut, her pencil frozen in the air. She couldn't believe they were asking *that*.

*Have you ever terminated a pregnancy?* she read silently. The words stared back at her from the page, cold and hard. How could they know to ask that question, and to spring it on her near the end? She felt her face getting red and she fought the urge to look around and see if anyone was staring at her, even though she knew it was irrational.

There's no way I'm answering that one, she thought at first. But the more she considered it, she realized that to answer truthfully would be the biggest "fuck you" to her dad she could think of at the moment. Let him suck on this report card, she thought with grim satisfaction, as she filled in the circle for yes, and quickly moved on, keeping the question booklet over the bubble sheet so Kelli or the guards sitting behind her couldn't read her answer.

At the end of the hour, Miss Richards and the two counselors came around and individually collected the questions and answers from each of them. Erica gave Brody an ironic little wave, but he pointedly ignored her. Anna wondered what the camp shrink would make of her responses, and what group she'd get put in. Not that it really mattered, because she didn't plan on being at Archstone too long, but she hoped one of the girls she already knew would be in it. Maybe not Kelli so much, but Erica seemed friendly, if crazy, and Stacey was at least smart, and that counted for something.

"Okay, cadets," Miss Richards said, clapping her hands together for attention, "the next part of today's diagnostic exam will begin right now. It's very different from the first and will require you to do some soul searching. In fact, some of you might have difficulty writing at first, but I assure you, that's a natural part of the process. Counselors Brody and McGathy will distribute the essay topic and two blank sheets of paper. You may write on both sides."

Once again, Anna was one of the last girls to get the

papers, and when she looked down at the question page, she was surprised to see just four words typed on it, right at the top:

*Why are you here?*

That's a hell of a good question, she thought as she gazed at it. She noticed very few of the other girls had started writing yet and many looked like they were thinking, just staring off into space. There are so many ways I could answer this, Anna thought. She didn't know exactly what the camp wanted or expected her to write, and she didn't really care. She guessed they wanted her to say it was all her own fault or something, but she decided to make an honest attempt to write down the series of events, as she saw it, that had led her to Archstone, including her secret abortion.

She was surprised by how quickly the words flowed onto the page. Time passed rapidly as she wrote about how nothing she ever did was good enough for her dad, and how he'd forced the abortion on her. Pretty soon both pages were full and she hadn't even made her handwriting big like she usually did when she had to write an essay for school.

From her vantage point in the back of the room, she could see a lot of the girls hadn't done so well. Some had only written a short paragraph, and she could see one of them had just made a bunch of drawings.

Miss Richards called time and the papers were collected. Anna noticed that when McGathy took hers, he didn't even look at her. To him she was probably nothing, just one in a long line of girls. He looked bored as hell with his job and was obviously thinking about other things. That might come in useful later on, she thought to herself. He seemed sort of absentminded, so maybe he'd inadvertently give her the opportunity she needed to escape.

"Okay, cadets. Class is over," Miss Richards said as the girls moved restlessly in their chairs. "We'll take you to the refectory for lunch now, after which you'll get a short break. Then we'll head over to the medical clinic, where each of you will receive a fifteen-minute individual session with one of the four camp psychologists. He or she will assess your immediate situations, and monitor your medicines, for those of you who are on them. After you've been assigned a group in a few days, you'll be meeting with your psychologist once a week, for an hour-long session."

One of the girls at the front of the class raised her hand and held it there. Miss Richards frowned at her. "Now's not the time for questions, Cadet Campbell. This isn't high school. When I'm talking, keep your hands down and your eyes up front, got it? There will be time for questions later today." The girl slowly lowered her hand.

Anna and the others were led from the classroom and back into the heat of the day. It had gone from what felt like ninety degrees to about a hundred, and the air was thick and wet. Miss Richards led them back to the refectory, where they had a silent lunch of PBJ sandwiches, potato salad, cottage cheese, and water.

Anna thought it was eerie to eat in such total silence. She was used to the noise and general craziness of her high school cafeteria, and she didn't understand why they weren't allowed to talk. Maybe it was punishment for the fight that had broken out between the girls and Brody? Or maybe it would always be like this. It wasn't as if Miss Richards or anyone else was talking or lecturing them, either. It was just dead silence, broken only by the sounds of plates being scraped with plastic forks, and girls chewing.

After lunch they were given a brief rest, sitting in their bunks, also under strict orders of silence, but because Brody and Ellis were up at the front, Anna was able to whisper with Kelli, Erica, and Stacey.

"What a long-ass day," Erica muttered. "I'm already beat."

"No kidding," Anna whispered back. She felt wiped out from the journey yesterday and the early morning exercises, and would have loved to take a nap.

Kelli leaned over the bunk and looked down at them. "I don't know how I'm going to make it through the rest of the day," she moaned.

"Oh, I'm sure this is nothing," Stacey whispered back from above Erica. "I get the feeling they're actually taking it easy on us, trying to break us in slowly."

"Yeah, the hike tomorrow is going to suck," Erica whispered up to her. "My legs are killing me from all those fucking jumping jacks. Why'd that bitch Laura have to cry?"

It wasn't her fault, Anna wanted to point out, but she couldn't find the energy. Besides, what did she care what Erica thought? "How long is the hike supposed to be again?" she asked instead.

"Christ, like ten miles, they said yesterday. It's nuts. My feet hurt just thinking about it."

"It's not nuts," Stacey said. "It's all worked out carefully to screw with our minds. You see, today they're taking it easy, letting us see how the camp works, and finding out all about us from those tests. Then they're going to use the information against us, to try to find our weak points and break us down. Remember what Adler said to that tall girl. It's his 'personal mission.' The hike is just a good way of tiring us out and making us malleable."

"So they can fuck with us better," Erica muttered.

"How do you know all this, Stacey?" Kelli asked. There was a note of challenge in her voice, as though she didn't like the girl. "Do you work here or something?"

"No. It's just pretty easy to put the pieces together if you're smart enough."

"Yeah, well, whatever," Kelli replied. She was about to say more, but Erica cut her off.

Addressing the question to Anna, she said, "What would you be doing right now if you weren't here? If you could be doing anything?"

Anna thought for a second, unsure of what to say because she honestly didn't know the answer, or why Erica was asking. "What about you?" she asked, turning the question back around.

"That's easy. Getting laid by a hot chick. Now back to you."

Anna didn't believe Erica's answer, because no girl could be such a one-dimensional sex machine. There had to be more to her story. Then again, she'd supposedly tried to kill her mom, so who knew how fucked-up she was?

Anna thought about the question for a moment. She definitely wouldn't want to be having sex, because she felt sticky and gross and bad about her body. What she really missed was regular life, just being at home in Atlanta, watching TV and chilling out with a beer, or a joint. Then maybe heading out and taking some photos with her Nikon. There was all kinds of cool, random stuff to see in the neighborhoods, if you knew what you were looking for. She supposed that would be her ideal day, as lame as it probably sounded to these girls. She decided to say it anyway, because she hated being put on the spot.

"That's cool," Erica nodded when Anna was done telling them. "I could definitely go for a beer."

"So you're into photography?" Stacey whispered down to her, sounding slightly impressed, or at least interested.

Anna suddenly felt embarrassed. "Yeah. I got into it at school. It was just something to do, you know?" She didn't want to reveal how much it meant to her, and how one day she even hoped to make it her career, because she didn't know these girls well enough and she didn't want to get laughed at.

"Stacey, what about you? What would you be doing?" Erica asked.

Stacey didn't need time to think at all. "I'd be on the computer."

"Doing what?"

"Probably IMing my friends about new software. And yes, it's fine if you think I'm a nerd. Everyone at school always did and it's the truth. I'm proud of it, actually."

No one said anything to that, though Anna thought it was a pretty good response.

"What about me?" Kelli asked. "Don't you guys want to know what I'd be doing?"

"Eating a Twinkie?" Erica asked.

"Fuck you," she hissed back. "As if you know shit about me. For your information, I'm not even hungry."

"Because you just pigged out at lunch."

"No, I didn't! Quit being so mean to me, Erica, and listen. What I'd be doing is swimming. That's what I like to do. Swim."

"Huh," mused Erica. "That's not such a bad idea, I guess. It's a shame this place doesn't have a pool."

Their conversation was eventually interrupted by the arrival of Adler, which got everyone's attention.

"Remember me, cadets?" he barked as he entered the room. "I'm back and I'm taking over from here." He conferred with Brody and Ellis for a moment and then nodded. "In the next three hours, each of you is going to meet with one of our psychologists. I bet all of you are looking forward to that! However, there are twenty-seven of you in this room, and only four doctors on staff, which means there'll be some downtime while you wait for your appointment. Because idle hands are the devil's plaything, you won't just get to laze around and chitchat. You're coming with me and Counselor Ellis to help prepare one of the gardens for planting. A lot of the food you'll be eating here is grown by the cadets, because it's too expensive to import provisions from America. So line up in your two rows again, A through M and N through Z, just like last time, and we'll take you out there and show you what to do."

Grumbling and bitching, the girls got off their bunks and stood up. Anna could only think that now it was a little past noon, the sun and heat would be even worse. They were bad enough, but it was the humidity that made it truly unbearable. Still, any opportunity to learn more about the camp meant a chance she might stumble across a future plan for escape.

The girls were led from the barracks in two groups and into the sunlight. The heat was as bad as she'd feared and by the time Adler had led her group to a patch of dirt, about twenty feet long and thirty feet wide, she was soaked with sweat again.

It *would* have to be Adler they were stuck with, Anna thought, wishing it was Brody or Ellis. They all stood at the edge of the dirt rectangle, which was next to a gray brick building, as Adler talked. The other group had been led away in a different direction to the opposite side of the building.

"Okay, cadets. In alphabetical order, each of you will be called by name to go inside this building and have a sit-down evaluation with the shrink. Nurse Wilson will come out and get you, and then she'll escort you back out when you're done. For the rest of you, when you're not in there with the doctor, you'll be out here with me. There's water over there—" he indicated a cooler sitting in the dirt, "—so if you're thirsty be sure to hydrate yourselves. Now, what kind of work will you be doing, you wonder? This field needs to be turned over and aerated, so vegetables can be planted a few weeks from now. As you've probably noticed, there aren't any shovels or hoes out here. That means you're going to work the old-fashioned way, with your hands."

He knelt down at the edge of the dirt patch. "Watch, because this is what you're going to be doing." He thrust his hand into the dirt, which was dark and deep, and stirred it around, almost like tossing a salad. Anna shifted on her feet. She was hot and bored, and nervous about seeing the psychologist, too. Could he or she really be any worse than Dr. Cochran, though?

"This is step one," Adler continued. "Turning the soil over. When the whole field is turned over, then it's time for step two, which goes like this." He stuck his fingers deep into the earth and made circular holes like the ones on a bowling ball. "This is how you aerate the soil, which refreshes it for future use." He stood up. "You better not be afraid to get your hands dirty, because that's what Camp Archstone is all about." He looked down at his watch. "Cadet Nichols, you'll be up first, but until Nurse Wilson calls you, get started with everyone else. All of you will work silently and efficiently, because you don't want to piss me off. You may begin."

Anna knelt down with the others and they started pushing the dirt around with their hands. Adler strode the circumference of the dirt plot, watching their progress. It seemed like pointless work to Anna, and she knew it probably was. Within a couple minutes, the door to the brick building opened and a nurse, a small woman dressed in white, called Emily inside. The door swung shut behind her and Anna wondered what was going on in there. She wished she wouldn't be the last one in the group to find out.

"This sucks," she whispered to Erica, who was working next to her.

"Yeah, typical bullshit. This isn't teaching us anything."

"It's just to keep us busy."

The two hours passed in an agonizing crawl, and Anna's back and hands were killing her. She watched as girls went in and out of the building and then returned and resumed their work. Some of them looked okay, but others had red eyes. Kara, of course, came out wearing a smile. Anna noticed that Laura and Alice had both really gravitated to the girl, and the three of them whispered back and forth like best friends. Unfortunately, Adler kept lingering near Anna's end of the field so she had to stay silent and couldn't talk to Erica more.

When Stacey got back from her appointment, however, Anna maneuvered herself over to her and started kneading the earth next to her. "How did it go?" she asked.

"Fine," Stacey answered. She didn't seem shaken up at all, which meant it couldn't be too bad. "It was just some old guy who told me my shoplifting was an attempt to get attention. I simply explained to him it was my attempt to get stuff for free. He seemed harmless enough."

"Yeah?"

"I think he wants everyone here to have just one central problem, because that's all he can handle. Clearly shoplifting is going to be my issue."

Anna started to wish she hadn't mentioned her abortion in her essay. Not that the shrink had had time to read it yet, but assuming he did, she knew he'd make her talk about it at some point. She wished it was a female doctor, too, not that Dr. Cochran had been any good, but it seemed easier to talk about her problems with a woman.

But who knew? If they had four psychologists on staff, maybe she'd get a different one from Stacey.

"How can a person even get to know us in fifteen minutes?" she asked Stacey as they worked.

"Don't worry about it. It's absurd. The whole thing is an insult to us."

She was going to ask Stacey more about it, and get a heads-up on what the therapist wanted to hear, but Adler declared there was too much talking, so they had to fall silent again.

Finally it was Anna's turn to enter the building and she passed Kelli on her way inside. "Good luck," Kelli said in a choked voice.

"Thanks," she replied as the nurse led her through the door and down a cool, dark hallway. She was taken into a large, wood-paneled room that looked like her dad's study.

"Hello, Anna," said the old man sitting in a comfortable leather chair behind a wide oak desk. "Come on in and have a seat." He gestured to a wooden chair in front of her.

Anna felt like she'd been slapped, because she recognized the old man immediately. It was Henry, the guy who'd driven her out to the camp. She was so surprised, it was hard to find her voice.

"You lied to me," she finally managed to say bitterly, as she remained standing in the doorway. And he'd been so nice to her!

"No, Anna, I didn't lie. Everything I told you was the truth." He spread his hands on the desk. "Please take a seat and we can discuss it. Everything you say in here is confidential, so you can speak freely to me."

She moved haltingly to the wooden chair across the desk from him and sat, mainly because she was so shocked and tired, not because she wanted to give in to his demands.

"You did lie," she said. "You never told me you were a shrink. Never."

He shrugged. "A sin of omission, perhaps, but a necessary one. I did tell you I worked at Archstone, didn't I?"

"Volunteered. You said you were a volunteer."

"I am. I volunteer my services to the camp for free." He smiled. "What, did you think I baked cookies for them or something? Just because I'm old and retired? No Anna, I really was an army psychiatrist for three decades, so I can be of more use here than that."

"You tricked me," she muttered. Weren't therapists supposed to encourage trust with their patients? There was no way she was opening up to this guy, ever.

"The reason I picked you up in the truck is because I heard you tried to run, and to be honest, I was curious about you. Not too many girls try running, surprisingly enough. I wanted to see if you were in a crisis situation and needed immediate psychological attention."

"I was fine."

"Yes, as it turns out, you were. You did quite well."

Anna hated the way he was assessing her, judging her. "You could have said something."

"Like what? That my name is Dr. Henry O'Connor, and I'm a psychiatrist?" He picked up a pen and tapped the desk with it lightly. "Somehow I don't think that would have gone down too well with you."

"Whatever." Anna looked away at the wall. There were framed photographs of the island hanging behind him, palm trees and beaches and sunsets. They were nice, but nothing special. She wondered if he'd taken them himself, and thought: I could do better. It gave her a momentary satisfaction.

Henry, or rather, Dr. O'Connor, began shuffling some files on his desk. "We only have a few minutes today, but we will, of course, be meeting over the duration of your stay at Camp Archstone. I've asked that I be assigned your case, even though your Biddle psychological profile test hasn't been processed yet—"

Anna interrupted him. At least it felt easier to ask questions here than outside with Adler. "Is it true they make girls stay here longer than three months sometimes?"

He nodded slowly. "Yes. But only in extreme circumstances. I wouldn't worry about it too much."

"And what about the torture box? This girl, Beth, she got sent there. Isn't that inhumane?"

"Was what Beth did to Counselor Brody humane?"

"No, but she was pissed off. Putting her in a box is just plain torture. You'd never be allowed to do that in America. That's why this camp is here, isn't it?"

Dr. O'Connor sighed. "You're a smart girl, Anna, but you're looking at this the wrong way around. I don't control the counselors, and neither do you. We've only got ten minutes left. Do you want to spend them talking about Beth or about yourself?"

"I don't want to talk at all."

"Then we'll spend a very boring ten minutes together, won't we?" He was smiling again, the asshole.

"I guess so," Anna said. A brief silence fell and she glared across the desk at him. Finally he laughed.

"A staring contest? I was always good at those, Anna. I promise you, I'll win."

Anna continued glaring.

"Listen," Dr. O'Connor said. "There are other issues we need to address, like the use of medication at Camp Archstone."

"I'm not on any medication," Anna replied, not understanding him.

"That might be the problem." Dr. O'Connor looked through the papers on his desk. "It says here you have ADD, depression, acting-out disorder—"

Anna was shocked. "What?! That's not true. Who told you that crap? My dad?"

"Dr. Melanie Cochran, from Atlanta, Georgia. She wanted to put you on Ritalin and Zoloft, but you resisted?"

Anna couldn't believe it. "I'm not taking any medication," she said firmly, suppressing a sense of fear. That was always something that had terrified her, being forced to take medications against her will, designed to make her into a brainwashed zombie. Her dad had got Dr. Cochran to prescribe them several times in the past for her, but she'd refused to take them, and no one could physically force her. Until now. She started to feel even more panicked.

"So you don't like taking strange drugs," Dr. O'Connor continued, "but in Dr. Cochran's report, it also says you drink, smoke pot, and experiment with ecstasy."

"That's different."

"How?"

She knew he was trying to get inside her head and it pissed her off because it was so presumptuous. He didn't know what living with her dad was like, or the pain of going through an abortion. "You wouldn't understand," she finally said.

"Are you sure about that? Has it occurred to you that over my thirty-plus years as a psychiatrist I've seen and heard pretty much everything? And that I might be equipped to help you?"

Anna sat there, silent, thinking that she was done talking.

Dr. O'Connor leaned back in his chair. "I'm not sure you fully understand the gravity of your situation, Anna. Your father has sent you here as a means of last resort. If you're not amenable to talking about your problems, there are things we can do to help you. . . ." He sighed. "I don't like to use it as a threat, but you should be aware I've been authorized by your parents to prescribe medication to help your behavior adapt—"

"I'm not taking any fucking medication!" She felt a rising sense of horror. She'd thought of Henry as a kindly, well-meaning old man. She wondered how she could have been so blind.

"You won't have much of a choice if I say it's necessary," he told her blandly. "The counselors will force you. They're more than happy to do it, because it makes their job so much easier." He paused. "I believe Counselor Adler takes a special pleasure in it. We have all kinds of drugs here, Anna, and not the kind you're used to. Klonopin and lithium, Prozac and Thorazine. Any combination might be the right one for you."

It was all too much for her. "I'll run!" she said suddenly, half rising from her chair. "If you try to make me take those fucking drugs, I'll run again! And this time you won't catch me!" Suddenly realizing what she was saying, she collapsed back into the chair. She'd just made it a whole lot worse for herself, and she knew it.

Dr. O'Connor was smiling. "Very interesting, Anna." He jotted something down on a notepad. "You see how these sessions can be useful, then." He looked at his watch. "Only two minutes left. Anything else you'd like to get off your chest?"

Anna wanted to tell him to go fuck himself, but now she was

scared of him, so she didn't say anything. She didn't know if he'd been serious about the medication, or just using the threat to make her freak out and admit that she wanted to run.

"Well, I'll tell you what," the doctor said. "When we meet again in a couple of days, I'll have read your test papers and essay, and I'll have a better idea of your situation. As of now, I don't see any immediate crisis, so there's no need to medicate you. Yet. But I'd advise you to watch your step and prove to me that you're willing to change. In terms of your desire to run, that's quite natural, although I'm afraid you're more apt to act on impulse than some of the others. However, I have all the faith in the world that Counselor Adler will prevent any escape attempts on your part, as he's quite vigilant."

At that moment, the nurse appeared in the doorway and said, "Dr. O'Connor, it's time."

"Ah, yes," he replied, looking up at her. Then to Anna he said, "Nurse Wilson will take you back outside." He stood up. "I'll be seeing you soon, Anna."

In a daze, Anna let Nurse Wilson lead her back into the sun and heat. She felt shell-shocked from her meeting with Dr. O'Connor. It couldn't have been as bad for the other girls. She wanted to tell Stacey and Erica about it, but there was no chance. She was the last girl out and when Adler saw her, he declared that their work was over. Counselor McGathy and his group had appeared from somewhere, too.

"Okay, cadets," Adler said. "Stand at attention."

They stood on the plot of dirt, Anna's whole body aching. She was still thinking about Dr. O'Connor, and vowed that no matter what happened, she wouldn't let them force any drugs on her.

"It's just past fifteen hundred hours," Adler said. "Now that we've got you warmed up, and the doc's checked you out, you get to do another activity." Anna prayed it would be something indoors, just to get a break, but Adler called out, "How many of you feel like a nice game of softball?"

Anna's shoulders slumped. He had to be kidding, she thought, but sadly, he wasn't.

"Form your two lines. You know the drill. First bunch goes with McGathy this time, and the rest comes with me."

"I don't even know how to play softball," the girl with the blue hair murmured.

Adler heard her and frowned. "What the hell are they teaching you at school these days? Anyway, for those of you who don't know how to play, you'll figure it out pretty fast. It's not a hard game to learn, unless you're mentally challenged. You stand at home plate, swing at the ball, and then run around the bases and try not to get tagged. Got it? Now move it and get into your lines."

They obeyed, and Anna's group followed Adler across the lawn at the center of the camp, past the American flag, and onto one of the grass fields encompassed by the chain-link fence. The field had a home plate area marked out on it, and three bases in a diamond shape. There were two rows of short metal benches on either side of home plate, and Anna's group walked to one side, while the first group walked to the other. There was a large bag of cheap vinyl gloves laying there and Adler distributed them to the girls.

Anna had never liked softball because it was boring, and she wasn't very good at it. She hadn't even played in years. Not that she was bad at sports in general. In fact, she played soccer and tennis, and always did well in gym class, but soft-ball was one of her least favorites. Playing it at a prison camp with a bunch of fucked-up girls only made it worse.

"This is modified slow-pitch softball," Adler declared as they huddled around him. "That means you have to throw the ball underhand, so it makes an arc in the air. Like this." He demonstrated with his arm. "You're going to be playing the other group, in case you haven't figured that out already. They'll be at bat first. The game will last five innings." Seeing some blank stares, he said, "Jesus, how many of you know what an inning is?'

Most of the girls, including Anna, raised their hands. "Good enough. There'll be nine players on the field from each team at one time, which means four of you will have to sit out at first. But don't worry, everyone will get a chance to play. I'll be pulling some of you out and replacing you at my discretion, mainly when you fuck up." He pointed at four cadets in quick succession, including Stacey and Kelli, but not Anna. "You guys look like the weakest players to me, so you'll be keeping the bench warm for now. The rest of you will be on the field."

Adler assigned positions to each of the players. Anna was sent way out to left field, which suited her just fine, and made her think Adler could sense she wasn't any good. Kara, maybe just because of her height, was the pitcher, and the other girls were scattered on the bases and around the outfield.

Anna didn't know the other girls in the outfield, and couldn't even remember their names. They were spaced far enough apart so that it was impossible to talk to them anyway. Erica was, unluckily for her, assigned to be the catcher.

"I don't expect you to be any good," Adler yelled at them, "but I expect you to give it your all! Anyone who doesn't will get two demerits."

"Let's play some ball!" McGathy called out.

The first girl from the other team came up to bat, and Anna noticed the bat was made out of hard, yellow plastic instead of metal or wood. How totally ridiculous, she thought, although she understood the reasoning behind not putting a weapon in some of these girls' hands.

The game began and it was total chaos, Adler and McGathy both yelling and everyone running around the field in disorder. Kara was a decent pitcher, and the first girl struck out. The next two did better, but the ball remained close to the center of the field, and they each only got a base. Then, just as Anna was starting to relax, the next girl got lucky and nailed the ball hard, right in her direction.

Oh shit, she thought, as she tried to get her glove up in time. She couldn't even see the ball in the sky because of the sun, but she heard it land behind her. Some of the girls started screaming at her as she groped for it, and she managed to throw it to Maria at second base, who fumbled badly before getting it to Erica. The focus of the action turned away from her again, but her heart was pounding. Fuck this stupid game, she thought. She really hated being the center of attention like that.

"Cadet Wheeler!" she heard Adler yell. "You're outta there. Same with you, Cadet Ruiz." Anna felt nothing but total relief as she walked across the field toward the benches, behind Maria. "You'll get another chance in a while," Adler called out, and she thought, God, I hope not.

As she was walking, she suddenly heard a girl hiss out of nowhere, "You suck!" from behind, and she looked around, startled and pissed off. Who'd said it? The only people close enough were Kara, on the pitcher's mound, and the girl named Emily, who was playing shortstop, and neither of them was looking at her.

Based on her previous observation of Kara's behavior, Anna had a pretty good idea of who had said it. What a bitch! She was pissed, but decided to let it slide. She wondered why it even bothered her, because she certainly didn't give a shit about softball, or any of these girls. Kara was seriously an asshole, that much was clear.

Soon she was back at the benches, with Stacey, Kelli, and Maria. Two other girls had been sent in for her and Maria.

"Welcome to the losers' club," Stacey said.

"Yeah, I hate softball," Anna told her, taking a seat on the bench, which had been heated by the sun so much it burned her legs.

"I hate all organized sports," Stacey continued, in her freakishly grown-up voice. "As a matter of principle."

"'Cause you're no good at them, right?" Kelli jeered.

"That's true." Stacey nodded, not even caring.

Anna looked behind them through the fence and at the trees beyond. It was interesting to note that no one seemed to be watching them too closely at the moment, though she supposed Adler or McGathy would notice if any of them got up and ran. And even if they didn't notice, there was no way to get through the locked gates and out of the camp.

"Gross, what is that?" she heard Kelli say. She followed the girl's gaze and saw a large, gray sand crab moving slowly past them along the edge of the field. It looked totally out of place, and kind of creepy, like a giant spider.

"It's just a crab, Kelli," Stacey said. "They're probably all over this island. Don't worry, it won't hurt you."

"I'm not worried," Kelli sniffed.

Anna looked back at the game unfolding on the field. Her team was losing, not that it mattered. It was the last pitch of the inning, and about time for them to go up to bat, which Anna was dreading, when something crazy happened.

A short, cute girl with dark hair was on the mound, and Kara was on her first pitch. Suddenly, and without warning, while the girl was still adjusting her grip on the bat, Kara swung her arm and hurled the ball through the air right at the girl's head. The girl had no time to move, and the ball struck her on the side of her face. She dropped the bat and clutched her jaw with both hands. Anna heard her begin to sob, and at the same time realized that neither Adler nor McGathy had seen what had happened.

"It slipped!" Kara yelled. "I'm so sorry! I didn't mean it." But she didn't look or sound particularly sorry. The game came to a halt and everyone stood still where they were. Long periods of calm punctuated by sudden violence seemed to be the way of the camp.

"Christ!" Adler swore, heading straight for Kara, while McGathy tended to Kara's crying victim.

"Cadet Parker, did you do that on purpose?" Adler yelled.

"No, no," she protested. "It was an accident. I wasn't trying to hit her. My aim's not so good."

Adler grabbed her by the arm hard and jerked her off the pitcher's mound. Anna saw she was smiling slightly, just at the corners of her lips, even though it looked like his grip hurt a lot.

"I told you not to fuck around!" he snapped, and even though Anna still hated him, she was glad he'd seen through Kara's bullshit. "You're going to solitary confinement." He grabbed his walkie-talkie in his free hand and barked into it for someone to come and take Kara away.

"That girl's crazy," Kelli said. Her flushed face looked vaguely horrified, but her voice sounded impressed.

"At least she's screwed up the game," Stacey added dryly. "We should thank her for that." And it was true that everything had come to a screeching halt and stayed that way, girls swaying in the heat and talking to each other, until a counselor Anna hadn't seen before came and took Kara off with him.

"'Bye, Kara," Alice called out, and Kara waved at her as she was escorted from the field, her perfect blonde hair bouncing in its ponytail as she walked. Anna figured if a couple girls got taken away each day, then soon there'd be no one in her class left.

The game finally resumed. The girl who'd been hit was only grazed, it turned out, and she sat on the other set of benches rubbing her cheek angrily. The rest of the game passed uneventfully. Anna struck out at bat each time she came up, partly deliberately, because she didn't want to run around in the heat. When she was put back in the outfield, the ball didn't come her way again. Her team lost, but no one cared, except maybe Adler, who made sure to tell them they were all fuckups.

After the game both teams merged and they were finally allowed to go inside to have dinner. Adler and McGathy watched over them as they ate. Anna didn't even feel hungry because of the heat and all the exercise. The enforced silence at mealtimes, which had seemed so weird to her at breakfast and lunch, was becoming more natural. She was hoping that after dinner they'd get to go back to their bunks and rest, and just hang out until bedtime, but she'd forgotten about Bible hour.

They were led from the refectory into the small chapel, where plastic chairs were arranged in a large circle. The girls took their seats, Anna noticing that two places were conspicuously empty where Beth and Kara should have been. Anna sat between Erica and Stacey, because they weren't in alphabetical order for once. Adler stood in the center of the room, holding a Bible he'd picked up from a lectern.

"Usually the time after dinner will be devoted to group therapy sessions," he said. "But tonight, and every Friday, we'll have a Bible study hour." He flourished his thick leather-bound Bible and held it aloft. "It works like this: I choose a place to start reading and then give the book to one of you. You each read twelve lines and then pass it to the person on your left, who continues reading. Now, I don't care if you're a Christian, a Muslim, a Jew, or a Hindu who worships cows, you're going to read from this book. You can all learn a whole lot from it about how to conduct your lives." He opened the Bible and handed it to a girl Anna didn't know, someone across the circle from her. "Tonight we'll start with the Book of Psalms. Cadet Dessen, you may begin with the first one."

So it was just like home after all, Anna thought. She supposed it didn't matter to Adler that she'd read the Book of Psalms at least three times before, back in Atlanta. The Bible hadn't helped her then, and it certainly wasn't going to now.

The girl started reading, and Anna sat there bored out of her skull. I just can't wait for this to be over, she thought. Most of the others looked like they felt the same way and were acting restless and twitchy. Alice was kicking her own chair with the backs of her shoes. The Bible moved around the circle slowly, all the girls reading in monotones, until it got to Maria. She took it from the girl next to her, and looked down at it, but she didn't open her mouth to speak.

Anna thought that maybe she couldn't read English, and felt bad for her. Adler didn't get mad, he just told Maria to hand the book off to the girl next to her, which happened to be the big, manly girl named Jennifer. Jennifer was chunky enough that she looked really uncomfortable in the narrow chair.

"Continue, Cadet Tully."

"Okay," Jennifer said, in the most unenthusiastic voice possible. They were on Psalm 15, about usury and bribes. She started to read slowly, stumbling over the words, and hit a snag pretty quickly on the word "tabernacle."

"Tab— Tab—" she stuttered, over and over, like a skipping CD. Anna thought she was about to choke. Some of the girls started laughing at once, including Alice and Kelli, and Jennifer glared at them, her chin trembling but her eyes blazing with anger.

"Tabernacle," Adler said loudly. "The word is tabernacle."

"Tab— Tab—" mimicked Alice under her breath, but everyone heard her, so even more of the girls started laughing. Anna just felt sorry for Jennifer, because it was bad enough to be so big, but to have a stutter on top of it made it harder for her.

Jennifer finally managed to get the word out and then she snapped, "I'm not stupid just because I stutter. Fuck all you bitches."

"Cadet Tully," Adler said tonelessly. "This is a place of worship. Surely I don't have to explain that to you. Your bad language just highlights your ignorance and disrespect. Now continue reading until I say you can stop."

Anna could tell Jennifer was upset, but the girl kept on plugging though the rest of the psalm. Mostly she did okay, but twice more words caught her out, and girls giggled at her stutter again. Anna noticed that Adler made no move to stop them. Finally when he'd had enough, he told her to pass the book onward, with a sigh.

Eventually the Bible came to Anna, and she read from it quickly and quietly, and then passed it along. She was starting to get sleepy, and at one point her eyes closed and her head started to lower on her chest until she snapped back awake. Fortunately Adler didn't catch it, or she knew he would have been all over her. Finally the book made its way all around the circle, and Bible hour came to an end. She couldn't believe it was only eight-something P.M., because it felt like three in the morning.

Adler and McGathy took them back to their bunks through the hot night air, where Counselor Ellis was waiting again to handle the night shift.

"You all better get a good night's sleep!" Adler declared on his way out. "Tomorrow's the big hike and you need to be rested. Today was nothing!"

Anna noticed neither Kara nor Beth had reappeared. She was so tired that although some of the girls whispered among themselves about the horrors of the day, she took off her boots and pants and fell asleep almost at once.

Sometime in the night she woke up to the sound of the front door opening, and she saw that Kara was rejoining them, released from solitary confinement, she presumed. She looked away, not wanting to catch the girl's gaze, because she knew there was something dangerous about her.

Anna fell asleep again, dreaming that she'd escaped the island, but she awoke back to the harsh reality of her new life on Andros.

## Chapter Four

# Beneath the Flowers

In the morning at breakfast, Miss Richards briefed them on the hike. Anna felt so tired that her head was heavy, and she just wanted to rest it on the table and shut her eyes. She noticed many of the others looked the same way, including Erica and Stacey. Kara looked surprisingly good for some-one who'd spent part of the night in solitary. There was still no sign of Beth.

"As you know, today is your first major hike, one of many to come, and the first day you'll be going outside the grounds of Camp Archstone. At oh-seven hundred hours, you'll begin your journey to Clayton Peak, a rock formation ten miles southwest of here. It's one of the most impressive and best-known landmarks on Andros. You'll be hiking there in your two groups, divided by last names, as usual. Counselors McGathy and Brody will be leading the first group down the Nevis River to the Andros River Basin." She traced the route on the map of the island. "Clayton Peak is just a quarter mile from there. The second group will take a different route, guided by Counselor Adler and myself. We'll be following the Blue Hollow Trail. It goes inland, deeper into the forest past Diver's Gem, one of the largest blueholes on the island."

Anna had no idea what a bluehole was because no one had bothered to explain it to her, and she was just a little too far from the map to see it clearly. It looked like a pond or small lake.

"The two trails take the same amount of time," Miss Richards continued, "so both groups should converge at the peak at seventeen hundred hours. This will be a challenging hike for all of you, especially those who are out of shape and overweight. You'll be hiking with full gear, and will be responsible for carrying a backpack filled with provisions, as well as a light sleeping bag that attaches to the pack. You'll also need to carry your own food and water for the journey, which means you'll be hauling quite a load. When you arrive at Clayton Peak, the counselors and I will help you set up camp, because we'll all be spending the night out there."

Glum faces greeted that pronouncement. Anna knew it would be difficult to sleep outside in the heat, with the insects. However, it might be harder for the counselors to keep an eye on them outside.

"Tomorrow you'll wake up at oh-five hundred hours, eat breakfast, pack your gear, and begin the journey back to Camp Archstone." Miss Richards glanced at her watch. "It's five forty-five now. You have fifteen minutes to clear your plates and get your backpacks and equipment. Counselor Adler will dispense them in the room next door."

After breakfast, Anna followed the others and got her sleeping bag and backpack. She was also given the necessary provisions to put inside, including sandwiches, energy bars, two water canteens, and a blank notebook to record her thoughts. Fully loaded, the backpacks were huge and heavy, and Anna had no idea how she'd carry hers for more than ten minutes, let alone on a twenty-mile hike.

When they got outside, Miss Richards was waiting for Anna's group with another lecture for them. Anna thought the lectures were probably meant to inspire them, but she just found them depressing.

"Girls, this trail is hard," Miss Richards told them. "There will be five twenty-minute rest stops along the way, one for lunch at twelve hundred hours and two on either side of it. You must keep pace with me and the rest of the group, or else you'll get left behind. I'm sure there won't be any stragglers, because I won't allow you to put in less than one hundred-and-ten percent."

Anna thought she sounded exactly like her high school gym teacher.

Adler, who was standing behind her, stepped forward and said, "You need to stay on the trail at all times. Consider Andros an environment hostile to spoiled brats like yourselves. If you leave the trail, there's a good chance we'll never find you again. This island is eighty percent mahogany and pine forest, with mangrove swamps in between, and most of it is unexplored. It's the largest island in the Bahamas, more than one hundred miles long and sixty miles wide, and like Miss Richards said yesterday, it's mostly uninhabited, except for the eastern coast. Any of you who leave the trail and are found will be severely disciplined and forcibly restrained. So if you feel like running off, I'd strongly encourage you to reconsider."

Anna got the feeling he was talking to her when he said that last part, but she was too tired to run again, so he didn't have to worry. At least not yet.

Miss Richards consulted her watch and picked up her own backpack, which Anna noticed was much smaller than the ones the girls were carrying. Anna could see the other group from her class already heading out through the gates and into the forest.

"Okay, cadets. Forward march," she said, and Anna's line began to move. Adler fell into step right behind her. She walked with her fellow inmates through the gates of the camp and down the driveway, and the gravel crunched loudly under her boots. Camp Archstone was so dismal and con-formist, she felt like she'd just joined the army or something. They turned off the gravel road and onto a narrow path that led into the woods.

At least getting out from behind the barbed wire is a step in the right direction, Anna thought, although she didn't know yet how she could use it to her advantage.

"Step it up!" Anna heard Miss Richards call from the front. "Pick up the rhythm, cadets. Feel it!" The line lurched forward clumsily. Anna was stiff and tired, hot and thirsty, too.

Within five minutes of beginning the hike, she was ready to sit down and rest. The trail was so narrow, it was barely a trail at all. The forest floor was lined with wet leaves, and palm fronds clawed at Anna's elbows from both sides of the path. Far above her, the treetops were so thick they blotted out the sun and allowed only a faint light to permeate the trail. The underbrush was heavy at the sides of the path, and wild purple orchids bloomed from rotting tree trunks. Some of the trees were covered with creeping vines that extended tendrils across the pathway, and technicolor mushrooms sprouted in patches under Anna's feet. It was still incredibly humid, even though Anna wasn't directly exposed to the sun anymore.

She took in all the visual stimuli and wished she had a way to record it. More great photos I'll never take, she thought dully, as she saw a colorful bird, maybe a parrot, fly past in the trees. Having her camera would have transformed the whole tragic, pointless experience into something worthwhile. She swatted at a mosquito and brooded.

Kelli was moving slowly in front of her, and she could hear her breathing hard. Sometimes Kelli stumbled and Anna had to avoid bumping into her. Anna could hear Adler's footsteps behind her and felt boxed in and claustrophobic. Once or twice she glanced back and saw his dark eyes staring, almost as if he were looking through her, like she wasn't there at all.

As Anna walked, she maneuvered her way over broken tree branches and around jagged rocks. She thought if her dad were right, and hell actually existed, surely it wouldn't be too different from Camp Archstone. It was going to be a long ten miles, that much was obvious.

Slowly and painfully, Anna and the girls moved farther from the safety of the camp and snaked their way deeper into the shadows of the forest. It had seemed very quiet at first, but as Anna walked, she picked up on all kinds of sounds. She heard constant birdcalls and squawks, and around her the trees buzzed with the noise of teeming insect life. The air was thick with mosquitoes, and small gnats swarmed greedily over her eyes and lips if she stopped moving for more than a second. The impossible heat didn't seem to bother them at all. Anna tried not to think about the other creatures that probably made their homes in the tangled underbrush. She was okay with lizards and sand crabs, but she didn't want to encounter any spiders or snakes.

The sounds of the forest were often drowned out by the noises the girls made, and by Miss Richards's occasional commands to drink water and keep moving. Anna's canteens, which hung from loops on the sides of her backpack, got heated by the sun and the water picked up the foul taste of plastic. Disgusting, she thought, but she drank it anyway.

All the other girls were having problems. Anna could tell Kelli was struggling more than she was, because the girl was gasping loudly for air. Anna was grossed out by the way her own body felt and smelled. Her tank top was soaked with sweat, and her feet were marinating inside her uncomfortable boots. I'd give anything to be back inside, she thought, cool and dry in the air-conditioning. This hike is insane.

The line of girls stopped after several hours for their first long break. They shed their backpacks and slumped on logs and rocks at the edge of the trail, making noises of exhaustion and discontent. Anna felt like she'd been hiking for days already. Her feet hurt from where the boots chafed her skin, and her legs felt shaky and unsteady.

"We're only partway there, cadets," Miss Richards said, walking up and down the trail in front of them. "You have to keep your energy up and make sure you stay hydrated." Most of the girls barely acknowledged her.

"So now you're too tired to act crazy!" Adler announced. "Is that right?" To Anna there was something pretty sadistic about his enjoyment of their misfortune. He took out his own water bottle and took a deep swig.

With such constant supervision, it was impossible for Anna to talk to the other girls, so she felt like she was alone. Not that she wanted to make friends, but at least Erica and Stacey could commiserate with her. She supposed isolation wasn't really a completely new feeling for her. Maybe she was just insecure, but even when she seemed totally accepted by her friends, she worried that no one really knew her, and maybe no one ever would. Anna had hoped for a chance at a real connection and relationship with Mr. Spate, but of course that had gone wrong in the worst possible way. And now her relationship with Ryan was going to get fucked-up, too.

To take her mind off it, Anna looked over at the other girls. Kelli and Stacey were sitting next to her, and they both looked like they were dying from the heat as much as she was. Kelli because she was too fat, and Stacey because she was too thin and scrawny. Erica looked fine.

Anna's eyes drifted onward to the other girls. Maria was perched on a rock sipping water, and Laura sat next to her, flushed and sweaty. Then there was Kara, her long legs kicked out in front of her and her blonde hair pulled back tightly. Anna had to admit she'd been fascinated by her from the start, the curve of her lips and her startling blue eyes. Kara had the kind of face you couldn't help staring at, a face designed for guys to desire and girls to be jealous of. Not that Anna considered herself bad looking, but Kara represented a more unattainable standard of beauty, like Cameron Diaz or something. Her time in solitary confinement hadn't seemed to affect her at all.

"Cadets!" Miss Richards called out, way too soon for Anna's liking. "Break's over. It's time to get moving." The girls grumbled, but got to their feet. Anna was ready for lunch, and for the hike to be over. She'd rather write a thousand essays about why she was a fuckup than do any more hiking. "Next stop is in two hours," Miss Richards declared. "So no slacking!" The hike began again.

As Anna settled into a fluid rhythm, her thoughts started to drift. Mr. Spate kept trying to come back into her head, and she wondered if she'd ever be able to get him out of there. She tried to speculate what he was doing right at that moment. Maybe he was in his darkroom, putting the moves on some other dumb high school girl.

What her dad didn't know was that it wasn't Ryan at all who'd gotten her pregnant, but of all people, her photography teacher. Someone she'd really trusted. Someone she'd thought had loved her.

Anna pulled back from those thoughts because they were too upsetting, and she didn't want to have a breakdown in front of everyone. There was a great, dark void inside her that the abortion had left, and she was afraid to explore it too much for fear it might overwhelm her.

She could think about her dad, though, and how much she hated him. When, or if, she ever got out of this hellhole, she was going to run away for good. She wished she could think of a way to hurt him as much as he'd hurt her. She could never go back to her school after being away for three months. In high school time, three months was like three decades. It would be too humiliating to come slinking back, because everyone would know where she'd been. How could she face them?

Anna had seen it happen before. In seventh grade, a popular girl named Stefanie had moved away with her family to Cincinnati for a year. When she came back everything had changed and she wasn't accepted anymore. Stefanie ended up making a whole new batch of friends, uncool kids she wouldn't have even talked to a year before. Anna didn't want to end up like that.

The minutes dragged past and she estimated they must have walked at least four miles total so far. She wondered what time it was. The camp didn't allow them watches, for some stupid reason. Anna's feet hurt a lot, especially her left heel, which was throbbing. How did they think this hike was going to help her grow as a person? It wasn't going to help her learn anything except how important comfortable shoes were.

"You're slowing down," Anna heard a voice say angrily behind her. "Don't slow down. Can't you keep pace with the rest of us?" It was Adler. She'd almost forgotten he was there for a second. She looked up and saw she'd lagged a few steps behind Kelli.

"Sorry," she muttered and picked up the pace.

"Don't be sorry, just do it right."

What a prick, she thought.

Right then, Kelli came to a sudden halt and Anna almost tumbled into her. The line of girls had stopped moving.

"Okay, cadets," Miss Richards's voice came down the path

to her. "Attention, up front. We had a storm here last week and there's some debris in the trail. Be careful. I don't want you hurting yourselves." The line began moving again, slower than before. Anna soon found herself climbing gingerly over splintered tree limbs. Knowing Adler was close behind compelled her to keep moving quickly. Sometimes she heard him muttering and cursing under his breath, and it made her happy to know he was suffering, too.

A few minutes later, Anna heard a loud snapping sound, and a girl in the middle of the line stumbled into the underbrush. Anna came to an abrupt halt and cringed, expecting Adler to knock into her, but he didn't.

"Miss Richards," a thin voice called out, sounding shaky. "I need help."

Anna stepped sideways off the edge of the trail to get a better look at what was going on, but it was hard to see over all the girls and their backpacks. Miss Richards was squeezing her way back past some of them to get to one who sat awkwardly in the brush. Anna saw it was Amelia, a girl with long brown hair and acne-spotted cheeks. She seemed normal enough, but Anna hadn't talked to her so far.

"What's wrong?" Adler asked brusquely, pushing past Anna on his way to the girl.

"I hurt myself. I slipped—"

Miss Richards knelt by the girl's side. "It's okay, Cadet Stevens. Let's have a look."

"Ew!" came another voice, one that Anna could tell belonged to Alice. "Check out her leg!"

"That's gross!" someone else cried out.

Anna jostled Kelli, but she still couldn't get a good view. She saw Kara leaning in to check out Amelia's injury, with that strange half smile on her face.

"Quiet!" Miss Richards commanded sternly. Adler bent down over Amelia, and Anna caught a glimpse of something red on Amelia's leg, probably blood. That's got to suck, Anna thought. The girl was starting to cry.

"What a pussy," Erica whispered loudly.

Kelli took the opportunity to sit down on the wet leaves, catching her breath, which gave Anna a better view. She and the rest of the girls clustered around the counselors.

"Can you get up?" Miss Richards asked Amelia.

"I don't know. It really hurts!"

Miss Richards stood and put a hand on her hip. Anna thought she looked worried. She conferred with Adler while Amelia moaned on the forest floor. Erica turned back to Anna and Stacey to report on the situation.

"Her leg is really fucked-up! It's all bloody, did you see? I think it might be broken."

Amelia's whimpers and moans turned into loud shrieks, because Miss Richards and Adler were trying to help her stand up. Fuck, I'm glad it's not me, Anna thought.

"Jesus, omigod, please!" Amelia was screaming. The girls looked on with curiosity. Some were sneering, while others seemed genuinely horrified at the unexpected development. Anna finally saw Amelia's leg for herself and realized what had happened. Part of a broken-off tree branch was sticking out of it, just above the ankle. Amelia had somehow skewered herself, and her orange pant leg had already turned dark red.

Anna felt sorry for the girl, but also grateful, because there was no way Amelia could continue with the hike. Now they'd all have to turn back to Archstone.

Amelia stood on one leg, supported by Miss Richards, tears coasting down her cheeks. "I stepped, and then I heard a noise— And then my leg— I don't know—"

"It's okay," Miss Richards said unconvincingly, as the girl leaned on her for support. "We'll take you back to camp and let the doctor take a look at it." The branch was still sticking out of Amelia's leg. Anna wondered why they didn't remove it, but maybe they were afraid the wound would bleed even more if they did.

Miss Richards talked into her radio for a while, but there was no response except static. Good, Anna thought. That meant they'd have to go back for sure. "Okay, cadets," she finally called out. "Change of plans. Gather 'round."

They obeyed, a lot of them whispering excitedly. Adler stood a little outside the group, watching them like a vulture.

"Cadet Stevens has injured herself, as all of you can see. I can't raise camp on the radio, so I'm going to take her back to Archstone for medical treatment myself. However, the rest of you will complete the hike with Counselor Adler as your group leader."

Some of the girls started cursing. Anna just felt like collapsing onto the leaves like Kelli. Still, at least it meant less supervision.

"Quiet! Nothing has changed. You'll continue on to Clayton Peak and rendezvous there with the other group, just as we planned."

"Amelia will be fine," Adler declared. "Though I doubt any

of you honestly care. We've lost a couple minutes here, but we can make the time up. We're going to meet group one at the peak at seventeen hundred hours, right on schedule. Amelia's accident should prove to all of you how seriously you must take this island. Miss Richards warned you to watch your step, and now you know why. Don't be stupid. Learn a lesson from it. Now, I want you to line up single file on the trail behind me, in order."

While he was speaking, Miss Richards had opened her backpack and taken out some white bandages. She wrapped them around Amelia's leg where they quickly turned red and did little to hide the bulge of the protruding stick.

"Forward march!" Adler commanded. "Come on, we don't have all day!" Reluctantly, the line started to move.

Anna stared at Amelia's leg as she passed. She didn't know how Miss Richards would be able to get Amelia back up the trail. She felt a flicker of fear for herself. Amelia's accident looked painful, and it had been completely unexpected. What if she got hurt out here? Now that Miss Richards was gone, she didn't really trust Adler to take care of her. I'd better be careful, she thought.

"The peak's not getting any closer!" Adler bellowed. "Unless you want to get lost, you'd better keep moving. I'm not slowing down for anyone, understand?"

Anna was relieved that at least he wasn't behind her anymore. With him up front, she was free to whisper with the other girls as they picked their way through the maze of broken branches.

"I'm glad that old bitch is gone," Erica whispered back to them.

"Did you see Amelia's leg?" Kelli asked, sounding a little dazed.

"Of course I saw it. All fucked up, like I said."

"Maybe they'll amputate it."

"Kelli, you're so stupid," Stacey replied, rolling her eyes. To Anna she looked like a little girl, a full head shorter than everyone else. "They'll just remove the branch, clean the wound, and suture it."

"How do you know?" Kelli asked. "Are you a doctor? What if she gets gangrene?"

"Shut up, both of you," Erica said. "You're getting annoying."

Just as Erica spoke, Anna's foot slipped on a rotten coconut and she flung out her arms to grasp at the trees. For a dizzying second she was afraid she might fall and end up like Amelia, but then she managed to recover her balance.

As her heartbeat slowed, it occurred to her that maybe getting hurt wasn't so bad after all. In fact, maybe it was the answer, because they'd have to send her home then. She turned the notion over in her mind for a second or two, but rejected it because she hated the idea of inflicting pain on herself, and there was no guarantee it would work.

"This is some boring shit," she heard Erica mutter loudly. "It's so goddamn hot out here!"

"No kidding," Anna whispered back. To her, walking through the forest was like wading at the bottom of a deep, green ocean, albeit an ocean that was over one hundred degrees. Glimmers of light penetrated the foliage like rays sparkling through the depths. Anna thought she might have liked this subterranean landscape more if she hadn't been a prisoner, and if she'd been allowed to bring her camera. She felt as though she were in a trance, like that strange realm between sleeping and waking. She was hundreds of miles from home, and felt a nervous energy that was equal parts homesickness and fear of what the future might hold.

"Halt!" she heard Adler call out.

The line stopped.

"I hear talking!"

Two girls near the middle of the line, Shelly and Jennifer, had been chatting about boys.

"There'll be none of that," Adler said. "You don't want to test me, so cool it. Keep quiet and stay focused."

Anna shifted, trying to ease the heavy burden of her backpack.

"God, I hate that guy," Erica whispered.

Anna nodded. "Me too."

They started walking again, even slower than before, climbing fallen trees, pushing branches out of their faces. The frame of the backpack dug into Anna's spine, and there was no way to make it comfortable. The trail virtually disappeared at one point and Anna was just blindly following Kelli. She thought at this pace it would probably take them all twelve weeks of camp just to reach the peak.

"Counselor Adler?" one of the girls called out. It was Lindsay. Her blue hair was now disheveled and grimy. "I have to go to the bathroom."

None of the girls laughed. The thought of the humiliation of stopping the line to squat in the undergrowth and pee in front of everyone just wasn't funny.

"All right," Adler said. The line ceased its motion. "You get two minutes."

"Counselor Adler?" the girl asked again, embarrassed. "My stomach . . . I think it was the melons at breakfast."

He sighed angrily. "Five minutes then. Move it."

"But I need toilet paper."

"What?!" He climbed back over a splintered branch to confront the girl. "You have a roll in your pack, dammit."

"I know, but my canteen leaked all over it. I guess I didn't screw the top on tight enough. I put it in my bag by mistake, and the whole thing flooded."

"There are no extra rolls," Adler said. His voice sounded cruel. "Just because you're careless doesn't mean that someone else has to come along and help you out. That kind of attitude is probably what got you sent here in the first place. You carry your own in this world, that's just the way it is. Use the wet roll to wipe your ass, or dry yourself the natural way. The forest isn't gonna run out of leaves."

Lindsay stood there, unsure and humiliated.

"Clock's ticking, Cadet Taylor."

"You can borrow my roll," Stacey called out, and the girl looked at her with relief in her eyes. Her gratitude was short-lived, however, because Adler blocked the transaction.

"Uh-uh. No way," he proclaimed. "No sharing. You have to take responsibility for your own actions. I'm sure it's hard for you girls to conceive of that idea, but that's how it works here."

Lindsay looked like she wanted to cry, but then something stopped her. Maybe she remembered how Adler had treated Laura the day before, Anna thought. Lindsay turned slowly and walked into the forest, out of view of Anna and the rest of the girls.

"Five minutes," Adler called out. "Then we're leaving you."

The girls waited. Anna's shoulders throbbed and her lower back ached. Surely it was almost time for another rest, or lunch?

Adler stared at the girls, particularly Kara. "I bet you didn't think you'd end up cooling your heels on Andros," he crowed. "None of the comforts of home out here. You better get used to it. This place is a walk in the park compared to juvie, which is where most of you were headed. Be glad your parents are rich." He smirked and glanced at his watch. "Two more minutes, Cadet Taylor!" he yelled.

A few of the girls swayed back and forth in the heat. Anna was surprised no one had fainted yet, and could only guess it was coming. She just hoped it wouldn't be her.

"Time's up," Adler finally said. "Line up, single file." It was hard to line up with so much debris in the path, but Anna did her best. Lindsay tumbled out of the forest and took her place in the line.

"I bet she couldn't even go," Kelli snickered.

The girls began their long walk again, down a nonexistent trail. Anna looked back at one point and saw only thick forest behind her. If she took off running, she could probably escape Adler and the rest of the group. However, she had no idea where she was, so running would be pointless. She could hear Adler's voice calling out to them from the front of the line.

"Keep up the pace! This isn't a stroll in the country, cadets." He was cackling. "Maybe some music will help you." He started to sing, military-style: "I'm a spoiled and selfish brat! My parents sent me off to camp!" He laughed again.

"Come on, sing along with me." No one sang. "What's wrong, girls? We got miles and miles to go." He seemed jubilant.

Anna stepped onto a fallen tree trunk in the path and jumped off. There was no fucking way she was going to sing along with that asshole.

It was then that she heard the sound, a sharp crack, much louder than the noise the tree branch made when it snapped and went into Amelia's leg. In fact, it was so loud, Anna's ears went fuzzy for a second. It sounded a lot like a gunshot, she thought.

"Get down!" Adler's shout came through the trees. All the fun had dropped out of his voice in an instant. Anna fell to her knees because she didn't know what the hell was happening, and she saw some of the other girls doing the same. "Dammit, get down!" he yelled again. The rest of the girls sank with their packs to the forest floor and crouched in the underbrush. There was a second cracking noise, and Anna jammed her fingers in her ears. Was someone firing a gun at them? At first she was too puzzled to be scared.

"Stay down," she heard Adler instruct. He sounded really concerned, and that made her worry, too. She'd been thinking maybe this was all part of some drill, a survival test or something, but the tension in Adler's voice seemed genuine. "Move toward the sound of my voice, and stay low!" Anna and the others began to find their way carefully to him, sneaking through the underbrush.

They must have been gunshots, Anna thought. She couldn't think of another explanation. Someone must be firing a gun in the forest, and close, by the sound of it. She felt very exposed, even though the dense brush engulfed her completely. Soon she was with the other girls, crouching in a big bunch around Adler at the base of a tree.

"What's going on?" Jennifer asked.

"Shhh!" Adler hissed. "Keep it down." His voice was low and insistent. "Some asshole's firing a pistol out there. It's not hunting season, so it must be a poacher. Maybe worse." His words brought home the reality of the situation, and Anna felt a surge of fear. Surely the forest was safe? The camp wouldn't risk taking the girls somewhere dangerous, would they?

Adler took out the radio he carried on his belt and spoke into it, but no one responded. "Shit!"

"What are we going to do?" Jennifer whispered. Her face was beet red and sweat dripped down her chin.

"Shut up, and let me think."

"Were they firing at us?" Laura whimpered.

"No more questions!" Adler snapped. "We're going to sit here and wait it out. Whoever it is will move on, and then we can continue our hike."

They sat in silence for several minutes that seemed like forever to Anna. Kara used the time to retie her ponytail. Adler finally rose to his feet when there were no more gunshots, and no signs anyone else was in the forest with them.

"You can get up now, cadets. It's okay. I'll report the incident when we get back to camp." He spat into the brush. "Fucking poachers."

The girls stood warily, all except for Kelli, who for some reason, remained cringing in the underbrush. Anna wondered what was wrong with her.

"Cadet Wardle, get up," Adler commanded.

"But I'm scared!"

"I understand that, but we're going to keep moving, and you're coming with us. You don't want to get left here, do you?"

"I don't want to get shot!"

"You won't get shot," Adler sighed, "but you *will* get five demerits if you don't get up and continue this hike immediately. Come on now."

"I'm tired of walking! I can't take it anymore. I need a break."

"That is not an option, cadet."

"But I can't do it!" Kelli wailed, her fat face breaking into tears. Anna felt a mixture of sympathy and revulsion. She was scared, too, but she wasn't going to pieces. Even Laura wasn't crying and freaking out. Didn't Kelli understand it was probably dangerous to stay where they were?

"I'm counting to three," Adler said. "If you're not on your feet by then, I'm going to walk over there and give you a big old kick in the ass. Now's not the time to fuck around with me."

Kelli was still crying and tried to hide her face in her hands.

"She's just scared," Stacey spoke out. "Can't you see that?"

Adler turned toward her. "Why are you always mouthing off, you little runt? Keep your trap shut unless you want some grief, too."

"I'm not afraid of you," Stacey replied calmly, but Anna noticed she looked away from him as she said it, down at the leaves.

Adler looked back at Kelli. "Last chance, Cadet Wardle." He began to count slowly. "One . . . two . . . three . . ."

Kelli made no move to stand up, but just sat there blubbering, so Adler walked over and stood behind her. She shrank away from him, but not quickly enough. He grabbed her under the arms and violently yanked her to her feet.

"Ouch!" she yelped. "You're hurting me! Stop it!"

Adler stepped back and slapped her twice across the face, hard. "Control yourself! Don't be so pathetic!"

Anna was stunned. There was a gasp from a couple of the girls, as Kelli's cries became big, gut-wrenching sobs.

"Hey, you can't hit her like that," Stacey said.

"Yeah," Erica jumped in. "What's your deal?"

"It's breaking the rules to hit us, isn't it?" added Kara, but she was smiling as though she were amused. It was the first thing Anna had heard her say since she'd gotten back from solitary confinement.

Adler looked enraged as his eyes darted back and forth between the girls. "You all better shut up and listen to me if you want to get out of this forest alive! I'm the boss here, make no mistake. I know this trail and you don't. Without me, you're dead meat. You'd better do as I say and cut out all this bullshit. You need to start walking and stop yacking."

Someone snorted with derision, but no one was brave enough to say anything else. Kelli continued to cry, but at least she was still standing up.

"Amelia's accident and some goddamn poachers aren't any reason for you to challenge my authority or lose your self-control. I slapped Kelli because she was acting hysterical. You need to stay calm and focused out here. Didn't I tell you Andros was a hostile environment? Didn't I?" He paused. "Now, we're going to proceed as planned, understand me?"

"Yes, sir," a few of the girls mumbled.

"Good."

It was then that Anna got the feeling something really bad was about to happen. She couldn't explain the sensation, and had only felt it a few times before in her life. It compressed her lungs, sucked the air out of her chest, and made her feel like she was floating a few inches in front of her own body. Adler continued to talk, but she wasn't hearing his words. She looked around at the other girls, sweaty with exertion and dirty from the grime of the forest. It was like she was seeing them in slow motion. She looked back at Adler and his mouth was open, just beginning a sentence.

It seemed like he was staring directly into her eyes when she heard the sound of the third gunshot. A red flower bloomed on his throat, right beneath his chin, and something sprayed out the back of his neck. Anna saw his eyes turn quizzical, puzzled, and his mouth remained open.

Some of the girls heard the sound, but didn't realize what had happened to their counselor. Anna was transfixed by how he stood there pale like a ghost, stunned as blood pumped down his shirt. She heard a thin screaming sound, like air being let out of a tire, and realized it was coming from his wound.

Anna felt like she was going into shock. Adler tried to speak, but no one was listening to him anymore. He crumpled to the forest floor, hands clutching his throat.

"Get down!" Stacey yelled, and then the voices all came at once, a chaotic jumble of terror.

"Run!"

"Look out!

"Oh my God!"

Another gunshot came, like the crack of a whip, and Anna's reflexes took over. She sprinted away from Adler and the group, running blindly into the forest, branches lacerating her face. Her flight set off a chain reaction, and the screaming girls fled, trying to get away as fast as they could. They scattered off the trail, some in pairs, but many alone. Anna only knew she had to escape the horror of what she'd seen.

The trees rushed by in a blur and she flung herself forward violently, sliding under thick vines and tearing back tree limbs. She ran for what seemed like miles, until she could run no more. Her legs burned and her chest heaved, and she felt like she was going to pass out. She collapsed into a pile of leaves below a huge, knotted tree, hidden from view, and stared out at the forest. What the fuck had just happened? It seemed like a dream, and she had to keep reminding herself it was real.

She looked down and noticed her hands and arms were shaking and covered with scratches, some of which oozed blood. Her face felt scratched up, too. She was surprised to realize she was still wearing her heavy backpack.

When Anna calmed down and recovered her breath, she struggled not to panic, but had the sinking feeling she was fucked. There was no sign of the person who'd shot Adler, but there was also no sign of anyone else. Anna realized she'd got completely lost in her frenzy to escape. Other than the whine of the insects and the cry of an occasional tropical bird, the forest was quiet, baking gently in the heat. A weird, pink plant bloomed to the left of her, emitting a sickly sweet odor, and twenty feet above was the green canopy of the treetops.

She was too scared to move, even though her position at the base of the tree was uncomfortable. She was terrified that whoever had shot Adler would keep shooting and accidentally hit her. She pressed her body up against the tree trunk. Its bark was gnarled and torn in places, and lichen grew on it in muted greens and yellows. She hid there, recovering her strength, and trying not to think about Adler's throat.

The more time passed, the more she realized she didn't know what to do. In fact, she had absolutely no idea how to survive in a forest on a desolate island. She hid until the sun began to move lower in the sky and the light filtered between the trees in abrupt angles. What would happen when it got dark? She hoped the people from the camp were already searching for them, and she wouldn't have to face that situation.

She realized that after what had happened she'd surely be sent home, and could dismiss the island as a fragment of a nightmare. She wondered what had happened to the other girls, and if any of them had been shot, too. She'd witnessed a fatal accident, maybe a murder, and the police would want to talk to her and ask her questions. The whole thing was impossible to believe.

Anna eventually decided she'd keep low and try to find her way back to the trail. She wasn't prepared to spend the night outdoors, especially if there was a man with a gun on the loose. She stood up and resettled her pack. Then she began to walk, a lone figure stumbling through the wilderness without any sense of direction.

Anna walked for hours. Her relief at surviving the shooting was giving way to a new set of fears. She'd never been lost like this before. No one knew where she was, and she couldn't find any semblance of a trail. The forest all looked the same to her, and there were no landmarks to rely on, just endless trees that stretched in every direction. She tried to look up at the sun, but the forest was so dense it was hard to get a position from it. She knew the sun would set in the west, but she didn't know where she was in relation to the camp. She just walked in what she thought was Archstone's general direction.

In the intense heat, she'd nearly exhausted her canteens, and she knew the remaining water wouldn't last long. She had a stash of four chocolate energy bars, two apples, and three liquefied peanut butter and jelly sandwiches in plastic bags. Her food and water would run out in a day. What if she were stuck for longer than that? She put the thought out of her head, rejecting it as inconceivable.

They know where we are, she thought. It won't take them long to find us, and then I can get off this fucking island for good.

As Anna walked, she considered her options, but there weren't too many. At one point she sat down on a flat rock and nearly started crying out of frustration and fear. Instead, she took out one of the energy bars and unwrapped it. It tasted like cardboard and chalk and she could only eat half. Her stomach hurt because of all the running, and because she was so scared.

It's going to be okay, she told herself. Don't flip out, and you'll be fine. But the forest was gradually becoming darker as the sun started to set, and the drone of the insects increased as nighttime grew closer. She felt rising terror at the prospect of sleeping outside alone, but she forced it down. She wasn't weak. If she could get through an abortion, and being shot at, she could get through this. She'd do whatever had to be done, like the people on *Survivor.* Or at least that's what she told herself. In reality, she felt scared out of her mind.

She resumed walking until it got so dark she couldn't see more than a foot in front of her face. So far she'd seen very few animals other than squirrels and lizards, but she knew a lot of creatures only came out at night. She'd heard about people lost in the woods who climbed into trees to sleep, but this seemed unlikely because there weren't any trees with large enough branches around her.

Anna looked around and found a hollow beneath a twisted mangrove tree. She felt reassured by the size and strength of its roots, so she settled at the base of it for the night, nearly enveloped by the massive roots, which rose high aboveground. Her haven had a thick odor of damp leaves and mold, but she didn't care. As long as she was hidden from view, she'd be okay. Or so she hoped.

She unrolled her sleeping bag and used her orange jacket as a pillow. She knew she needed sleep, but it was completely impossible given the circumstances, and her eyes constantly scanned the gloom of the forest. At night everything seemed much worse.

Please let me get out of here, she prayed inwardly. Please let them find me as soon as fucking possible.

She wondered if the person who'd shot Adler was still out there. She shuddered and curled up in her sleeping bag, too scared to close her eyes. The image of Adler getting shot kept floating back into her mind like she was reliving the moment. How could her dad have sent her to a place like this? Didn't he care about her at all? She thought about how all the people who mattered to her, Ryan and all her friends, had no idea where she was, or what she'd just seen. Anna felt very alone.

She was bone tired, but didn't fall asleep until it was light, and then she slept only for a few hours. When she awoke, a scrawny figure she recognized was standing over her, calling her name.

**Chapter Five**

## The Bluehole

"Anna," the figure said, its tiny frame backlit by the sun so it was just a dark silhouette. "Come on, wake up. Are you okay? You look pretty bad."

"Stacey?" Anna sat up, blinking the sleep away. She rubbed her eyes hard. Her sense of relief at seeing Stacey was overwhelming. Thank God, Anna thought. Thank fucking God someone's found me.

"I got water if you need it." Stacey held out a canteen and Anna drank gratefully. "There's plenty of water for us now. We found a bluehole, a freshwater one not far from here."

"We?" That meant there had to be others.

"Maria, Erica, and me. Everyone scattered and ran after . . . after what happened." Anna realized Stacey couldn't bring herself to say it. "Erica and I ran together for a while and ended up at the bluehole. Then last night Maria wandered in and found us."

Anna wiped her mouth on the back of her arm.

"We haven't found anyone else yet," Stacey continued. "We turned the bluehole into our campsite. Erica and Maria are there right now, but I went looking for food. All we have are coconuts, and there are supposed to be pineapples and bananas on Andros. So you're okay, right?"

"I guess so." Anna felt dazed, but Stacey didn't seem to notice.

"Good. Me too. We slept in shifts last night to keep guard. It must have been hard out here all by yourself."

"Yeah," Anna said, getting to her feet. "I didn't sleep until early this morning." Her hair was a tangled mess with bits of leaves in it, and her arms and legs ached. Her neck was so stiff it was hard for her to turn it and she tried to massage the pain away. The forest was saturated with that weird green glow again.

"If we stick together we'll be all right. There's no point looking for the trail, or trying to hike out of here. If we just camp at the bluehole, the rescue team will find us."

Stacey sounded so sure of herself, it was comforting. "You think so?"

"I know they will. Erica wants to try walking east to the coast, where the towns are, but that's not a very smart idea. I think the best thing to do in an emergency like this one is to stay put. We're not too far from the trail, and if we start running around in the forest, we'll get even more lost. We have lots of water, but other than fruit, food will be hard to find. I guess we can live off it if we have to."

"I'm glad you're so calm," Anna said. Honestly, she thought Stacey was a little too calm. How could anyone be so calm after what they'd seen? "I'm totally freaked out," she admitted, "I mean, after what happened. It didn't seem real, like a movie."

"I know, but it's very real. We have to stay sane and think straight so we can get out of here."

Anna was relieved Stacey had her wits about her, and she supposed it made her feel better about the situation. It was funny, though, Anna knew, because in real life she'd probably never hang out with a girl who looked like Stacey. But here in the forest Stacey was a lifesaver.

"Thank you," Anna said.

Stacey looked back at her. "For what?"

"For finding me."

Stacey smiled. "No problem. Let's get your stuff." She helped Anna pack up her sleeping bag, and Anna strapped it to her backpack and hoisted it over her shoulders. It felt even heavier than yesterday. As the two girls walked through the forest, Anna was suddenly afraid Stacey might not be able to find her way back to the others at the bluehole. "You know where you're going, right?"

"Of course. I've got an excellent sense of direction."

"I'm glad to hear it, because I sure don't. Everything looks the same out here."

Stacey nodded. "You just have to know what you're looking for."

The island seemed less menacing to Anna now that Stacey was with her. Neither of them talked about the shooting yet, maybe because it was too scary. Anna tried not to think about it. Along the way, they stopped at a tree thick with large scarlet berries that hung from its limbs like grapes. It stood out from all the other foliage.

"I think these are marsleberries," Stacey said. "I remember reading about them when I researched Andros. They're safe."

Anna was a little skeptical. "Are you sure?"

"No." Stacey grabbed a bunch and pulled them off, staining her hands red. She held some out to Anna. "Why don't you try one and see what happens."

Was she serious? "I think I'll pass. I don't want to get poisoned or anything."

"Suit yourself." Stacey took a couple berries, tentatively put them in her mouth, and chewed. "They're okay. Kind of bitter." She swallowed. "They taste a lot like cranberries."

"I think I'll hold out for the pineapples and bananas," Anna said. "God, why did you want to come to this place? I think I'd rather go to juvie for eight months."

Stacey grabbed some more berries. "I'm not the type of girl who could go to juvie and come out okay. I'm too small. Besides, I like to travel and I'd never been to the Bahamas. Now I can say that I have."

"Fuck, I don't think it was worth it."

"I guess not." Stacey put the berries in the back flap of Anna's pack. "We'll take these back for Maria and Erica. They're probably starving."

"Do you think the person with the gun is still out there?" Anna suddenly asked.

Stacey frowned and licked her palms. It was like she didn't want to think about it, either. "I don't know. I hope not."

"I guess there's not much we can do if he is."

The two girls continued walking in the morning heat. Stacey took a notepad out of her pocket and scribbled something in the blank pages. Anna had forgotten about the notepads. They'd each been given one in which to write down their most intimate thoughts.

"What are you doing?" she asked.

"I'm making a map. I'm marking down where the berries are so we can come back here if we need to. It's good to know where the different food sources are located."

There's no fucking way I'm going to live off berries, Anna thought. "Don't you think they'll find us soon?"

"Sure I do, but it's good to be careful."

"They're going to send us back home after this." Anna almost grinned at the thought, but the smile faded quickly when she remembered the shooting. "They can't make us stay after what we saw, right?"

"Let's hope not."

"You don't think they would?"

"Probably not, but anything's possible. I'm sure this isn't the first bad accident that's happened out here."

"It's more than just some accident," Anna said.

Stacey didn't reply to that.

When they arrived at the bluehole, Anna realized she'd spent the night less than half a mile from where the other girls had made their camp. The bluehole turned out to be a smooth, oval pond, roughly fifteen feet across at its widest point. To Anna, it looked like it had been scooped out of the ground by a giant spoon. The edges were lined with flat, gray rocks, which gave way to black mud and green grass. Trees surrounded the bluehole, and their branches hung down over the water, the leaves nearly touching the surface and providing shade from the sun.

On one side of the bluehole was a large pile of rocks, with a sheltering ledge that extended outward five feet above the ground. Anna could see three green sleeping bags spread out beneath it at the edge of the water, and realized that was where the other girls had spent the previous night.

"Hey!" Stacey called out when she and Anna arrived. "I'm back!" Maria was startled and jumped up, followed by Erica, who'd been dangling her legs in the blue water. "Look who I found."

"Anna!" Erica yelled back. "You made it, girl!" Anna dropped her pack on the ground, relieved to be rid of the weight, and ran to hug Erica. She was elated to see another friendly face after such a rough night. With Erica, Stacey, and Maria around, more of her fear started to subside.

"This shit is crazy," Erica said. "Can you believe it?" She noticed the scratches all over Anna's face and arms. "What happened to you?"

"I don't even know. I just ran as far as I could and then I stopped."

Erica laughed. "Same here." She paused. "So you slept outside last night by yourself?"

"Yeah, and it sucked. I can't believe no one's found us yet."

The girls sat at the edge of the water and talked about their predicament. The surface of the bluehole was placid and undisturbed, like a sheet of glass. For some weird reason, none of them talked about the murder. It didn't make any sense that they wouldn't, except whenever Anna was about to bring it up, she held back. Perhaps it was for the best, because here at the bluehole they were sitting ducks if somebody wanted to hurt them.

"We found some marsleberries," Stacey told Erica and Maria. "Don't worry, they're safe. I tried them myself." She opened the flap of Anna's pack and passed them around. "Now we have something to go with our coconuts and PowerBars."

Erica bit into one and made a face. "Disgusting."

"They're not so bad," Stacey remarked.

"They taste like shit. I want a cheeseburger and fries or something, not some nasty-ass berries."

Anna's mouth was watering at the thought of food. "I could go for some chocolate," she said.

"Yeah," Erica said excitedly. "And coffee and cigarettes, too."

Stacey smiled, but refused to get caught up in their daydream. "I think you guys are out of luck."

"Shit."

Anna noticed that during all their bantering, only Maria remained quiet. She tried to catch the girl's eye, but Maria kept looking away from her. What was up with that girl?

"She doesn't talk," Erica explained when she saw that Anna was staring. "Haven't you noticed yet? Stacey tried to get her to write stuff down, but she refused. We're not sure what her deal is."

"Maybe she just doesn't have anything to say," Stacey said.

"Maybe she's in shock?" Anna asked, but she knew that didn't make sense, because she'd never heard Maria talk, not even during Bible hour.

Maria smiled enigmatically at her.

"Maybe." Erica stood up. "Well, I've got plenty to say, like this island sucks and I'm ready to go home. I can't believe what happened to us. What the hell are we going to do?"

"We probably won't be stuck here too long," Anna said optimistically. "Someone's going to come and find us." This was her fervent wish, and she hoped if she repeated it enough then it might come true. She also knew it was in the best interest of the camp to find them fast, or there'd be a lot of angry parents for them to deal with.

"I think we should start walking," Erica said. "We can use the sun to find our way east to the coast, or we can look for the trail we were on."

"We'll never find the trail," Stacey said. "Be realistic. It was barely there to begin with. And we know the coast is east, but I'm not sure how our latitude affects our sense of direction. We don't know how far inland we are, either. This island is sixty miles wide, and that's a huge distance. And some of the island is just swamp that would be impossible to get across."

The girls fell silent and Erica looked like she was sulking. Stacey had brought them all down, Anna thought. Still, she was so grateful that Stacey had rescued her, she didn't want to criticize the girl for being pessimistic. "Maybe we can make a fire?" Anna proposed. "A signal so they know where we are?"

"Brainiac here already thought of that," Erica replied, gesturing at Stacey, who was now busy scrutinizing the map she'd drawn in her notebook. Maria watched, but kept her silence.

"We don't have any matches," Stacey explained to Anna, looking up from her work, "and I tried rubbing two sticks together, but I couldn't make anything happen. It's physically possible to start a fire that way, you know. I just couldn't do it. And none of us wear glasses so we can't do the *Lord of the Flies* thing, either."

*"Lord of the Flies?"* Anna remembered being assigned the book freshman year, but she'd just skimmed plot summaries online. Too boring, and all about twelve-year-old boys.

"They used the fat kid's glasses to focus the sun's rays."

"There's nothing to cook anyway," Erica complained. "If there was something to cook I'd figure out how to build a fire. I'm so starving I could eat a whole fucking pizza, a large one with pepperoni and mushrooms, and extra cheese, and I usually never eat crap like that."

"Maybe we can keep looking for pineapples," Stacey said.

"That'd be cool," Anna replied, although she really just wanted to sit and rest.

Erica stood up, rolled her head on her neck, and peered at the canopy of green. "I'm getting a really bad headache from the stress. I need some aspirin and caffeine, or a Percocet. You ever tried those? They're great for hangovers and PMS. I used to steal them from my mom."

It seemed weird to be talking about such mundane stuff like headaches after what they'd seen. "I still have a few PowerBars left," Anna volunteered.

"Those things suck, but thanks anyway. Maybe Maria wants one?"

Anna offered one to Maria, who just shook her head and lowered her brown eyes. Anna wondered what she made of the whole mess.

"Hey Stacey, you know what?" Erica asked. Anna thought Erica was acting kind of hyper, maybe as a way to deal with her anxiety.

"What?"

"Maybe Maria can't talk because she's missing her tongue. That's something we didn't think of yet. Hey Maria, you do have a tongue, right?"

"Oh, I'm sure she can talk," Stacey affirmed. "She just chooses not to for some reason."

A cloud of pink butterflies drifted in from the forest, flitted over the surface of the water, and then disappeared. Anna thought about her camera again. The scenery here was beautiful, but Adler's death had tainted it beyond belief, and she couldn't shake the feeling that more bad things were going to happen to them before they got rescued.

The girls spent a leisurely day at the bluehole, splitting coconuts on rocks and eating the white meat within. Anna tried to eat her sandwiches, but they'd transformed themselves into sticky goop. Several times the girls stripped to their underwear and swam in the water to cool off. Anna noticed that Erica had black tattoos all over her back, including a Queens of the Stone Age pitchfork logo on her shoulder.

Erica caught her staring, so Anna called out, "Nice tattoos."

"Thanks, man." Erica waved back at her. "My brother's best friend did some of them for free."

Anna had always wanted a tattoo herself, just a little red heart on her hip or on the small of her back, but she was scared of both the pain and her dad's reaction. He'd practically gone ballistic when her mother had taken her to get her ears pierced, and she'd been twelve already. Mr. Spate didn't like tattoos, either, and had said only sailors and rock stars should be allowed to get them. She hadn't known if he'd been serious or just joking around.

The bluehole was cooler than the air, but still warm, and to Anna it felt like being engulfed in a giant, relaxing bath. The temperature of the water and the gentle motion of swimming soothed her aching muscles and made her feel sleepy.

At one point Anna and the girls thought they heard the faint sounds of a helicopter above them, but although they stood on top of the rock ledge yelling and straining to look, they couldn't see anything through the branches and leaves. Anna realized, in an ironic way, she'd gotten exactly what she'd wanted, and escaped from Camp Archstone. There were no more stupid softball games, Bible readings, or threats of being medicated, only the island itself to contend with.

It was shocking to think that it was already Sunday. It was the first Sunday she could remember that her dad hadn't dragged both her and her mom to church with him. Tomorrow the school week would start and probably everyone would be talking about her disappearance. She wished she could hear what they'd say. It would be sort of like attending her own funeral. Probably some bitch would be hitting on Ryan already, Anna mused, and it took a lot of effort not to think about what Mr. Spate would be doing.

When dusk finally came, the light gently draining from the forest, Anna felt surprised and dismayed that they hadn't been found. Surely they hadn't wandered that far from the trail? She remembered what Adler had said about Andros being mostly unexplored wilderness, but Stacey was smart and Stacey thought they'd get found soon, so Anna believed that they would. She was pretty bummed at spending yet another night outdoors, although it wouldn't be as bad now that she wasn't alone.

At night the island thrummed to life like an engine, and the noise of the crickets became a mechanical drone. It was impossible to keep all the gnats off her, so eventually she gave up. Anna thought at least now she'd have a good, if horrific, story to tell for the rest of her life. It was strange how all the books and movies about people stranded in the wilderness were usually about men. Didn't girls have wilderness disasters, too? Maybe most girls were smart enough not to get stuck in the middle of nowhere, she finally thought.

Anna huddled in her sleeping bag under the rock ledge, next to the other girls. They hadn't forgotten about Adler and decided they'd take turns keeping watch during the night, just in case. Anna would go last and Stacey first.

The darkness made the island spooky again, and Anna knew it would be hard to sleep. She stared out from the safety of the ledge across the bluehole and into the forest. A strange phosphorescent glow came from some of the trees, and it reminded Anna of the night-vision feature on her dad's videocamera, grainy and green. Occasional birdcalls punctuated the crickets, as did more ominous sounds that Anna tried hard to ignore.

"I'm surprised we haven't heard more helicopters," she said to the others, lying in her sleeping bag, staring up at the underside of the ledge. None of them had fallen asleep yet.

"Maybe they're looking in the wrong place."

"Maybe the trees are too fucking thick," Erica said. "I think we're gonna have to walk out of here and find a trail."

"I don't know," Stacey said, turning around. "I think we should stay put for now. That's the smart thing to do." Anna trusted Stacey enough to agree with her.

"Hey, you know what's funny?" Erica asked, after a moment of silence had elapsed. "Even though I've been bitching all day, it's actually not so bad out here. I mean, I'm pissed off I can't get any french fries, or a pack of smokes, but this is the first day in my whole life no one's been yelling at me and telling me what to do. At home everyone's on my case twenty-four seven. And I've got three little brothers, so the house is never quiet."

"I wish I had brothers," Anna said. "Or a sister. Just someone to take the heat off me."

Stacey nodded. "I know what you mean."

"You're an only child, too?"

"Yeah."

"From my perspective, you guys are damn lucky," Erica said, and then she laughed softly. "I'd sell my brothers if I thought I could get any money for them."

Stacey smiled. "I bet Miss Richards would be shocked to see we're not fighting each other," she said. "She probably expects that we've turned into savages by now."

"We could always cook and eat Maria," Erica cracked. "Mmm, tasty." Then she added, "Just kidding, Maria."

Anna let her mind wander and her exhausted body relax. She was glad to be with these girls, and not any of the others. She hoped they'd all be found tomorrow. It had only been a day and a half since she'd entered the forest, but it seemed a whole lot longer.

She drifted off to sleep, and woke up a few hours later, sweating.

She'd been having a nightmare about being lost again, all alone. In her dream, Adler was still alive, and he was chasing her through the trees and the underbrush. She fell down and he cornered her, stepping from the shadows, the wound on his throat still streaming blood. But when she looked at his face more closely, it hadn't been Adler at all, but Mr. Spate instead, so what the fuck did that mean? When he'd smiled, his teeth were stained red.

Anna didn't sleep again because she was too freaked out, but got up and sat with Erica, who was keeping watch. When Erica went to sleep, Anna stayed up alone, and observed the sunrise through the trees. It came slowly at first, a gradual increase of light that caused parrots and macaws to start squawking, followed by other birds. Then the sky got reddish pink, and the trees became highlighted by its glow. It was beautiful, and she longed for her camera. The sunrises back home never looked like this, not that she'd been up early enough to see one in years.

In the morning, all four girls were tired and sore. The heat was already unbearable, even early in the day. Maria got up and sat on a rock, staring into the forest, lost in her own world. Erica lay in the sun while Stacey bathed in the blue-hole. Anna felt bad for Stacey because her body was so bony and underdeveloped, it looked like she hadn't even gone through puberty yet. Still, Stacey was probably the smartest one there, or at least the most together.

Anna needed to cool off, too, so she climbed down to the

bluehole to join her. "I barely slept," she said as she got into the water. "The island gave me really bad nightmares."

"Same here. What did you dream about?"

"Adler." Anna didn't need to say anything more because Stacey just nodded.

The girls dogpaddled back and forth, making ripples that traveled across to the opposite side. Anna wondered how deep the bluehole was, because it didn't seem to have any bottom. There were gray and yellow fish in it, too, tiny ones that darted back and forth in schools. She and Stacey swam several lazy laps before they got out and sat drying in a patch of sunlight on the rocks.

"I thought I heard something in the forest last night," Stacey told Anna. "Maybe a girl from the camp, someone lost. It sounded like they were calling for help. Did you hear anything?"

Anna was surprised. "No. Why didn't you wake us up?"

"I wasn't sure if it was real. It might have just been a bird, or my imagination, and I didn't want to scare anyone."

"It would have been okay," Anna said. "Definitely get me if you hear anything like it again."

"Sure. It sounded like it was to our left, but I couldn't really tell. I actually want to have a look and see if anyone's nearby, like when I found you. Want to come with me?"

Anna thought for a second before answering. "Yeah, I guess. I don't want to get lost, though."

"We won't go far, I promise."

"Okay." Anna smoothed back her wet hair. "Hey, do you think they'll find us today?"

"I hope so." Stacey put on her tank top. On the rock ledge Anna saw Erica stretch and turn over.

"How could they not? It'd be crazy. I'm sure our parents are going nuts already."

"If they even know what's happened to us," Stacey pointed out.

"They must, right? When we didn't meet up with the other group, I'm sure the counselors realized something was wrong."

"I just think it's strange we haven't heard another helicopter."

Anna had already thought about that some more. "Maybe they're searching for us on foot."

"Maybe."

Stacey's apparent lack of confidence made Anna depressed. She found it unbelievable that somewhere out there the world continued to go about its business as if nothing were wrong. What was everyone doing? If her mom and dad knew she was lost, then they were probably on their way to the island, if they still cared about her at all. If they didn't know, then her dad was probably locked in his study writing, and her mom was out with friends. It was now Monday morning, so Mr. Spate was getting ready to teach one of his art classes. She pictured him in his gray sweater and brown shoes, wire-frame glasses halfway down his nose. What the hell had she been thinking when she'd found him sexy? It was that whole older man thing, she supposed, but it seemed so stupid now.

After a late breakfast of coconuts and the last of the energy bars, Anna and Stacey left Erica and Maria at the bluehole to venture into the forest. They'd only been walking for a few minutes, Stacey writing urgently in her notebook, when Anna heard a rustling noise from behind a tree and froze. It sounded too loud to be a bird or a lizard.

"What was that?" she asked, thinking it might have been a mistake for her to come with Stacey. At least she'd been safe at the bluehole.

Stacey stopped walking and let her notebook fall to her side. "I don't know."

The two girls remained silent and still. Anna heard only silence, but she didn't relax. After what had happened to Adler, she didn't know if she'd ever completely relax again.

"It's just an animal," Stacey remarked, but she sounded a little unsure of herself. "I think it's okay."

"I hope so." Anna and Stacey began to walk forward again, more slowly than before.

"You know, supposedly they have pigs here, wild boars," Stacey said. "And flamingoes, too. One guidebook said there were flamingoes all over Andros, but I haven't seen a single one."

"Me neither." Anna swatted away a fly. "They sure have a lot of insects, though. When I get back to Atlanta, I don't think I'll ever want to go outside again." *If* I ever get back to Atlanta, that is, Anna thought.

"Hey, can I ask you a question?"

"Sure."

"It's kind of personal."

"That's okay. I won't answer if I don't want to."

"Why did you get sent here? Was I right about the boys? I didn't mean to be presumptuous when I said that, it's just that you seemed different from a lot of the other girls at the camp."

For a moment, Anna was tempted to tell Stacey exactly what had happened, the whole truth, including the part about

Mr. Spate, because it would have been interesting to get her perspective on it. But Anna held back. She'd never told anyone about that part. She felt fairly comfortable with Stacey, but knew enough about girls not to trust them completely, especially with her darkest secret.

"It still hurts a lot to talk about," Anna explained cautiously, being honest but vague. "I screwed up and got pregnant. My dad made me get an abortion, even though he's super religious, and then I didn't think straight for a while and started partying kind of hard. He has no tolerance for anything, so he finally went over the edge. I think he just wanted to get rid of me."

Stacey nodded. "I thought it was something like that. I don't know why. I hope you don't mind that I asked. Sometimes I talk without thinking and then everyone says I'm rude. It's a character flaw, I guess. I just get so curious about things."

"It's okay." Anna had met a lot of girls far ruder than Stacey. They continued walking, eyes peeled for signs of life.

"Hey Anna?"

"Yeah?"

"Can I ask you something else?"

"Sure." Anna mentally prepared for another personal question, but this time Stacey caught her off guard.

"Do you think Adler's dead?"

It was the first time the issue had been raised so bluntly, and Anna thought the answer was pretty obvious. She wished Stacey had brought it up while they were back at the bluehole, however, rather than out in the forest. "Yes. I saw him fall down, and it looked like he couldn't breathe. His throat was all bloody. I don't remember anything after that because I heard more gunshots and that's when I started running."

Stacey rubbed her forehead. "I've never seen anyone die before, have you?"

Anna shook her head. "No way."

"I saw my granddad's body at his funeral, but that was different. He died of lung cancer because he smoked three packs a day for forty years. It wasn't like what happened to Adler."

"I've never seen any kind of dead body before," Anna said. All four of her grandparents were still alive, if barely. Her grandfather on her dad's side was a sad, old man who sat in a recliner and watched the Weather Channel all day.

When Anna thought about Adler she felt cold and empty. How could someone be alive and talking one second, and a piece of meat the next? Even an asshole like Adler probably didn't deserve such a violent, crazy death. It just didn't make any sense, and Anna marveled at how it had been so sudden and random. Death was never talked about that much at school, or even in church, so she wasn't sure how she was supposed to deal with it. She'd never known anyone who'd died, and she'd never been to a funeral.

"Who do you think shot him?" she asked Stacey.

"Who knows? I read that the Bahamas are often used to smuggle drugs and weapons into Miami, so maybe it had something to do with that. Probably a poacher, though, just like Adler said, although I don't know what he was hunting."

"Me neither," Anna said. All the talk about the shooting was making her feel nervous again. "This place is way too dangerous for a wilderness camp."

"You know why Archstone's here?" Stacey asked. "It's so they can avoid high taxes in the U.S., and get around a lot of laws, too. I figured out that a lot of these wilderness programs are located outside America because—"

Stacey's words were interrupted by a low, moaning sound of pain that was unmistakably human.

"Wait!" Anna whispered, startled and afraid. "Do you hear that?"

Stacey stopped walking and listened closely. "It's coming from over there, from behind that log," she whispered back. The two girls stared at a huge, rotting log that rested in front of a cluster of mangrove trees. Anna couldn't see what was beyond it, and she really didn't want to.

"Should we look?" she asked softly, hoping the answer would be no, but knowing in her heart that they'd have to.

"I think so."

"Are you sure? We don't know what it is."

"It sounds like someone's hurt. We can't just leave them there. Remember when I found you?"

"But what if it's a trap? What if it's the poacher?" The girls stood and listened to the sound, which had now become a faint whimpering. Definitely human, Anna thought. And it sounded female. Shit.

"We can't ignore it," Stacey finally said. She took a step closer to the log, and then another one.

"Fuck, I'm scared," Anna whispered. It was like the scene in every bad horror movie where the victim climbs the dark staircase, or opens the closet door. Let's go back! Anna wanted to scream, yet she didn't. It could be one of the girls, she knew, and if that was the case then she wanted to help, just like Stacey had helped her. Nothing was worse than being alone on the island.

Please don't let us find anything bad, she prayed, as she took a deep breath and followed Stacey.

The girls walked close enough to the mangrove trees that Stacey could grab some branches above the log and pull them back, revealing a dark hollow. Anna breathed a sigh of relief when she saw that lying there in the underbrush was Lindsay. The blue-haired girl was filthy, her face smeared with dirt, and her body covered in leaves. Anna also saw her clothes were torn and she had a thick, purple bruise across her forehead and left temple.

"She's hurt!" Anna said.

At the sound of Anna's voice, the girl's eyes sprung open and she reared up. Before Anna and Stacey could react, she leapt at both of them and Stacey stumbled backward onto the forest floor, letting the branches snap back in the girl's face. What the fuck? Anna thought as she tried to back away. Lindsay pushed the branches away and burst out of the hollow, trembling with nervous energy.

"Where is he?" she shrieked. Her voice was hoarse, like she'd been yelling for days. She shot a look of hatred and fear at Anna. "He's close! Closer than you think! We have to start running!"

"It's okay," Anna said, trying to soothe the frantic girl, whose blue hair was nearly black with mud. She wondered if the stress of the island had driven Lindsay crazy, because that's how she was acting. Stacey picked herself up off the ground, looking surprised.

The girl looked back and forth from Anna to Stacey. She

had the wide, staring eyes of a caged animal about to attack. "You're going to die!" she proclaimed. "Both of you! Do you really want to die? Someone's after us, and he's not going to stop until we're all dead." She worked herself into a frenzy, clawing at her face with her chewed-up nails. "Oh my God!"

"Who's after us?" Stacey questioned. "Can you just calm down and talk? We want to help you."

"The man with the gun! Haven't you been listening? Didn't you see what he did to Counselor Adler?"

The girl's words made Anna's blood run cold in the heat of the forest. Even though the girl seemed irrational and crazed, she was saying the very things Anna had feared hearing.

"Have you seen him?" Stacey asked, and Anna could hear the tension in her voice. "What does he look like? Where is he now?"

"I see him all the time, don't you understand?" Lindsay shut her eyes. "Wherever I go, he follows. He's tracking me like game! Sometimes I wish he'd just get it over with and shoot me right in the head. I haven't slept in two days and I haven't eaten, either." Her voice rose to a wail. "I just keep running around in circles waiting to get shot!"

"Come back with us," Stacey said, interrupting the tirade. "Erica and Maria are with us, too. We found a bluehole and you'll be safe there."

Lindsay gave Stacey an angry stare. "I can't go with you," she explained, "because you're going to die. I don't want to die, so I'm going to keep on running as long as I can. He can't catch me if I run, that's the rule."

"We can help you," Anna said, but she knew her words would have little effect. "Just don't flip out, okay?"

"No one can help me!" The girl balled her hands into fists. "No one. Don't you get it?"

"Please," Stacey said.

"You're just two stupid bitches too dumb to save your own lives. Now get out of my way before I make you." There was no mistaking the absolute certainty in the girl's voice, and Anna glanced over at Stacey helplessly. They shared a look that said, What a psycho!

"You're being really irrational," Stacey told the girl, still trying to reason with her. "Come with us and we'll protect you. You'll be much safer with the four of us than on your own in the forest, don't you see the logic in that?"

"I can't hear you," Lindsay said. "You're already dead!" Before they could do anything, she strode past them, breaking into an awkward jog, and Anna watched her disappear between the trees.

"At least we tried," Stacey murmured, when the girl was out of view.

"She's lost her mind," Anna said, feeling like she'd been punched in the stomach. "I can't believe she freaked out like that."

"Me neither. But maybe she was unstable to begin with."

"What'll happen to her now?"

"Nothing good."

Anna took a deep breath. "Do you really think she saw someone? Do you think someone's after us? Or is she just crazy?"

"I don't know."

"She seemed pretty crazy, right?"

"Very."

"So what the fuck should we do about it?" Anna rubbed her arms, trying to dispel the goose bumps. "Was she telling the truth?"

Stacey gave her answer some thought. "I'm not sure. We know someone really shot Adler, but I doubt anyone's hunting us. It just sounds too absurd. I think Adler got hit by a stray bullet. Lindsay seems to be suffering from a mental breakdown."

"I really hope so, or we're in a shitload of trouble." Anna tried not to sound panicked, but it was very difficult to keep her voice steady.

"All we can do is stick together and hope they find us soon. It won't do any good to get upset."

"I know, I know." Anna attempted to swallow her fear. "Listen, I think we need to head back to the bluehole and tell Erica and Maria what we saw."

"Agreed."

"I'm really scared, Stacey. We're going to be all right, aren't we?"

Stacey nodded. "Of course we are. Better than all right."

The two girls turned back the way they'd come, Anna following Stacey's lead. Without Stacey's unerring sense of direction, she knew she'd be lost in the forest. Anna was much more on edge now, thinking about the man with the gun and what Lindsay had said. Yesterday, Anna had mostly managed to forget about the possibility that whoever killed Adler might come after them, because it seemed so unlikely. But she knew there were evil people in the world who did awful things for no reason at all, other than the thrill of it. Girls got kidnapped, raped, and murdered all the time, and that was in America where they had police. Anything was possible out here in the wilds of Andros, and it wasn't a comforting thought.

When Anna returned to the bluehole with Stacey, glad to be back on familiar ground, another surprise awaited her. As they came in sight of the familiar rock formation, Anna was shocked to hear new voices echoing loudly through the forest.

"They found us!" Anna exclaimed, feeling elated. "Fuck yeah!" She could hear talking and laughing, happy sounds that promised a quick escape from the island. "Stacey, come on!"

She and Stacey ran forward and burst out of the trees together, eager to see who'd arrived to rescue them.

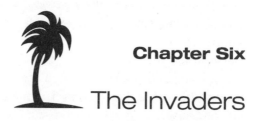

## Chapter Six

## The Invaders

There were two shocks, actually. Both came at once for Anna, and made her feel vertigo, like she was standing on the edge of a cliff, contemplating a jump. The first shock was that there were no rescuers, just a ragged crew of girls sitting like gulls on the rocks by the water. The second shock, and Anna didn't know why it should affect her in such a way, was that Kara sat in the center of the group.

"Oh, here they are," Erica said, grinning at Anna and Stacey as they tumbled out of the trees at the water's edge. "Look who turned up while you were gone."

"Hey there," Kara said, as though she were welcoming Anna and Stacey to her own private domain. Shouldn't it be the other way around? There was an awkward moment while the girls looked one another over. Anna hadn't forgotten what Kara had whispered to her during the softball game.

"It's Stacey, and, um . . . Ann?" Kara asked sweetly.

"Anna," she corrected.

"Oh, yeah." Kara fixed her with a contemptuous blue-eyed gaze. "The one who was late to camp. The one who tried to run away." She gestured to the two girls who had journeyed with her. "Laura and Alice. You remember them." The girls said hello in a chorus.

It was the first time Anna had a real chance to look at either of the girls in detail. Laura had one of those perfectly upturned noses, but she didn't look cute because it failed to match the rest of her face. It just looked like a nose job, Anna thought, and not a particularly good one. In addition, the girl's eyes were a bit too wide, giving her a permanent expression of surprise that was framed by her blonde hair.

On the other side of Kara sat Alice. Her curly brown hair was disheveled and hung over her eyes, making her look like a cocker spaniel. They were two of the girls Anna was least eager to see again.

She and Stacey took their seats on the rocks.

"I'm glad you found us," Stacey said to the newcomers, although Anna didn't think she sounded glad at all. Girls who looked like Stacey usually didn't get on too well with girls who looked like Kara, and Anna sensed a personality clash on the horizon. "We were out searching the forest. We found Lindsay, but she took off."

Kara rolled her eyes. "That girl's crazy." Laura and Alice tittered in unison. "I sat next to her on our first night, in orientation. She told me she does crystal meth and that's why she got sent to Archstone. She's a loser."

"Are all of you okay?" Stacey asked.

"Yeah, but we're really tired. We've been hiking all day while you guys were just sitting here resting and hanging out."

Anna saw the whole dynamic of the group was altered now that Kara and her companions had arrived. She felt a little unsure of herself, but knew she had to speak up. "Do you know anything about what happened on the trail? To Counselor Adler?"

Kara fixed her with those unblinking blue eyes. "What do you mean?"

Kara knew exactly what she was talking about, Anna thought. The question was merely intended to make her feel stupid, so Anna didn't respond.

Kara flipped back her hair. "Adler got shot, didn't he?" Alice and Laura giggled again. "Maybe someone mistook him for a pig. That would be a pretty easy mistake to make. Were you scared? I bet Stacey was."

Stacey ignored Kara's barb and said, "Lindsay told us she saw the man with the gun in the forest. She said he was chasing her, and that he wanted to kill her. She was really upset."

Laura shrugged. "Like Kara said, she does drugs." Her voice had a squeaky tone that made everything she said sound annoying. Anna also noticed she glanced back at Kara after speaking, as if seeking confirmation.

"Did you see anyone else out there?" Stacey asked Kara.

"No." She leaned back on the rocks. "We've just been walking, trying to get out of this fucking forest."

"Kara knows how to get us out," Erica spoke up, sounding excited. "You were all wrong, Stacey. Kara says if we stay put we're just going to die out here because the island's too big to get searched. We need to start walking east, just like I said yesterday." She pointed. "To the towns."

Stacey frowned. "That's not east, Erica. Besides, we could be thirty miles away from the coast. Are any of us in the condition to hike thirty miles? And what about water? We have a freshwater bluehole right here and those are rare on Andros. We might get stuck without water, and then what?"

Kara smiled. "You just have to trust me, that's what. Everyone else does. No one wants to sit here and wait. It's boring." Then, in a complete nonsequitur, "I just turned seventeen, you know. I'm the oldest."

"I think it's stupid to walk any farther," Stacey contended, determined not to let Kara win the argument. "The farther we go, the harder it'll be for the rescuers to find us."

Kara looked at Anna. "What do you think, Ann?"

Anna didn't know, because so far she'd been letting Stacey make most of the decisions for her. And she hated the bitchy way Kara deliberately kept saying her name wrong. "It's Anna, not Ann, and I think Stacey's probably right. We're safest here. I spent a night out there by myself and it sucked. The bluehole is better than the forest."

"But if we find the coast, we'll get home so much faster," Erica added. "It's lame to just sit around and do nothing. Kara says we're probably only a few miles away from a town or something."

Stacey stared Erica down. "And her logic is based on what? Blind hope? Certainly not on intellectual prowess. We're at least twenty miles from the coast. At least. And there aren't many towns on Andros. I studied the map in the cafeteria, so I know."

Kara got irritated. "Look, we need someone to make decisions and act like a leader. We're never going to agree on anything unless someone's in charge, now that there are seven of us. Well, six and Maria." Alice and Laura giggled on cue. "That's too many opinions. We'll never get anything done."

"We're not a bunch of boys," Stacey retorted. "We don't need a team captain to boss us around. We had that back at Archstone and see how well that worked. Now he's dead and we're on our own."

It struck Anna as grimly funny that out in the middle of nowhere, far from any kind of supervision, they should be debating the necessity of an authority figure. She was annoyed Erica had sided with the newcomers, but maybe Kara's beauty had somehow blinded her.

"We could be a democracy," Anna offered, trying to defuse the situation. "We could vote on our decision to stay here or go." She was afraid for a second both Kara and Stacey would hate her idea, but Kara smiled.

"Okay then," Kara said, seizing on the proposal with apparent glee. "I actually think that's a great idea. Let's vote. I say we rest here for a while and then hike out to the coast first thing tomorrow. Who's with me?"

"I am," Alice said.

"Me too," Laura added.

They were acting like her little disciples, Anna thought. Ready to do whatever she said.

Kara nodded. "Awesome. Anna?"

She realized that she suddenly wasn't sure. If she thought Kara would leave and take Laura and Alice with her, then she definitely preferred to stay at the bluehole with the others. But she knew Erica would probably leave with them, and Maria didn't talk, which meant it would be basically her and Stacey. She considered Stacey a friend, but she had an irrational fear that if she didn't follow the majority of the group, she, Stacey, and Maria might get overlooked and left behind. They'd only heard a helicopter once, if that, which meant the bluehole probably wasn't in the target search area.

Anna became aware that the others were looking at her. Maybe there was some way she could talk to Stacey about it alone. "I don't know. Can I abstain?"

"It was your idea to vote!"

"I know, but I just can't decide. I'm not good at making decisions like these." Anna wanted to support Stacey, but she also wanted to maximize her chance of escape and not get stuck in the wilderness. Everything looked the same to her in the forest and she felt overwhelmed. "Give me a few seconds and then I'll decide."

"Sure, sure, I understand. Take your time." Kara's voice was honey sweet but extremely phony sounding.

Anna hated Kara's arrogance, but she was careful not to display her true feelings. She sensed Kara would be dangerous to have as an enemy, and she could tell Stacey knew it, too.

"What about Maria?" Kara asked, turning to peer into Maria's eyes. "Maria, do you want to stay here and live in the trees like a monkey, or do you want to find the coast and get back home?"

There was no response.

"She's retarded," Alice snickered. "Let's just leave her."

"She can hear, right?" Kara asked Stacey. "She's not a Helen Keller?"

"She can hear, and she can see, too. Maybe she just doesn't like you."

As if to confirm Stacey's judgment, Maria stood up abruptly, brushed some dirt off her orange pants, and walked away.

"Retard," Alice said again, like it was the funniest word in the world.

Kara looked at Erica. "What about you? What do you want to do? Head east, right?"

"For sure. If that's where the people live, that's where I want to go. I'm ready to get moving."

"Then it's settled. Four votes for leaving, including mine. We'll set out tomorrow when it gets light."

"Who said we have to stick together?" Stacey asked. "You don't speak for me and Anna."

"Suit yourself," Kara replied. "You and Anna can stay here with Maria and a pile of coconuts if you want. What do I care?"

"We *will* stay, and while you're blundering around in the forest, we'll get rescued and taken back to America. The farther you go looking for the coast, the more lost you're going to get. We'll be just fine."

"I didn't say I was staying," Anna said suddenly. She liked Stacey, but she still wanted to have a voice of her own. She didn't like the way both Stacey and Kara were making assumptions about her actions.

Stacey glared at her, taking it the wrong way. "You're making a big mistake."

"Don't be childish, Stacey," Kara instructed. She'd taken

on the tone of an aggrieved parent. "Anna can make up her own mind."

"Stacey, you're just too scared to come with us," Alice taunted, like she'd been waiting for the right moment to attack her. "Just admit it."

"At least I have an IQ of more than fifty."

"Then what are you doing here if you're so smart? You're stuck on this island with the rest of us, so fuck you."

"Please, please," Kara said, sighing dramatically. "Here's the deal. Whoever wants to stay can stay. Stacey's right. We're not a bunch of boys and we don't have to play follow the leader. Laura, Alice, Erica, and I will leave tomorrow morning. I know we're close to the coast, a day's walk at the most. I can lead you there, if you want, and we can get out of this fucking jungle and back to civilization. Anna, if you decide to come, we're happy to have you. You too, Stacey."

"Thanks," Stacey replied sarcastically.

"We'll rest here for the night and get our packs ready for the trip. By tomorrow we'll be safe and sound." Kara stretched out her long legs. "Hey Alice, can you go fill my canteens for me? I'm thirsty after all this bitching."

"Sure," Alice said, eager to please, like a puppy with its master.

Anna wasn't sure why Kara had such a hold over Laura and Alice. It wasn't just that she was older than them. Maybe it was Kara's looks, and she was undeniably hot in a Paris Hilton, rich-bitch kind of way, but looks shouldn't matter much in the middle of a forest without any boys around. Anna realized more than anything else it was Kara's attitude. There was a strong force to her personality, as though she exerted some kind of gravitational pull. Anna knew that girls like Kara were trouble, and if you weren't careful you could get sucked into their orbit and soon your whole life revolved around them. Then, once they had you as a best friend, they started to get spiteful and play mind games.

"So it's safe to swim in this pond?" Kara was asking Stacey.

"It's not a pond. It's a freshwater bluehole."

"Whatever. I just need a bath."

Kara stood up, stripping off her orange tank top to reveal the white bra beneath, and a perfectly tanned torso. She unhooked the bra and tossed it onto a nearby rock. Anna stared despite herself, impressed by Kara's self-confidence, if nothing else.

Kara unbuttoned her pants and slid them down. "There's something about the feel of water on bare skin, don't you think?" Anna thought she sounded as though she were auditioning for a role in a movie. "Anyone want to join me?" She peeled off her panties, placed them delicately on the rock, and stepped naked into the bluehole.

Anna was torn between hatred and envy for girls who looked and acted like Kara. Where did they get the confidence? Were they just born with it?

"It's warm!" Kara called out. Alice, Laura, and Erica soon stripped to their bare skin and joined her in the water, total followers.

Stacey shot Anna a helpless glance. Their bluehole had been invaded.

"I hope you decide to stay, Anna," Stacey said softly. "They're going to get lost out there."

Anna sighed. "I guess I haven't made up my mind yet, but I'm starting to think we should go with them, as much as that sucks. We've been here more than a day, and there's no sign anyone's looking for us. I don't know how long I can live on coconuts and berries without getting sick."

"You *do* want to be found, don't you?"

"Of course I do," Anna said, feeling irritated. Stacey was being almost as domineering as Kara. "I hate this fucking island." It was draining to be around girls all the time, Anna thought. Girls talked too much, or maybe they were just too analytical about everything. She felt like no matter what she did or said, she was going to get criticized. "I just don't want to be out here any longer than I have to."

Stacey stood up. "Well, I'm going back to that tree to get some more berries. You want to come?"

Anna shook her head. She knew Stacey just wanted to get away from Kara. "I think I'll stay here this time. I'm kind of tired."

Stacey shrugged. "Okay." She grabbed her backpack and quickly headed off into the forest alone. Anna knew Stacey was annoyed with her, but there was nothing she could do about it.

A few minutes later Kara said something to the other girls, and then got out of the water and put her underwear back on. She walked over to Anna, sopping wet, and sat down next to her on the rocks.

Uh-oh, Anna thought, wondering what the girl wanted.

"Hey, babe," Kara said.

"Hey." Anna brushed some hair away from her face. Kara made her nervous.

"So why do you hang out with that girl?" Kara asked. Anna

knew she meant Stacey and considered the absurdity of the question before answering. It wasn't like there was room for cliques at the bluehole.

"I don't, like, *hang out* with her, Kara. We just found each other in the forest and stuck together."

"Are you going to stay here with her? I mean, with her and Maria?"

"I still haven't decided."

"You should come with us. I bet if you come, Stacey and Maria will, too."

Anna wondered why everyone was so concerned about what she did. Should she feel flattered by their attention, or manipulated like a pawn? "Why does it matter?" she asked Kara. "We're going to get found eventually, no matter what we do. There's probably a hundred people searching for us already."

Kara looked up at the canopy of trees. "But we're free now, Anna. Wouldn't you rather take action than sit around, wasting away at this pond? What if it takes weeks for anyone to find us? Can we survive that long?"

"It won't take weeks." The thought of spending much more time in the forest made Anna feel very uneasy and frustrated. "We're not that far from the camp. I don't even understand why it's taking this long."

"That's my point. We don't know how long it'll take for all of us to be found. That's why we have to walk out of here ourselves."

"Maybe."

Kara grinned. "Fuck, I know you ran away on the trip down to Archstone. I thought you'd have more balls."

More balls, Anna mused. Now there was an expression you didn't hear girls say to each other very often. "I just want to do what's best."

"I know what you mean. Really, I do. But listen, I want to have you around." She gestured at the girls in the water. "It gets kind of boring with Alice and Laura. They're so young, and Erica's a lesbo and has a crush on me, so that's awkward. And we're the oldest, or at least I think we are. How old are you, anyway?"

"Sixteen."

"A sophomore?"

"Yeah."

"Well, I'm a junior, or was, or still am. Whatever. So yeah, we should be the leaders." Kara smiled. "And not to be vain, but we're the best looking, too." What did that matter? Kara was interrupted by screaming from the bluehole. "See what I mean? Little girls. I bet they're still virgins."

"Help me!" Laura shouted from the water. "I can't breathe!" Alice and Erica had teamed up and were splashing her. Laura grabbed hold of a tree branch and tried to drag herself out of the bluehole, but Alice dove down and pulled her legs so she fell back into the water.

"I'm gonna drown! Stop!" Laura yelled, stark fear in her voice. Alice and Erica didn't care and continued to tease her, swimming around like sharks. Kara was watching with a big grin on her face. Anna recognized that smile because she'd seen it before, when Adler dragged Beth out of the barracks back at the camp, and after Kara had thrown the softball at the girl's face. Anna knew that for all her beauty, Kara got off on violence.

Laura finally managed to climb out of the bluehole, and she sat at the edge, flat chest heaving, eyes wide. "You almost drowned me!"

"We were just playing," Erica called out, still in the water. "Don't be such a wimp."

"Yeah, Laura, you pussy," Alice added.

Laura got up angrily and stomped to higher ground, as if she were afraid the bluehole would reach out and suck her back in. Alice and Erica whispered about her back and forth in the water, giggling, while Laura pointedly ignored them.

"I'm hungry," Kara said, turning her attention away from the bluehole now that the violence was over. "I'd kill for some french fries. What about you?"

That was easy. "I want Ben & Jerry's." Anna was starving for all the junk food she tried so hard to deny herself at home.

"What flavor?"

Her mouth watered. "Chocolate fudge brownie."

"That'd be good. Their cookie dough ice cream is better, though."

No it's fucking not, Anna thought. She felt a drop of water fall on her arm and she looked up at a sliver of sky through the trees. It was an ominous shade of greenish gray, and branches were beginning to wave in the wind.

"Fuck, that's just what we need," Kara muttered. Erica and Alice climbed out of the bluehole and started putting their clothes back on. Within seconds, beaded drops of water started to fall from the forest ceiling.

The rain became a torrent as the sky opened up, and the girls took refuge under the rock ledge to watch the downpour. Only Maria remained outside, sitting on a rock across the bluehole, getting soaked, but seeming to enjoy it. Anna worried about Stacey because she was still somewhere out in the forest alone. Anna hoped the rain and the dark skies wouldn't fuck up her sense of direction. Maybe I should have gone with her, she thought.

"This sucks," Laura said. "I hate thunderstorms." She was still pouting about getting teased in the water. The girls slouched against their sleeping bags and backpacks, watching Maria get wet from the safety of the ledge.

"Is that girl retarded?" Alice asked. "Who sits in the rain like that? And why doesn't she speak?"

Kara smiled. "Maybe she can't speak English, did you think of that?"

"Yeah, like my mom's maid back home," Laura agreed, trying to get back in their good graces. "She's lived in America for fifteen years and she still only speaks Mexican. What a moron."

You're the moron, Anna thought, but she didn't say it. She couldn't afford to alienate any of these girls yet.

"Maria belongs in the jungle," Alice said, and she laughed meanly.

Anna stared out at the rain, which was coming down in thick sheets, and considered how badly their situation sucked. She'd been so eager to escape from the camp, but now that she was free there was nowhere to go. She wondered where Stacey was and hoped she'd get back soon. Stacey was the only girl that Anna could really relate to, especially now that the others had arrived.

Anna didn't have to wonder about Stacey for long, because a few seconds later she emerged from the trees to the left of the bluehole and scurried under the rock ledge. Her clothes were soaking, her hair was in wet strands, and her eyes were huge in her narrow face. She looked completely terrified.

"What's up, babe?" Kara asked laconically.

Stacey sat down and wrapped her arms around her bony knees, struggling to catch her breath.

"Are you okay?" Anna asked with concern.

Stacey had been running hard and her pants were splattered with mud. "I saw him," she finally gasped. "A man. Out there in the rain."

Her words silenced everyone and the girls exchanged frightened looks. Stacey was shivering, but not from cold. "I was working on my map," she said, the words coming in staccato bursts between breaths. "I was on my way back when it happened. I don't think he saw me. At least, I hope he didn't."

"You're probably just seeing things," Kara declared loudly. "You got scared out there in the rain by yourself." She intended to sound belittling, but Anna could detect the fear in her voice, so it didn't work.

Stacey's chin jutted out. "I know what I saw. There was a man out there."

"It was no one," Erica burst in. "Right? I mean, c'mon, Stacey. Don't scare us like this."

"I'm not trying to scare you, I'm just telling you what I saw. He was sitting in a tree with his back to me. It looked like he was watching something."

"Maybe it was an Indian?" Alice asked. "Don't they live in trees?"

It was almost a guarantee that anything she said would be stupid, Anna thought.

"No. Besides, I think he was white."

"It could have been a hunter."

"Yeah. What if he was a hunter and could have rescued us?" Kara asked. "Then you really fucked up."

"And what if he was the man who killed Adler?" Stacey brushed wet hair out of her eyes. "The man I saw looked weird, like there was something wrong with him. I didn't want to get shot."

"Weird how?" Anna asked.

"I don't know. He just seemed creepy. Maybe it was because he was hiding in a tree."

"Maybe he's a pervert," Laura murmured. Anna looked at her and saw that her face had gone very pale. "Maybe he's going to find us, and do things to us. Sexual things."

"Jesus, shut up. Are you a fucking wacko?" Erica asked in irritation.

"Listen," Kara said. "There's no need to scare everyone, Stacey. We can't do anything about it if someone's out there. Are you sure he didn't see you?"

She nodded. "Pretty sure."

"Then we'll stay here tonight, just like I said. We can't go anywhere in the rain anyway. We can keep watch from the ledge and make sure nothing bad happens. Then in the daylight we'll head for the coast. We're going to be fine, but all of you need to stop acting like little babies and just stay calm."

"I don't want to get shot," Laura said, and Alice told her to shut up.

Anna felt more frightened than she had since the first

night alone in the forest. She believed Stacey one hundred percent. There was a man out there, nameless and faceless, waiting to do them harm. She realized the noise of the rain was constant and it would be hard to hear someone sneaking up on the ledge from behind.

Anna felt a flash of anger at herself for getting sent to Andros. She could have stopped partying for a while, cut back on drinking and getting high, yet she'd needed some way to deal with the pain of the abortion, some sort of remedy. If only her dad weren't so mean and unforgiving, they could have worked things out. It'd serve him right if I got killed out here, she thought bleakly. Then he'd be sorry.

Anna heard a pathetic choking sound and realized Laura was crying.

"Cut that out," Kara spat. "You're thirteen, not two."

"We're going to die out here." Laura sobbed, hugging herself. "They're never going to find us. I want my mom."

"We need to stay focused and not give in to our fear," Kara told her.

"We're all scared," Stacey added.

"Suppose there is a man," Erica said, after a pause. "What do we do if he finds us? We should have a plan."

"We're probably safe here," Anna said, to assuage her own terror. "With the rain and the rocks, no one can really see us. I think we'd see him first, and there'd be time to run, right?"

"Yeah," Alice said.

"You can't outrun a bullet," Laura cried, wiping her eyes on her sleeve. No one responded to that one.

Thanks, Laura, Anna thought.

It suddenly occurred to her that they were all forgetting

someone. "Hey, where's Maria?" she asked. "I don't see her anymore." The girls turned to stare out into the rain, but there was no sign of the dark-haired girl.

"She was right there just a minute ago," Erica insisted, sounding puzzled. "On that rock."

"She's not there now."

"Shit."

Now Anna was really starting to worry.

"I'm sure she's okay," Kara said. "Let's not panic. Like Alice said, she's probably at home in the jungle. She probably went to the bathroom, or to get coconuts."

In this rain? No way, Anna thought.

"What if she's not okay?" asked Laura's trembling voice. "What if that man's got her?"

"You're such a crybaby," Kara fumed, but it didn't make Laura stop talking.

"What if he's watching us, stalking us? Waiting for the right time to get us, one by one. What if he's—"

"What if, what if," Alice mimicked. She was sitting slightly behind Laura under the ledge and she kicked her hard in the back, which only caused Laura to start sobbing again.

"Why would you even think that?" Erica asked Laura. "Adler got shot, not one of us."

"Laura, you're getting hysterical," Kara said. "We can't act like a bunch of silly little girls. That's how everyone would expect us to act, weak-minded and afraid of every single shadow. If you don't cut it out, I'll make you go stand in the rain alone."

"I won't! You can't make me!"

"Yes, we can," Alice said. "So shut up, bitch."

Laura didn't completely fall silent, but she lowered the volume and started mumbling to herself instead of weeping.

Anna scanned the forest through the downpour for any signs of Maria, but there were none. She was concerned about Maria's disappearance, but she wasn't about to go looking for her in the rain. Laura's panicked words echoed in Anna's head. Why would anyone want to hurt them? Anna wished she knew what was going on because she hated feeling like a victim, passive and helpless. Her dad and Mr. Spate had both played on those tendencies and it made her feel sick. They were still safe at home and she was stuck out here, potentially with a psychotic gunman.

The girls waited out the rest of the rainy day hiding under the rock ledge. Maria didn't reappear, but neither did the man with the gun. Night fell and the rain continued to beat down loudly on the ledge. In the morning the forest was dark and gloomy, as if the sun had decided not to rise. Anna had barely slept, and her neck and back ached. The damp had seeped into everything, her clothes, her sleeping bag, and even her skin itself. The scratches all over her body and face weren't healing and had begun to pucker at the edges. She worried they were going to get infected and leave scars.

Anna felt worse than she ever had in her life. Her stomach pulsed angrily with hunger, like a knife stabbing her in the belly, and she had a gross taste in her mouth. She stank, and she knew her breath smelled bad, too. Her fingernails were chipped and torn, imbedded with dirt.

Anna sat with the girls, glumly under the rocks, watching the rain continue to fall. They didn't talk about Maria. Anna noticed only Kara still looked refreshed and beautiful in the morning, as though she existed in a separate universe from the others. How typical, Anna thought. Maybe Kara was actually from another planet. She bet Kara was the kind of girl who didn't even need to diet to stay thin, or at least claimed that she didn't.

"So are you coming with us?" Kara asked Anna. "As soon as the rain lets up, we're heading east."

Anna nodded her head. Since Stacey had seen the man, everything was different and there was no way she was staying at the bluehole. "I'll go with you." She bet Stacey wouldn't want to stay anymore, either.

"Stacey?" Kara asked. "What about you?"

"What if Maria comes back? Shouldn't we wait for her?"

"But what if she doesn't? Who knows where she's gone? We can't make any decisions based on her."

Anna knew what everyone was thinking, that maybe the man had gotten her somehow, but that was impossible. No one had seen or heard it happen, and they'd all been right there watching. Maria had disappeared into thin air.

Stacey thought for a moment. "Well, I guess I'm not going to stay here alone," she finally said. "That wouldn't make any sense. I'll go with you, although I want you to know statistically our best chance of rescue is to stay put. We have shelter and water. I don't think the trip to the coast will be easy. We might even run into the man I saw out there."

"I'm glad you're coming," Anna said. She understood Stacey's capitulation. Anna wouldn't want to stay at the bluehole by herself, either, even if it was supposedly the smart thing to do. Because of the rain and the threat of the man with the gun, Anna now hated the bluehole and its surroundings.

Its perfect contours seemed mockingly out of place on such a hazardous island. And if there were people still searching for them, as Anna assumed there were, the rescue teams were obviously looking in the wrong place.

"I bet we'll be home by tonight," Kara asserted. "Tomorrow morning at the latest."

"I hope you're right," Stacey said, but her tone made it clear she didn't think it would happen that way.

When the rain finally eased, slowing to a light drizzle, the girls filled their canteens at the water's edge, prepared their backpacks, and rolled up their sleeping bags. Soon they left the bluehole behind them and walked through the maze of trees, heading east. Anna was pretty confident they were heading in the right direction.

God, I hope we get out of here soon, she thought. Fuck this shitty place. She knew it was possible they could be lost in the forest for at least a couple more days. Anna wondered if the others were as nervous as she was. If Kara felt the same way, she certainly didn't show it.

"It shouldn't take us too long if we keep up a good pace," Kara called out, sounding eerily like an echo of Miss Richards. Yet it was nearly impossible to move faster than a crawl because the trees grew so close together and the underbrush was a thick tangle.

They made slow progress for many hours, but then the rain started up again and soon the girls were drenched. They kept walking because they had no other choice. Anna followed along blindly, dreaming of food and hoping the rescuers would find them soon. Before anyone else did.

## Chapter Seven

# The Caves

The girls finally stopped moving and huddled together in the downpour. The rain was coming down sideways, the forest so dark it seemed like twilight. Trees waved in the wind and leaves fluttered from the canopy. Anna felt battered by the elements

"We need to get out of this rain!" Erica yelled, stating the obvious. A peal of thunder came from above and Anna looked up nervously. Leaving the bluehole was beginning to seem like a huge mistake.

"I want to go back," Laura whimpered. "I can't take it anymore, all the trees, all the rain." Her voice was trembling with fear.

Alice sneered. To Anna she looked like a goblin with her matted hair, and the rain dripping off her face. "Is Baby scared?"

"No."

"Liar."

"Quit it!" Kara said. "We need to make a new plan."

"Yeah, come on," Anna added, but Alice wouldn't let the argument drop.

"Are you gonna start crying again?" she taunted Laura. "Scaredy cat, scaredy cat."

"Shut up, Alice," Stacey said.

"Just try to make me," she spat quickly, and then turned back to Laura. "You're such a fucking waste. I wish you'd get shot, too."

Laura's face contorted. "Why are you being so mean to me?" She brushed at the raindrops falling on her too-perfect nose. "Can't you just get off my case? Of course I'm scared, and I know you are, too!"

"You're ugly, and you're stupid, and all of us hate you. You're a fucking wimp."

"And you're a bitch!" Laura suddenly rallied. "You've got your nose stuck so far up Kara's ass you can't see straight!"

"We need to stay united—" Stacey began to say, but right then Alice stepped forward and shoved Laura as hard as she could. Laura flew back into the underbrush and sprawled there in the mud, her mouth a perfect circle of surprise. Oh no, Anna thought.

"Stupid ho," Alice said. The other girls stared at her. She wiped rain out of her eyes and spat on the ground. "What?"

"Why'd you do that?" Stacey asked, over the rain. "Laura didn't do anything to you."

"Yes she did. Besides, I just felt like it."

Laura didn't even try to get up, she just lay among the branches and leaves, sobbing. Rain spattered her dirty face.

"She's really losing it," Erica observed. "Alice, you probably shouldn't have done that, even if Laura is a pussy."

"She's a crybaby. She's weak, and she deserved it. She's lucky I didn't smack her in the face, the dumb bitch."

Laura was still weeping, her eyes scrunched tight. Anna pitied her, but also felt frustrated because the rain was coming down hard, and her wet bra was chafing her skin.

"Laura," Kara said. "Get up. We need to find shelter. I'm getting soaked, and I don't like it."

Laura didn't respond.

Stacey knelt down by her side in the underbrush. "Laura, it's okay. We're going to get out of here fine. Alice didn't mean it, she's just scared, too."

"Am not!" Alice yelled. "I'm not scared at all."

Then you're crazy, Anna thought. Laura's sobs were subsiding, but her eyes remained shut. To Anna it looked like she was having a breakdown just like Lindsay. What was up with these girls? "Come on," she muttered.

Laura opened her eyes and stared up at them. "I can't go on," she said, her words almost getting drowned out by the rain.

"What?"

"I can't do this anymore."

Kara sighed. "Why'd you have to push her?" she asked Alice. "Look at what you've done. Laura was fine yesterday." Alice didn't answer. Kara was the only girl she seemed afraid of.

"We have to keep walking," Erica called out to Laura. "We'll get to the coast soon and everything'll be okay. Don't give up now."

Anna saw Laura smile thinly at Erica's encouragement. "You know what?" Laura asked. "Today I had my period. My third one ever. It got all in my pants but I didn't want to say. I had to put toilet paper up there."

Why would Laura even say that? God, she was really losing it. Alice giggled, but no one else did. For once, even Stacey didn't know what to say. The rain fell heavily down on them.

Laura continued speaking. "My belly hurts, my head hurts, my legs hurt, and my feet hurt. I can't take one more step. I'm so tired, I just can't do it."

"We all need rest and sleep," Kara said. Rain cascaded down her face, beading on her chin. "But we can't give up, not when we're so close. I bet we're just a few hours from the coast, and we could be even closer."

Laura shut her eyes again. "I think I'm going to stay here for a while. You guys go on without me."

"No way," Anna exclaimed, shocked that Laura sounded serious. She couldn't imagine anything worse. "Not in this weather. You'll get sick. And what about the man with the gun?"

Laura didn't answer. Kara wiped the rain off her own face and peered down at Laura. "You know we can't stay here with you. We have to keep moving and get out of this rain. We really will leave you here if you don't get up."

"Yeah, Laura, don't be so fucking stupid," Alice said, but the other girls shot her dirty looks so she fell quiet.

"I can catch up with you later," Laura said. "I just need to rest for a while."

Anna felt numb despair. Laura had cracked up. "That's ridiculous! You'll get lost and never find your way back. Our only hope is to stick together."

"She's right," Stacey added.

"We can't make her come with us if she doesn't want to," Kara snapped. Unfortunately, Anna knew Kara was right. It was hard enough to get through the forest already, and it would be impossible to carry someone, even a small girl like Laura.

Stacey stood up. "We can't leave her. I refuse. She might die."

So it was down to this again, Anna thought. Stacey versus Kara.

"Let's vote," Kara said. "We're a democracy, right? If it wasn't for the storm we could stay as long as we wanted, but we need to go look for shelter. We can come back for Laura when it stops raining."

"If she's still here," Stacey said. "If we can find her." She was trying to get Laura to sit up, but she wasn't having any luck.

The forest flashed with lightning, followed by another boom of thunder.

"Let's go!" Alice yelled. "Laura's a moron! Why wait for her? We don't need her."

The rain was pelting them now, coming down so hard it hurt. It was one of the worst storms Anna had ever been outside in.

"I vote we go, too," Erica cried. "I'm drowning out here!"

"Okay," Kara said, over the noise of the rain. "Let's do it, then." She bent down to Laura. "We'll come back for you, girl."

"I'm sorry, Laura," Erica called out. "See you soon."

"Sorry," Anna muttered, wanting to do more. If she could think of any way to get Laura back on her feet, she'd do it.

Only Alice said nothing as they stood around Laura helplessly.

Stacey took out one of her canteens and some berries and placed them on the ground next to Laura. She leaned down and whispered something in her ear. Then, to Anna's horror, they left Laura all alone in the underbrush, out in the rain.

"She'll be okay," Erica said to Anna as they trudged through the downpour. "Right? All she has to do is head east and she'll be fine."

Which way is east? Anna wondered. She frankly had no idea. She realized their abandonment of Laura was a turning point, because none of them had done the right thing. It was partly Laura's fault for collapsing, she told herself, and not keeping up with the group, but now they were down to five when yesterday there had been seven of them. She wondered how many would be left at the end.

They have to find us soon, she thought. I don't think we can take it much longer.

The girls walked in the direction they thought was east, even though there was no sun to guide them. To Anna it seemed like they'd never find shelter, like there would be only trees reflected endlessly in their desperate eyes. Finally Anna spotted something beyond the foliage, a tall pile of craggy, gray rocks similar to the ones at the bluehole. "Look up ahead!" she yelled, over the din of the rain. "Do you see it?"

"Where?" Erica asked.

"Over there! See?"

"Let's check it out!" Kara said.

Anna and the others headed toward the rocks, which loomed up like a monolith behind the trees. Maybe it indicated they'd found another bluehole? But when they got there, Anna saw that they hadn't. Instead it was just a spherical pile of rocks, like a giant cairn. There was a lip that stuck out on one side resembling the shell of an amphitheater, with an opening in the center that led down into the ground.

"It's the mouth of a cave," Stacey called out, just as Anna realized the same thing.

"Let's go inside!" Erica yelled.

The girls climbed into the opening, where they were protected from the rain by the rock ceiling that curved out above them. Anna looked behind her into the depths and saw that the cave extended deep into the ground, sloping gently down like a long, dark tunnel. Something about the cave gave her the creeps, but Kara, Alice, and Erica seemed elated, giggling and talking, and Anna was glad to be out of the rain.

Kara tried to reassert a semblance of authority. "Let's wait here until the storm passes," she declared.

"You mean, *if* it passes," Stacey said. "Storms can last three or four days on Andros in the spring. We might be stuck here that long."

"What a know-it-all," Alice remarked.

"At least we don't have to worry about water," Anna pointed out. The rain was coming down so heavily it seemed like it might never stop. All her wet clothes stuck to her body. "We should put our canteens out to collect it."

Stacey nodded. "That's a good idea. Then when it stops raining we can go and get Laura."

Alice stood up and walked the circumference of their circular enclosure. She seemed bored without Laura around to tease, Anna thought.

The rain was running down into the opening of the cave, so the girls retreated farther into its mouth to find a dry area. The rock walls were damp and marbled with something white, so they looked like sides of beef. Whenever anyone said anything, the words echoed back and forth, audible over the rain. Anna noticed that unfortunately the roof of their enclosure wasn't perfectly sealed, so drops of water occasionally came down on her head.

Kara and Erica were shuffling and talking until Stacey spoke loudly and cut through the racket. "Hey, shut up! Shut up for a second."

"You shut up," Kara retorted.

"No, seriously. I think I heard something."

The girls quieted down and waited, Anna hoping it was nothing.

"It's just your nerves," Kara said.

"Listen," Stacey insisted. "It sounded like a scream."

"I don't hear anything." Alice kicked at the wall of the cave, dislodging a piece of rock that skittered to the ground.

"Stop that."

A second later Anna heard it, too, the very faint but unmistakable sound of someone crying out in pain or terror. She got cold all over, because it sounded like Laura. I knew we shouldn't have left her out there, she thought.

"What the fuck is that?" Erica whispered. "Is that Laura?"

"Jesus, I don't know."

"Shut up!"

And then, much louder, but still a distance away, came the report of a gunshot. Anna and Stacey stared at each other with terrified eyes. Even Kara looked scared. The screaming sound had been abruptly silenced.

Anna thought she was going to pass out. Her worst fears had been realized in an instant. The man had found them, he was real, and he was out there. He'd just shot Laura, and was coming for them next. Erica clutched at Anna and she clutched back.

"Oh no," Anna breathed. The girls stared out at the forest from within the mouth of the cave, petrified.

"Someone's stalking us!" Alice said. She sounded surprised at her own fear, or maybe she just couldn't imagine herself worthy of being stalked. Anna felt like she was inside a nightmare.

"We don't know what we heard, so don't panic," Kara said, in a voice that was very panicked. "It could have been a hunter shooting an animal."

"I don't think so," Stacey whispered. The girls turned toward her. "I think it was Laura. Even if it wasn't, we can't take any chances. We need to go deeper into the cave. If it's the man with the gun, he won't find us in there. He might not even know we're out here at all. We have to hide, that's the only answer."

Anna nodded and so did Kara. "Okay," they whispered.

Holding hands, the girls moved down the narrow opening that led into total darkness. The thought of going into those unknown depths terrified Anna, but nothing was as scary as the idea of being shot. Laura might be dead now, she realized. This was a life-and-death situation. She'd heard that stupid cliché so many times before, but it had never held any meaning for her. Now it was the scariest phrase in the world, and it meant absolutely everything. I don't want to die here, she thought, as she slowly followed the chain of girls into the cave.

The tunnel was only narrow for the first few seconds and then widened into a larger space. The other girls were mostly invisible to Anna, although when she turned back the way she came, she could see the faint, gray light of the outside world filtering through the tunnel. She stood there, slightly stunned. Someone coughed.

"Hello?" Anna whispered.

"Shhh," she heard in response. Stacey's hand tightened on hers.

"Are we all here?" It was Kara.

"Yeah."

"What the hell just happened?" Erica asked. As Anna's eyes adjusted to the gloom she could make out faint shapes. The cave was very dark and damp, and the air smelled musty. Her heart was thumping in her chest. She could still hear the rain outside and an occasional rumble of thunder.

All of the girls remained standing nervously at the edge of the cavern, watching the gray rectangle of light that came from the tunnel. At any second Anna expected to hear another gunshot, or see a shape appear at the opening.

A girl suddenly screamed and Anna spun around, disoriented. Everyone started gibbering with fear.

"Who's there!"

"Fuck!"

"What was that?"

"I'm okay, I'm okay. It was me," Erica said sheepishly. "Fuck. Something got on my arm. I think it was just a spider."

Just a spider? Anna instinctively brushed at her own arms and hair, even though there was nothing there.

"So what do we do now?" Alice asked. She made it sound like a philosophical question. Anna looked around at the gray shapes in the darkness.

"We wait," Kara replied.

"For how long?"

"I don't know, Alice. As long as we have to."

"I hope Laura's okay," Anna said.

"Me too," Erica replied. "Even though she was crazy to stay out there by herself." She paused. "You know, if someone's hunting us, that really pisses me off."

Kara sighed. "We don't know what's going on."

Anna wondered for a moment if it were possible they'd all imagined the gunshot, like a mass hallucination. She knew that wasn't the case, though. The gunshot had been loud and real.

"So we wait," Stacey said.

Anna saw a gray shape bend down. It was Kara. "I keep stepping on something," she complained. "There's something on the floor." Anna heard rustling noises, a snapping sound, and then, shockingly, at the same instant, the room was illuminated with pale yellow light.

"Oh my God," Anna breathed, as she gazed around at what was inside the cave.

"Holy shit!" Erica said. "Look at all this stuff."

Kara was holding a flashlight, which lit up the cavern, and Anna was stunned by what she saw. The space was large, maybe thirty feet by twenty, with walls of gray rock and a low, dark ceiling. Opposite the short tunnel they'd climbed down were four separate openings that led to further catacombs. She realized they were still just at the entrance of a huge, complex system of caves.

But the most shocking thing of all was the fact that the cave wasn't empty. As insane as it was, Anna saw they were indisputably inside someone's home.

"God," Kara said. "Someone actually lives down here." She shone the flashlight around, pinpointing different items as the girls stood still in their places. "Look at this crap. Can you believe it?"

It was the last thing in the world Anna had expected to find. Two red sleeping bags lay on a plastic sheet against a rock wall, next to a tiny wooden table that also held a battery-powered lantern. There was a pile of pillows on a cardboard box, and a stack of paperback books. At the foot of the bed was a large, clear plastic container that appeared to be full of food. There was a stock of tins beyond that, stacked neatly against another side of the cave. There were bottles of water and root beer, and several more sealed plastic containers. A portable stove sat at the foot of the sleeping bags, and there were two white garden chairs in front of it.

"What do we do now?" Anna breathed.

Alice walked over to the container of food before anyone could stop her. "I'm going to open this thing up and eat!" She pried off the clear plastic top and it fell to the ground.

"No, wait, we need to think," Stacey said, but Erica was already following Alice. Anna felt her mouth watering as the smell of food reached her nose. Whatever was in that container was going to get eaten, even if this was someone else's home and someone else's food. Anna followed the girls and sat down next to it, digging through the contents like it was Christmas, too starved to exert any self-control.

"This stuff is fresh! There are oranges and apples, and bread."

"Snickers bars and Kit Kats!" Alice sounded like a little kid.

They found a can opener and opened some of the cans,

too. There was a frenzy of eating, the girls gorging like bulimics on a Friday-night binge. The food tasted so good to Anna it was almost unbearable. Only Stacey restrained herself somewhat, nibbling a pack of sugar cookies. She switched on the lamp, so the cave was much brighter, but there were still patches of shadowy darkness in the corners.

"Fucking unbelievable," Erica effused, between mouthfuls of miniature prepackaged chocolate donuts. "Who do you think lives here?"

"Could be a hunter's lodge," Stacey said. "Or a poacher's." She paused. "Of course, you realize it could be where the man with the gun lives."

She said this last part casually, but it had been exactly what Anna was thinking. "Maybe we shouldn't have eaten all this stuff," she said.

"Too late now."

"This place could also be a fisherman's getaway," Kara proposed. "Maybe it's a sign we're near the coast."

"Whoever lives here isn't home," Alice said. "So who the fuck cares?"

Stacey sighed. "Well, if this place belongs to the man with the gun, he'll come back here eventually. Just so you know."

"But we can't go outside," Kara said, "so we might as well make the best of it. We're stuck." She peeled off her wet top. "We should get out of these clothes, too."

"We need to look in those tunnels back there." Stacey gestured to the four openings in the opposite wall. "We can hide in one of them if someone comes in here. Maybe there's even another way out." The girls stared with apprehension at the dark holes.

There's no fucking way I'm going in there, Anna thought. Spiders and bats lived in dark places like those, and she didn't need any more nasty surprises.

But after the girls had sated their appetites, they decided to cautiously investigate. None of the girls was any more eager than Anna to go inside them, so they just shone the flashlight into their depths. The caves were empty, and two of them had further openings that led mazelike to still more caverns. Anna speculated the caves went on forever, deep into the fabric of Andros, and the thought made her shudder. She couldn't wait until she was off this terrible island.

The girls turned their attention back to the main cave. They'd left a mess from their feast, which they were careful to clean up at Stacey's suggestion that they leave as few indications of their existence as possible. Afterward, they unrolled their sleeping bags and prepared to rest. Anna took off her wet tank top and pants. Stacey found some thick, white candles in a box and Anna and Kara lit five of them, placing four around the circumference of the room, and one in the center. The cave danced with light and the girls cast shadows on the rock walls. Now that they had matches, Anna hoped that when it stopped raining they could try to light a signal fire outside. She wasn't exactly clear on the plan anymore, because they didn't have a good one.

The five girls sat around the center candle in a circle on their bags and tried to work out their next move. They decided if the man came back, or if they heard any suspicious noises from the opening of the cave, they'd grab the flashlight and candles and flee back into one of the tunnels, as far as they could go. They'd decided upon the one on the left, because it was the largest. Heading into those depths wasn't a very comforting idea, and Anna had images of being trapped down there blind in the dark, but it was their only option. She hoped it wouldn't come to that. Then, in the morning, if the rain stopped, they would venture out of the caves and try to head east again, hoping the man with the gun had lost them during the night.

Anna curled up in her sleeping bag next to the other girls and took comfort in the fact that they had a plan. Even though it was kind of early, they were so exhausted they needed to sleep. Stacey had taken the first watch, and was sitting up, writing in her notepad by candlelight. She'd turned the lantern off to save its batteries, but left all the candles burning, so the cave remained filled with a warm, yellow glow. Anna worried that somehow the man with the gun would see the flickering light through the opening of the cave, but she knew the curve of the rock walls would make this impossible.

While Kara and Erica chatted about what they'd do when they got home, Anna turned over and stared up at the veins of white in the ceiling. They had a strange shimmering cast to them that made them look like spiderwebs. Another great photo wasted, Anna thought. She tried to figure out how she'd take the photo if she had her Nikon with her. She'd need a wide aperture and a slow shutter speed to capture the contrast of the shadows, and maybe a density filter, too. At least Mr. Spate had taught her something, unlike most of her teachers at school. He'd actually taught her way too much, she thought, but that was another story.

Had she asked for it? She knew if she ever told, that's

what everyone would say, that her jeans were too tight, her skirts too short. The typical crap people always said. She wondered if they wouldn't be at least part right. Maybe she'd had a crush on Mr. Spate to begin with, but she didn't remember it that way. Her memories were all tangled up with her emotions and she couldn't straighten them out. How weird was it that she still thought of him as "mister"? Outside of class, he'd always made her call him Greg, but in her mind he was forever Mr. Spate.

The day they first kissed, they were in the school darkroom together, just the two of them. It was a slow Tuesday afternoon, and she'd stayed late to work on a photograph for the high school art show. Mr. Spate was helping her develop it, and he said it was her best yet, said it showed a real eye for detail.

Anna wasn't sure if the photo was anything special. It was a shot of the sun setting behind a bridge over Lilac River, two streets down from her house. She'd taken it in color, but she was only learning how to develop in black and white, so the print looked indistinct and blurry.

That Tuesday afternoon, Mr. Spate was standing behind her in the red glow of the darkroom, supervising. She'd felt a hand on her shoulder, a light touch that surprised her. She'd turned around to see him smiling back. He was standing right under the little red lamp, bathed in its glow, a handsome devil.

"Anna, there's something I need to tell you," he said, "but I don't know how to say it." Her pulse quickened. She turned back to look at her photo soaking in the tray of developer. It was almost time to put it in the stop bath.

"Forget about that," he said, noticing her concern. "We can

print another one." The hand on her shoulder tightened. "I just can't stay silent anymore about my feelings. They're driving me crazy, and I think you might feel the same way."

Anna felt paralyzed, like she couldn't breathe, both excited and nervous.

"Anna?"

"Yeah?" she managed to reply, turning around to look at him. His expression was serious, his eyes open and warm.

"I'm think I'm falling in love with you."

There. He'd said it. She'd known he felt something for her, but she didn't know it was love. She seriously felt lightheaded for a second. Then it was her turn to say something.

"I . . . I . . ." is what she managed, groping for words to express her feelings. She didn't know how she felt. She felt something for him, that much was sure, but she couldn't articulate such a weird sensation. She thought he was hot, and it was awesome he was so into her, but was it love?

Looking back from her vantage point on Andros, she knew it wasn't. She'd thought he was handsome and smart, in a way none of the boys her own age were, not even Ryan. He was older than her, nearly thirty-two, which meant he knew a lot, not just about photography, but life in general. He'd worked as a photojournalist in his twenties and traveled the world, and his photos had been printed in newspapers and magazines in a bunch of different countries. He'd tried to make it as a fine artist for several years after that, but it hadn't worked out. Supposedly he was at her school because somehow he discovered he loved teaching, not because his work had failed to sell. She'd seen through that bullshit excuse even then, but it hadn't mattered to her.

That day in the darkroom Anna had said, "I'm in love with you, too." They'd stared at each other under the red light and then he'd taken her in his arms. She didn't think anything could possibly feel so good as his touch. He kissed her gently on the lips and she returned his kiss, their hands moving over each other's bodies.

The kiss was the culmination of weeks of flirting, and the beginning of everything else that happened afterward. Lying in the cave on Andros, Anna wished they'd never gone further than that one delicious moment. But in the following weeks, they'd started meeting in the darkroom, in Mr. Spate's car, and finally in his apartment on the west side of town. He introduced her to things she'd never known about. She understood what they were doing was forbidden, and the knowledge made her tryst with him all the more exciting.

Trying to forget, Anna rolled over and attempted to force herself to sleep. It wasn't fair that she had to pay the price for mistakes both of them had made. Were all men such jerks?

Anna felt safe in the cave with Stacey keeping watch. It was surprising to her that other than her dad, Ryan, and Mr. Spate, the world she'd left behind barely impacted on her thoughts at all. All she wanted was to be safe and dry, and off the island. She shut her eyes and must have fallen asleep because when she opened them again, she saw the candles were burning lower and two had gone out. She wondered if it was her turn to keep watch yet. She looked to see who was guarding the tunnel opening and felt a moment of panic when she realized that no one was. After Stacey's watch it was supposed to be Erica's.

"Anna?" a voice whispered in her ear, and she jumped.

"Keep quiet. Don't move." It was Stacey, crouching low in the shadows between Anna and the wall.

"Is it my turn?" Anna whispered back, disoriented. She saw the other girls, slumbering bundles in their sleeping bags.

"No. I thought I heard something outside."

Shit! "What did it sound like?"

"Footsteps."

Anna felt the hairs on the back of her neck begin to rise. "Stacey, are you sure?"

"No."

Anna listened hard and heard nothing. She was wide awake now. "Can you still hear it?"

"It stopped right before I woke you."

"Maybe it was an animal."

"Maybe." The tone of her voice indicated Stacey didn't believe it. "It's possible my mind's playing tricks on me."

"What should we do?"

"I don't want to scare everyone, but I think we should go and wake the others up."

"Definitely."

"But I don't want them bitching and making a lot of noise."

Anna nodded. She picked at the scabs on her face nervously. Even if no one was there, she knew she'd never be able to fall back asleep that night. "Let's do it one by one."

"Okay."

Anna slipped out of her sleeping bag and crouched next to Stacey on the cold floor of the cave. She put her pants and tank top back on. "It's worth it, right? Even if it's nothing?"

"I think so. We can relax if no one's there. Have a party. Play truth or dare."

Anna was struck by a perverse urge to giggle, but she managed to fight it back. It was rare for Stacey to make a joke. Anna felt terrified, but alive. "Let's do it."

Anna and Stacey got up and moved silently to each of the girls, rousing them gently in turn. When Anna touched Kara's shoulder, she jerked and kicked out her legs.

"It's okay," Anna said. "You need to get up." Kara mumbled something and opened her eyes, and they moved on to Alice.

The girls got dressed, and soon all of them were sitting up, staring at the opening that led to the forest as nervous minutes passed slowly. After a while, when no further sounds came, the mood changed from tension and anxiety to plain fatigue.

"I'm going back to sleep," Alice muttered.

Erica sighed and lay back down. "False alarm, I guess."

"How come it's always Stacey who hears things?" Kara grumbled, burrowing into her sleeping bag.

Her comment was followed almost immediately by a faint crackling noise from outside, and she sat right back up again. It was like Kara's comment had jinxed them. Anna realized that something, or someone, was definitely out there beyond the tunnel. The girls turned stricken faces to one another.

Please don't let it be the man with the gun, Anna prayed. Let it be anything but that. Then she realized she didn't want it to be a wolf or a bear, either. It's nothing, she told herself. Just a squirrel or some other furry little creature. Maybe a lizard or a rat. Not the man with the gun.

But her worst fears were confirmed as she listened to the sound resolve into footsteps.

"See!" Stacey whispered. "I told you! There's someone walking around out there. Aren't you glad I woke you up now?"

"Oh God," Erica blurted, and Kara told her to shut up.

"The hole," Stacey said. "The left one, like we planned. I've got the flashlight."

Kara nodded.

"Let's bring the candles," Anna said, picking up the one closest to her. Melted wax had cascaded down its base so it looked like a frozen waterfall. I can't believe this is happening, she thought, trying to stay calm.

She got up and all of them quickly headed toward the opening in a state of controlled panic. They left their sleeping bags and backpacks behind, because there wasn't enough time to grab them. Anna thought if it were a person, he'd realize pretty quickly someone had been in the cave. And unless he was really stupid, he'd be able to figure out exactly where they were hiding. Still, there was little else Anna could do but follow the others through the opening and into the space beyond. Soon she was crouching in the darkness with her terrified companions.

Stacey turned off the flashlight and the space was lit only by Anna's candle. It was smaller than the cave they'd slept in, and had dark openings on all sides that seemed to lead to absolute blackness. The ceiling was so low that Anna couldn't stand up straight, and she noticed only Stacey was short enough to stand.

It was funny, Anna thought, but in the dim candlelight the girls all looked the same to her. You couldn't tell Stacey was probably a nerd back home, or that Kara was gorgeous. Those distinctions ceased to matter anymore because everyone's face was the same shade of yellow-gray.

"Snuff out that candle, Anna," Kara said urgently. "We don't want to be seen."

Anna blew the candle out and plunged the girls into velvety darkness. A candle was still burning in the center of the larger cave, and they could peer through the opening of their tunnel and see it flickering. From their vantage point they were able to observe a large portion of the cavern without being seen.

Anna knelt on the wet floor and watched nervously, hoping they were all overreacting and would soon be able to reemerge.

"If it's the man with the gun we'll have to go even deeper," Stacey whispered, which was the last thing Anna wanted to hear.

"It's way too dark," Erica replied. "Who knows what's back there?"

Anna was starting to feel claustrophobic, and she didn't know how long she'd be able to contain the feeling. The walls of the cave seemed to be contracting, pressing in on her. She put her hands to her temples and rubbed her eyes.

"Oh fuck," Erica said suddenly, and Anna's heart sank.

Time seemed to slow down as she peered back out the opening and saw a man emerge from the shadows, as though their terror had conjured him up. He'd stepped out of the tunnel at the other end of the cave and was standing very still. It was hard to see him with only one candle burning, but he looked big. Anna was afraid to even swallow in case he heard it.

"Is it him?" Alice whispered softly.

"I can't tell," Stacey whispered back.

"Shhh," Kara cautioned. "He doesn't know we're here."

The man took a step out of the shadows, toward the candle in the center of the cave. In the low light, and at that distance, it was impossible for Anna to see his features clearly, and he wore a baseball cap that further masked his face. He took off a green poncho and tossed it on the floor at his feet. He was tall, she could see that, but at least he wasn't carrying any sort of weapon, which she took as a positive sign.

She watched as he glanced down at their abandoned items, their sleeping bags, their clothes. Anna's feet were cold on the wet clay. She'd fled the cave so fast she didn't even have her shoes on. Only Stacey had remembered hers; the others were all barefoot.

The man seemed puzzled. He turned his head to look back the way he'd come, and then he turned to look at the openings, including the cave in which the five girls hid. He scanned it, trying to peer into the darkness.

The man walked over to the candle in the center of the room and picked it up. Anna could see him more clearly now. He was wearing a camouflage jacket and dark pants. He was heavy and disheveled, with matted black hair poking out from under his green hat. She couldn't see his eyes. Was he the murderer? The man with the gun? It was impossible to tell. He definitely didn't look like someone who was there to rescue them. There was something about him, the way he stood, that made her feel afraid.

"Do you think he'll just leave?" Alice whispered.

"No."

"Shut up or he'll hear you," Anna whispered back.

The man continued to scan the caves, his head moving back and forth like he had all the time in the world.

"What if he comes this way?" Erica asked.

"Then we go deeper."

The man glanced over at the container filled with food and the stack of cans.

"What's he doing?"

Anna wished they'd stop whispering because the man might be able to hear them, and then it would all be over. Anna was struck by the certainty he'd search the caves and find them. This same thought must have occurred to Stacey because Anna felt her tugging at her shirt.

"Let's go. We have to go deeper. Come on."

"Okay."

The girls tried moving in a silent line into one of the larger holes at the back of their cave, but it was impossible to see in the dark. Anna was too afraid to relight her candle in case the man saw. Besides, she realized she'd stupidly left the matches behind, and the flashlight was definitely too bright to turn on. She huddled together with the other girls, watching the man again.

He'd switched on the battery-powered lantern and was over at the stack of supplies. He clutched a can, which he tossed from hand to hand, and then he picked up a metal can opener from a cardboard box. It appeared as though he were lost in thought. He looked in the direction of the girls and then took a step forward.

He knows exactly where we are, Anna thought, with the clarity of true fear. He lives here, he can tell somehow. And now he's going to find us.

Sure enough, the man walked right over to the cave where they were hiding. Anna shrank back against the wall, hands feeling desperately for an opening, but she couldn't find one. Jesus, please, she thought, her heart pounding as she broke into a cold sweat.

Then the man did something very strange. He knelt down in front of their cave, just a few yards from where they hid in the dark. He pulled back his arm like he was bowling, and then he rolled the can into the cave. It stopped a few feet from Anna's bare foot. She could hear her own ragged breathing and tried to hold her breath. She stared at the can, which lay there, dented. There was a clatter as the man tossed the can opener after it. What the fuck?

None of the girls spoke or moved. The man was so close to them, but Anna knew the darkness prevented him from seeing them. The silence was oppressive, and Anna wondered what the man was going to do next. If he was indeed the man with the gun, then it would be something terrible. And if he wasn't, if he was just a crazy hermit or a hunter without a license, he might still be angry his space had been invaded. There was no telling what a man like him might do alone in the forest with them, especially if he was pissed off. Anna wished they had weapons to defend themselves, but it was too late for that.

The man stood, peering into the darkness. Anna knew he had candles, as well as the lantern, and probably another flashlight somewhere. He could easily pick something up and come into the cave. He was deliberately trying to frighten them by keeping them in the dark.

The man rubbed his belly and then, without warning, started to laugh. He put his hands on his sides and laughed and laughed until it turned into a coughing fit. Then he spoke.

## Chapter Eight

# The Kiss

"Hey girlies," the man said. His voice was thick and slow. "I gave you a treat, and where's my thanks?" He mumbled something to himself that Anna didn't catch. Then he said, "I know you're there, sitting in the dark, feeling scared and lonely. Don't you like peaches? One little can for five little girls won't last long at all." He sneezed, and Anna jumped. "Bless me. I must be allergic to your sweet perfumes."

Oh my God, Anna thought. He sounded mentally ill, maybe completely deranged.

He sat down clumsily on the floor in front of the cave in which Anna and the other girls hid.

"I can see you've helped yourself to my food and water, and you know what? That's okay. I thought those peaches might make a nice dessert for you. There's no way out of that cave, by the way. Those little holes in the back are dead ends. The only way out is the way you came in." He sneezed again and wiped his nose on the back of his sleeve. "You can come out anytime you want. I won't hurt you. My name's Leod. That's not my real name, you know, but it's what everyone calls me. This is where I've been living for the past month or so. I think I'm being pretty calm about everything, considering you're in my house." He snickered like a madman. "I'm not mad at you. Honest. I haven't had any visitors in a long while."

The more the man talked, the more afraid Anna felt. There was something really wrong with him, like a crazy, homeless person who kept up a constant dialogue with himself.

The man stood up. "Come out when you're ready, girls. I'm going to make some food now, because I'm hungry." He walked away from them slowly to the other side of the cave.

"What the fuck are we going to do?" Erica whispered. "I think he's whacked."

"That doesn't mean he's dangerous," Stacey replied. "We just need to analyze the situation."

"How does he know there are five of us?" Anna asked.

"He's been watching," Kara said. "He's probably the guy who's been shooting at us."

Erica shook her head. "Fuck."

"Listen. Hear that?"

The man was singing to himself as he prepared his meal, and his eerie, low-pitched voice echoed across the cavern.

"What a freak," Erica whispered.

Alice scowled. "He sounds like a retard."

"We need a plan," Stacey told the others. "Retard or not, he thinks he's got us trapped."

"You and your plans."

"We could rush him," Erica suggested. "Take him off guard."

"He's a big guy. Does anyone want to risk that? He could really hurt us if he wanted to."

"We can't attack him," Anna said. While the others were talking she'd been thinking. The man was still singing and mumbling to himself like a mental patient. He hadn't hurt them yet, but who knew what he was planning? There wasn't any need to trigger potential rage by attacking him. "He wants us here," Anna said. "But that doesn't mean he's going to hurt us."

Kara frowned. "Says who?"

"He hasn't done anything bad to us yet. In fact, he gave us peaches. He obviously knows where we are, so there's not much point hiding. I think we should just walk out there and be honest with him." Anna could barely believe what she heard herself saying.

"Bitch, are you crazy?" Erica whispered, but Stacey was nodding.

"Listen," Stacey said. "I don't trust this guy at all, because he's really strange, but Anna has a point. If we come out, maybe we can get past him to the tunnel and into the forest. He's so big, we could probably outrun him."

"Unless he's the man with the gun, in which case he could start shooting."

"I don't see a gun, and he hasn't shown any signs of violence yet. I think it's worth the risk. Besides, he could shoot us in here just as easily, right?"

"So we'll come out," Kara asserted, like the idea had been hers to begin with. "And when we get the chance we'll make a break for it."

"Okay."

"Deal."

Even Alice voiced her agreement.

Anna thought that everyone, including herself, sounded preternaturally calm. It was taking a lot of effort, because inside she was scared shitless. She knew they couldn't screw up if they wanted to make it safely out of the caves.

The man still had his back to them, preparing his food. It looked like he'd made himself a sandwich, and Anna heard the sound of a soda can being opened.

"So we just walk out there? Into the cave and confront him?" Erica asked.

"I guess so," Kara said.

Anna's stomach clenched up. "On the count of five?"

"Sure."

"Ready?"

The girls whispered the count together, and when they got to five, Stacey turned on the flashlight and they filed out of their hiding place and into the cave. I hope this is the right decision, Anna thought nervously.

The man turned around. He didn't appear particularly surprised to see them. In one hand was his sandwich and in the other was a can of root beer. The girls stood and stared at him across the cave.

"Howdy," he said. Now that Anna was closer to him she could see there was something wrong with his face. He had a weird indentation on his forehead, like a dimple, that his cap failed to hide. His nose was flat and slightly misshapen. She also noticed the left side of his body seemed rigid and awkward, too, like maybe he'd had a stroke and never fully recovered.

"My name's Leod," he said. "But I guess I told you that already." He stood stiffly, watching them, and they stared back, unsure of what to do. Anna realized no one wanted to make the first move. Leod took a bite of his sandwich and chewed it slowly. "I'm glad you came out of that cave on your own. I thought you would, given time." He paused. "Well, speak up, girlies. Don't be shy." His eyes located Kara, and they lingered on her chest before moving down to her legs.

"We need your help," Kara said. "We're lost."

Leod raised his eyes to meet hers. "I know that. No one comes here on purpose. Of course you're lost." His eyes looked weird, slightly askew, like there was something broken inside him. He was the kind of guy people crossed the street to avoid, Anna thought. A genuine creep.

"Can you help us?" Stacey asked.

"Sure, sure," Leod said excitedly, still looking at Kara. He took another bite of his sandwich and washed it down with a swig of root beer. "I'll help you real good."

Anna and Stacey exchanged apprehensive glances. Leod's words weren't setting their minds at ease.

"Do you have a telephone?" Kara asked. "We need to call nine-one-one."

"They don't have nine-one-one on Andros," Leod replied. "Besides, I don't have a phone anyway. What would I need with a phone?" He was acting like Kara's question was absurd.

"We have to get to the coast and find help," Kara plowed ahead. "We've been lost in the forest since Saturday."

Leod took a step closer. The closer he got, the bigger he seemed. "Saturday? Boy, that's a long time. I can help you, though, 'cause I know where the coast is. We're a long way from it, but I know how to get there. Say, where do you girlies come from?"

"Camp," Stacey said quickly, before anyone else could answer. "We were on a field trip and we got lost."

"Huh." The response seemed to satisfy him. He took another shambling step toward them and followed it with a sip of root beer.

Anna recognized that their plan had been pretty fucking poor. It would be impossible to get past this lumbering creature and out the narrow tunnel that led to the forest. She hadn't realized how truly massive he was until they'd come out into the open.

"So you'll help us?" Kara asked him. "We need help right away, like, right now."

Leod's face abruptly darkened, and even in the dim light Anna could see a frown crease his scarred forehead. "I can't do anything right now!" he snapped. "Not until Jume comes back. I thought you understood. He makes the decisions around here." The girls shrank back, and Leod sighed. "I'm sorry. I thought I explained already, but I guess I forgot." He sounded petulant. "Jume's my best friend."

"When is he coming back?" Alice asked, annoyed. Anna thought that was definitely the wrong attitude to take with this guy. Leod seemed pretty insane, and he was possibly the man who'd been shooting at them. She wanted to grab Alice and shake some sense into her.

"We've been out here for days. You have to help us," Kara added and Leod scowled again.

He tore into his sandwich and chewed violently. Then he

smiled. His face was like a baby's, Anna thought, rapidly displaying all kinds of emotions. "Jume will be back soon. He's just checking on some things. Don't you worry."

"When he comes, you'll help us then?"

"Sure, if that's what he wants. I let him do the thinking around here. It hurts too much when I try to think. Say, girlies, what are your names? You haven't even told me yet."

The girls introduced themselves one by one, starting with Kara. Anna thought about giving a fake name, but then she realized it didn't matter if this guy knew who she was or not. The only important thing was that he didn't hurt them.

"You have some pretty names all right, but Kara's the prettiest," Leod said. Of all the girls, it was obvious to Anna that Kara fascinated him the most. "Kara's a real pretty name." His eyes lingered on where her breasts pushed out her orange tank top. "How old are you, girlie?"

"Seventeen."

Leod nodded and didn't say anything else, but he seemed satisfied. His weird eyes passed over the others, and Anna looked away when she felt them on her. She knew what he was thinking about, what he wanted.

"Hey, you know something?" he exclaimed in his odd-sounding voice. "I bet you're tired. I bet I ruined your beauty sleep. Don't mind me. You can lie down again, go back to sleep."

Leod's offer wasn't too enticing, Anna thought. It just made him sound even more like a psycho.

"We're not tired," Stacey protested. "It's almost morning anyway."

Leod frowned, confused by the lie. "No, it's not."

"Yes, it is."

Leod looked puzzled. He brought his arm up as if to take a sip of root beer, but then brought it down again, like a broken robot. Then his face brightened. "If it's morning, I bet you're hungry for breakfast! Eggs and bacon, not cans of peaches!"

"Actually," Anna said, "we've eaten, remember? All we want now is some fresh air. It's cold and dark in here, and we want to see the sun. If you don't mind, we were thinking of going outside for a minute."

"Yeah," Alice said, and for once Anna was glad to hear her speak up.

"Fresh air," Leod mused, chewing the inside of his cheek. "I don't think so. The sun's not even up yet and it's still raining. Let's just stay inside until Jume comes back. He'll be mad if I let you get away without introducing him."

"But we really want to go out," Anna pleaded.

Leod looked nervous. "I'm afraid I can't let you. Not until Jume gets here."

"Leod, I have to go to the bathroom," Erica said. Smart thinking, Anna thought, because he'd have to let them outside for that. "You don't want me to go in here, do you?"

Leod smiled. "First cave on the right. That's my bathroom. It's a good thing you didn't pick that one to hide in. That's where I go when it rains. There's even some TP back there for you."

Anna felt despair, and she didn't know what to try next. They'd talked about running out of the cave, but it didn't seem likely now that they stood only a few paces away from the man. Who'd be the first one to act? It seemed like he'd just grab them on the way out.

"You can't do this," Alice said to Leod, stepping forward.

"Alice, shut up," Erica whispered. "Don't say any more to him."

Alice ignored her. "You're acting like an asshole," she continued, walking right up to the man. She was either very brave or very stupid, and Anna knew for sure which one it was. "Are you, like, a retard or something?"

Anna couldn't believe what she'd just said, and she wondered if Alice had lost her mind.

"Alice—" Stacey cautioned, but it was too late. Alice made a sudden break for the opening that led to the outside, revealing her strategy, as dumb as it was. Leod turned, much faster than his size and clumsiness seemed to allow for, and he dropped his half-eaten sandwich and can of root beer.

One second Alice was running and it looked like she might even make it, and the next, Leod was in her path. In the confusion, the other girls started running, too, but Leod spun Alice in front of him, effectively blocking the only exit. Anna slipped sideways around the edge of the cave, trying to keep as far away from Leod as she could. She stumbled over something and realized it was her boots. She grabbed them. The girls were all screaming and yelling, and Leod was screaming, too.

As Anna watched, Alice flailed at Leod's torso until he finally brought a fist down on the top of her head. He hit her only once, but the dull thwacking sound reverberated through the cavern, and Alice released her hold. She fell face down and rolled up into a ball, clutching her head.

"I told you to stay put!" Leod screamed. Anna stopped trying to run and stared at him with fear and dread. The others did the same, Kara breathing hard as she leaned against the cave wall. "Didn't you understand?" Alice writhed on the floor as Leod looked around at the girls. "Look what you made me do."

"She's really hurt," Stacey murmured at last, horrified.

They were prisoners now, Anna realized, captives of this lunatic. The man was going to keep them down in the caves forever. No one knew where they were, so no one was going to rescue them. Anna realized it was likely the man was indeed the shooter, had set everything up in advance, and killed Adler just to hunt them down like animals. Lindsay had been right!

"I told her not to run," Leod said, pulling at his shirt. "If she'd listened, she'd be all right. Why did she try to run away? Jume will be so upset with me."

Alice began to crawl across the wet floor, over sleeping bags and strewn clothes, toward the back of the cave. Stacey moved over to her when she reached the wall, and knelt down to help the injured girl. Leod shuffled nervously from foot to foot.

"She's not really hurt, is she?" he asked.

"You could have killed her," Stacey said. Her voice trembled slightly and Anna could tell she was making an effort to hide her fear. Anna was amazed Stacey even had the strength to speak at all. Anna's legs were shaking so much it was hard to stand up.

"She'll be okay." Leod looked down at his spilled root beer. "You," he said suddenly, gazing at Erica. "Tattoo girlie. What's your name again?"

"Erica."

"Oh yeah, right. Go get me another root beer. You know

where they are." It was clear he didn't want to move away from the entrance. "Do it!"

Erica walked stiffly to the pile of cans and got one out, as Anna, Stacey, and Kara watched.

"Bring it here," Leod said. "I won't hurt you."

Erica walked over to Leod and held it out. Leod took the soda and opened it as she quickly retreated to the safety of the wall. He drank from the can and licked his lips as his eyes found Kara again. Anna could see what the promise of those eyes held, and she was glad they weren't directed at her. She dropped her boots to the ground and slipped her feet into them.

"I feel bad I hurt your friend," Leod said to Kara. "I didn't mean to. Now I want you to make me feel better. Come over here and give me a kiss, little girl. Make it wet." He said the words in such a nonchalant way, Anna thought she must have misheard.

Evidently so did Kara because she asked, "What?!"

"I want a kiss from you because I'm feeling bad. I haven't kissed a girl in eight whole years. Now I want one from you, and I want it on the lips."

"No way," Kara said, before she could even think about it. A split second later, Anna could tell she regretted her abrupt rebuttal, but it was too late.

Leod's face contorted into a grimace of pain. "Yes! A kiss! Now!" His left hand balled into a fist. "You think I'm stupid, but I'm the one in control now."

"Hey Leod," Stacey called out softly, trying to distract him.

He looked in her direction. "Yeah?"

"What if we make an exchange?"

With a mounting sense of horror, Anna wondered what Stacey had in mind. She knew Stacey was smart, probably the smartest of all of them, and if they were going to get out of the cave in one piece, it would most likely be because of her.

"I'm listening," Leod said.

"If we do something for you, then maybe you could do something for us." The light flickered in her dark eyes.

"What do you mean?"

"Well, if you want a kiss, maybe you could give us something in return."

"I don't want a kiss from you. You're ugly, and you're way too small."

"But you want one from Kara. What would you do for us if Kara gave you a nice big kiss on the lips?"

Kara looked totally revolted, like she was about to vomit. "No way," she whispered to Stacey, before Leod could even respond. "No fucking way."

Leod heard and looked hurt. With his brow puckered, the shiny dimple on his forehead was accentuated by the candlelight.

"Kara, think about it," Stacey said, maintaining a soothing tone. "If you do something nice for Leod, he might do something nice for us." She spoke slowly and clearly so Leod could understand. Alice was slumped at the edge of the cave, moaning and whimpering about her head, but everyone ignored her. They had to deal with Leod first.

"Wouldn't it be nice if Leod helped us out?" Stacey continued. "Leod, what could you do for us if Kara gave you a kiss on the lips? Would you let us go outside for a moment? Just one minute or two? We won't run away, because there's nowhere to go."

Leod was deep in thought. "You mean an exchange," he finally said. "Like a game. Well, that's a fun idea, but I'd need more than a kiss to let you go out." He paused. "A lot more."

Anna saw Kara shudder involuntarily.

Stacey pressed on. "How much more, Leod?" What was Stacey up to?

"You know. All the way." Anna felt a rolling wave of repulsion at the thought. This guy was as much of a sicko as he looked.

"All the way?"

"Yes. Sex."

Stacey kept her face blank. "Then you'd let us go outside?"

Leod suddenly smiled, lost in thought. "I sure would."

"Do you promise?

"I promise."

"I won't do it!" Kara said loudly, scowling at Stacey. "I'd rather die than do that with him." She didn't look so pretty now, Anna thought uncharitably. In fact, Kara looked terrified, and to be honest, Anna was terrified for her. A tear came down Kara's cheek and she swiped at it angrily.

Leod looked serene, like a big, fat Buddha who'd secretly gone insane. "If Kara gives me sex, then I'll let you all go," he proclaimed. "Jume will understand that. I haven't had sex since before my accident. Girls don't like me anymore because my head looks funny and I act strange. I lost part of my brain, you know. The doctors said I was a miracle."

"We like you," Stacey said, as though she were talking to

a child. "But what if Kara doesn't want to have sex with you? Sex is a really big deal for girls. Maybe we can make another kind of exchange."

"No," Leod said, his voice hard-edged. "I like the deal we just made. You promised and I agreed. I want to have sex with Kara, and I'm going to."

Erica took a step forward. She'd been very quiet so far, but now she was about to speak her mind. "I'll do it, Leod," she said. "If you want. It's nothing to me." She looked at the other girls, who were staring at her with gaping mouths, but she ignored them. Anna had no clue what Erica was doing, or why. What the hell was she thinking?

"Leod, we need to talk for a moment," Stacey interrupted, before he could answer. "I mean just us girls. Will you give us a second?"

"Sure." He sipped his root beer and blinked, his eyes like lumps of coal.

The girls clustered at the other end of the cave, away from Leod and the tunnel leading to freedom. Alice was still lying on the floor, badly injured, but there wasn't time for her yet.

"Erica, are you nuts?" Kara hissed.

"We obviously can't trust this guy," Stacey whispered. "He has no intention of letting us go."

"We need to come up with some other plan," Anna said, trying not to show how shocked she was by Erica's offer. "Maybe this Jume guy will come back and help us."

"You don't understand," Erica told the group. "I'm planning to fake Leod out and kick him in the balls. It's something I did once, when this asshole tried to rape me after a party. That's one of the reasons I hate guys so much. I kicked him so hard,

I think I ruptured something inside him. I know I could do it to Leod."

Anna didn't think it sounded very likely, given that Leod was twice Erica's size.

"He might hit back," Stacey warned.

"We're totally fucked anyway."

"Maybe it would work," Kara said. "You could kick him, and then we could all jump him at once. We could grab cans and hit him on the head with them. His head looks fucked-up already."

Stacey looked from one girl to another. "We'd have to time it right."

Jesus, Anna thought.

"When he's on top of me," Erica insisted. "Do it then. Hit him on the head when he's distracted and I'll kick him in the balls. Then we can run out." The plan sounded way too dangerous to Anna, but it was too late to think of anything else, because Leod was getting agitated.

"Enough talk," he called out from across the cave. "Kissing time."

"So how about me?" Erica yelled back. "We talked it over. Kara here, she thinks you're ugly, but I don't."

"You don't?"

"No, I think you're kind of cute, like a teddy bear. I'll do it with you. Does that sound like a deal? Then afterward you can let us go outside."

"Sex. With you." Leod looked like he was figuring out the cost of some astronomically expensive purchase. He finally grinned. Anna saw that some of his teeth were black and rotted, up to the gumline. "Okay, tattoo girlie. You're not so bad. All the way, right?"

"Right. But only if you let us out afterward."

"Sure, sure. I'll let you out."

Erica slipped off her tank top, revealing a bra stained with sweat and dirt. She turned back and whispered, "When he starts kissing me, grab the cans. Then beat the hell out of him." She arranged her face into a smile and walked across the cave to meet Leod.

Anna knew their plan had little chance of success, but it was their only hope, so they had to make it work. She didn't know how she'd ever repay Erica for saving them like this.

Erica sat down on a sleeping bag in the center of the cave. "Come over here, Leod." She stretched out her legs in a parody of a provocative pose. "Do you like what you see?" She unbuttoned her pants and slowly pushed them down to her ankles.

Leod shambled over to her and stood, looking down. In doing so, he moved away from the opening of the cave. He kneeled and caressed Erica's dirty hair with a massive paw. Soon they were kissing, his big body straddling hers.

"Let's go," Stacey whispered and the three girls crept around the edge of the cave to grab hold of the cans. Only Alice remained behind, still slumped on the ground.

"Hey!" Anna heard suddenly whispered in her ear. It was Kara. "Look!" Leod was down on all fours, embracing Erica, and the path to the tunnel was completely clear. "We can sneak out now! We can run!"

It was one of those terrible moral choices Anna always worried about encountering, the sort of choice that let you know what kind of person you were. She knew she should follow through with the plan they'd all formulated, but on the other hand she didn't know Erica that well, and her own life was at stake. Yet she also knew she couldn't live with herself if she abandoned the girl. She just couldn't be as cold as Kara. "Don't," she whispered. "We need to help Erica."

"Fuck that!" Kara hissed. "I'm going for it." She slipped away from the wall toward the opening.

What happened next was unexpected. Leod must have glimpsed Kara's shadow moving across the wall because he arched up, screaming.

"No!" he yelled, and in an instant he was off Erica and grabbing at Kara's legs. He caught her right foot and jerked it out from under her so she sprawled on the floor of the cave. Leod crawled up her legs and got on top of her, pressing her down as she screamed and struggled to get away. It was like something out of a horror movie.

"Run!" Erica yelled, and Anna realized there was still an opportunity for her and the others to escape. Erica scrambled past Leod and Kara to the opening that led outside, and within seconds she was through it.

Fuck, Anna thought, and made a dash for it herself. She could hear Stacey right behind her. She didn't know what Leod was doing to Kara, but she hoped Kara could fend for herself. Anna's hands scrabbled at the limestone walls as she tore through the opening and into the narrow tunnel that led to freedom.

Just as she was about to tumble out of the mouth of the cave and into daylight, she heard Erica yell. "Anna! Look out! There's a man out here!"

"Jesus!" Anna screamed, tumbled, and then tried to regain her footing in the narrow space. Erica had managed to escape, but Anna couldn't get up in time. She caught a glimpse of Erica running away through the trees, but her own path was blocked by a dark shadow. Anna had no choice but to reverse her direction and fall back into the cave, knocking Stacey over in the process.

As Anna got shakily to her feet, she saw Leod still bent over Kara, a nightmarish scene. Kara's clothes were torn and she was face down in the dirt. Leod was pressing a hand on the back of her head, trying to muffle her screams. His pants were off and his face was grim and red as he tried to force himself on her. Anna couldn't tear her eyes away. He looked up in surprise as she and Stacey tumbled back into the cave.

Now there's a photo, Anna thought crazily. One for the high school art show indeed.

"Leod!" came a voice, deep and harsh. The man who'd prevented Anna's escape stepped out of the tunnel and into the cave behind her. "You shit for brains, what's going on? What are all these girls doing here?"

Leod leapt off Kara, a stricken look on his face. He did an awkward shuffle as he tried to pull up his pants.

"It's nothing, please don't be mad," he implored. "We're just having some fun. Please, Jume. Don't be mad at me." His hat had fallen off in his frenzy and Anna saw deep indentations in his head, like his skull had been crushed and put back together again. "I'm sorry, Jume, I'm so sorry."

"Oh, I'm not mad," said the man, stripping off a raincoat. He was tiny, maybe five foot four at the most. But where Leod was flabby and soft, this man was made of wire, all muscles and tendons. He wore a cap, and was dressed in a similar fashion to Leod, green camouflage pants and a jacket. His face was sharp and craggy, with bristly stubble painted across his cheeks and chin. He looked mean, small and mean, Anna thought. His thin lips were very red, almost like he was wearing lipstick.

Jume gazed at the girls and at the mess in the cave. He looked down at Kara's body and then up at Leod with a tight smile. "It seems like you got some explaining to do."

## Chapter Nine

# Jume

"He tried to rape her," Stacey said, pointing at Leod. Kara was on her hands and knees, sobbing. "If you hadn't gotten here, he would have done it."

"He's crazy!" Anna exclaimed. "You've got to help us. Please."

Jume made a curious motion in the air with his hands, like he was trying to calm her down. "I don't have to do anything," he replied finally. Anna realized Jume was shorter than her, even though he was wearing boots. She was still afraid of him.

"They just turned up," Leod said. He shuffled away from Kara, pants still down at his ankles. "You told me, if anyone finds us, keep them in the caves until you get back. I was just doing what you said."

"Nice job," Jume replied, sarcasm dripping from his voice. "So you've had your fun then." He had a strange way of speaking, Anna noticed, putting the emphasis on every other word, which gave his speech a sing-song pattern. Jume looked over at the girls. "You're a fine mess. Dirty and wet. Where'd you all come from?"

"Field trip." Anna marveled at how Stacey could still sound so cool.

Jume wasn't buying it, though. "There're only two schools on Andros and both of them are for natives."

"We're from a wilderness camp," Stacey said. "Camp Archstone. We were hiking and we got lost, and now we need your help."

"That's a lie." There was no anger in Jume's voice, and none visible in his eyes. In fact, there was nothing in his eyes at all. To Anna, his face seemed like a mask he manipulated into human expressions, with no real emotion behind it. He had the dead, flat eyes of a shark, glittering in the candle-light. "Did Leod hurt anyone?" He looked down at Kara. "Other than her?"

"He hit Alice on the head," Stacey said.

"Leod gets funny sometimes. He can't control it. Did he tell you about his accident? Or why we're living down here?"

"No."

Jume paused. "Are you sure?"

"We're telling the truth," Anna pleaded. Jume was obviously a paranoiac, in addition to being a pretty scary guy.

Leod struggled forward. "Aaron—"

"Goddamn it, don't say my real name." Jume didn't even raise his voice. "And zip up your fly while you're at it." Jume looked at the girls and pointed back at Leod. "I bet he told you things he shouldn't have. I can sense it."

Anna and Stacey shook their heads.

223

"I can always tell a liar. Always. A person's eyes move to the left. It's subconscious. You know what we're doing here, right? There's no reason to be dishonest."

"Leod didn't tell us anything," Stacey said.

"Excuse me," Anna broke in, hating the thin, weak sound of her own voice. Jume fixed her with his dead eyes. "Can you just tell us how to get out of here? We don't want to make any trouble for you. We just want to get to the coast, where the towns are. We don't care what you're doing here, really. We just want to get back home."

Jume paused. "Did someone send you to spy on us?"

"No." Anna's mind teemed with awful scenarios. Perhaps these two men were ex-convicts, hiding out on Andros. Maybe murderers. She prayed that Erica would make it to a town and bring back help in time.

"No one sent us," Stacey told Jume. "We're just lost."

Anna was struck by the impossibility of trying to convince him they were telling the truth, because he seemed determined to disbelieve them. "Please, just let us go. We don't even know your names, and nothing bad has happened yet. Not really. We won't even mention we've been here."

"What about her?" Jume said. He was referring to Kara, who sat sobbing on the floor, all the glamour drained out of her. "And her." Alice was a silent body, lying dazed in the corner. "Think they'll keep quiet for long?" His mouth was a tight line. "No way. And one of you got out and ran away. I'm going to have to find her. She won't get far if she doesn't know the forest. I can't let any of you talk, don't you see?"

"We could make up a story," Anna implored, inwardly begging the man to relent.

"There'd be too many questions. You'd tell."

"They said bad things to me," Leod interjected. "They forced me to hurt them. Please don't be mad, Jume. I'm awful sorry. They tried to run away from me."

Jume stared him down. Even though Jume was a whole head shorter, it was clear Leod was very afraid of him. "Leod, you've got us in the shit now," Jume said. "The Mendoza Brothers are due in an hour."

Leod twisted his hands nervously. "You weren't here. You were late. I didn't know what to do."

The Mendoza Brothers, Anna thought. Who were they? What did it mean?

"I was out hunting," Jume explained to Leod as the girls looked on. "Hunting things that bleed. These girls are pretty damn lucky. Today anything suspicious within thirty miles of here gets shot." As he said the words, a silver pistol appeared in his right hand. Anna stared in amazement. It was like a magic trick. One second his hand had been empty, and the next there was a gun in it.

Now there's no denying it, Anna thought. He was the man who'd been hunting them.

Jume saw her reaction and grinned.

"You don't need to hurt us," Stacey begged. "We can be rational about this whole thing."

"Hurt you?" Jume asked. He gestured with the pistol. The gun had made everything seem much more real to Anna. Terrifyingly real. "That's not a bad idea, but I've got a better one. The Mendozas don't like blood and guts, so I can't afford to scare them. Four bodies is four too many, so I'm going to let you live for now. But you're going to be our guests for a while. I'm going to put you in one of the back caves with Leod as your guard, and if I hear any noise, I'll come down there and make you wish you'd never been born. I'll make what Leod was doing to your friend look like nothing." He pointed at Alice and Kara. "Now get those two on their feet, pronto."

When Alice and Kara were standing, supported by Stacey and Anna, they were herded into the opening that was second from the left, next to the cave they'd hidden inside earlier. Leod and Jume walked behind them, holding the flashlight and the lantern. It reminded Anna of being on the hike with Adler breathing down her neck, only this was a thousand times worse. Had that hike only been less than four days ago? It didn't seem possible.

Anna kept reminding herself that this was really happening, that it wasn't a TV show or a movie. In a movie everything would be explained, and everything would work out okay, but real life was just chaos and confusion. She realized there was no guarantee she'd live. Jume seemed to be the man who'd shot Adler and Laura, so he could easily shoot her.

Jume guided Anna and the girls down through a tunnel and into yet another cramped cave. He made them sit on the wet clay floor in a semicircle around the lantern.

"Remember, no talking. No trying to escape. You'll be signing your death warrant if you do. I kill people all the time, and guess what? It takes nothing to pull a trigger, except an index finger, that is. *Bang,* and you're dead, understand?"

The girls nodded. Kara wiped at her eyes.

"Leod is going to watch you. I'm going to find your friend who ran out, and then clean things up in preparation for our visitors." Jume glanced at Leod as he climbed out of the opening. "Don't touch any of them unless they deserve it."

The girls were alone with Leod again. Alone with a madman, Anna thought. She wasn't sure which one was worse, Leod or Jume. At least Leod didn't have a gun, and fortunately he only seemed interested in Kara. Once Jume had left, Leod resumed leering at the girl, and she bunched up in the corner, as far away from him as she could get. Alice looked semicomatose, like she could be suffering from a concussion. She'd been very quiet since Leod had hit her.

Anna watched Leod warily as he stared at Kara with his glazed eyes. They were all silent for a long time. Anna could see no way to escape. There wasn't even any way to talk among themselves without Leod hearing.

"Boy, Jume's mad," Leod said at last. "I don't like it when he gets mad at me. We're best friends, you know." He sighed. "I don't feel too good." He swung his ruined head toward Stacey. "Can we make another exchange? Another deal?"

"No. Deals are over," Stacey replied. To Anna, it sounded like even she was close to giving up.

"Why?"

"Because you're crazy," Kara spat.

"And because you broke the rules," Stacey added.

Leod got flustered. "No, I didn't. You said I could get a kiss. On Kara's lips."

"No, Leod. You know that wasn't the deal. Besides, you did much more than kiss her, and you hurt Alice's head, too."

"I didn't mean to."

"Yes, you did," Kara hissed from the back of the cave, eyes filled with anger. "You're a monster. You tried to rape me."

"No, no, just kissing," Leod said, nonsensically. He faced the hard eyes of the girls and looked away. "You be quiet now or I'll hit you, all of you. You're just girlies and I'm a man."

"You're not a man," Kara continued, "and Jume knows it. You're just a filthy, disgusting, retarded monster. That's why he keeps you down here in the caves like an animal."

Anna wished she'd stop talking. The last thing they needed was to incite him to violence again. "Cut it out, Kara," she said.

"Jume lives here, too. He loves me. He looks after me." Leod was starting to get angry. "He trusts me, too. After my accident I wasn't good for anything else, that's what he said. I had to come and work for him. I had to do things, special jobs. Don't you understand?"

"No."

"Kara, don't provoke him anymore," Stacey told her. "Look what he did to Alice."

"At least he didn't try to rape her!" Kara yelled, losing her self-control. "He's a monster!"

"Kara, please," Anna implored, but it was too late.

Leod leapt to his feet, knocking his head on the low ceiling of the cave. "Jume loves me! He looks after me! I'm like a brother to him!"

Anna heard rapid footsteps and Jume appeared in the entrance. She was almost relieved, because Leod looked ready to start hitting them.

"Aw, Leod," he said. He sounded almost sad. "Come with me. You're riling them up. Girls, you're testing my patience. I really don't want to hurt you, but I'll blow your brains out if I have to. It's your decision." He paused. "I took care of your friend, by the way. I found her in the forest not far from here and shot her in the head. I didn't have time to drag her body back."

Anna didn't know if Jume was telling the truth about Erica or not, but she felt terrified. She couldn't believe Erica might be dead.

"We'll be quiet," Stacey said softly.

"Okay then. Leod, come." Jume disappeared and Leod followed him with a backward glance at Kara. The four girls were now alone.

"Kara, you have to keep it together," Anna said. "These guys are criminals or drug dealers, or something else bad. Terrorists maybe. We need to figure out how to escape before they shoot us."

Stacey was nodding as Anna spoke.

"There is no escape," Kara said despondently. "We'll be stuck in this place forever, until we're dead." Anna wondered if Kara was mad at her and Stacey for running out and leaving her with Leod.

"My head," Alice moaned. They turned to look at her. It was the first thing she'd said in a while. "It hurts so much."

"You'll be okay," Stacey told her dismissively. Anna knew they had much bigger problems to worry about than Alice. Turning back to the others, Stacey said, "Listen, if they were going to shoot us, they probably would have done it already. There's a big difference between smuggling drugs, or whatever they're up to, and premeditated murder."

"He shot Adler, didn't he?" Anna asked. "And Laura? Maybe Erica, too."

"We don't know that for sure."

Anna thought at this point Stacey's hyperrational tone had

to be a cover for her own fear and anxiety, and also an attempt to keep them all calm. She knew there was nothing in the world to stop Jume from shooting all four of them and leaving their bodies to rot in the caves.

"I'm not planning on dying in here," Stacey continued, looking around at her companions. "This whole experience is one big test. A much more difficult one than Camp Archstone planned for us, but still a test. If we stick together and come up with a plan, we'll survive."

"Thanks for the pep talk," Kara said, "but you're deluded, bitch."

Anna noticed that despite her words, Kara seemed to be calming down, perhaps reassured by Stacey's logical approach and also the absence of Leod.

"I feel sick," Alice croaked, and she threw up noisily in the corner. The stench of her vomit soon filled their small enclosure.

"Great," Kara muttered.

Anna could hear echoes of Leod and Jume talking, and noises that sounded like they were moving things around. Whoever the Mendoza Brothers were, she had a pretty good idea they weren't likely to help her and the other girls. "What do you think they're doing out there?" she asked Stacey.

"I think a drug deal's going down, but I'm not sure."

Anna wanted to laugh. It sounded like a line from some bad cop flick, or *CSI: Miami.*

"They're both too stupid to be criminal masterminds," Kara pointed out. She seemed to be slowly recovering from Leod's attack.

"I don't know what to think," Anna said. She put her head in her hands for a moment. If Jume hadn't shot them, then maybe he wanted them alive for some other purpose.

"Put yourself in their shoes," Stacey said. "It's more work for them to kill us than to let us live."

This didn't sound too convincing to Anna. I might not get out of this okay, she thought starkly. She'd seen Jume's face, and Leod's, too, and she could describe them well. Would Jume risk letting them go free? He couldn't, she understood. Both he and Leod were probably going to kill them, maybe rape them first, and just the thought of it made her want to throw up, like Alice had.

She sat with the others, nervously in the dark, and many minutes passed. Her legs kept falling asleep, but there was too little room to stretch them out. Alice lay on her side, eyes shut, taking shallow breaths. At some point the voices in the main cavern multiplied, and Anna realized the men Leod and Jume were waiting for had arrived.

She'd spent so long being scared that now she was just numb. The men would either hurt them or let them go. The resolution was out of her hands, which gave her an odd sensation of freedom amidst the dread. She wished she could use the feeling to empower herself somehow, but she saw no way out of her predicament. The only time she'd ever felt the exact same way was right before her abortion, when she and her uncle had gotten out of the car at the clinic and seen protesters waving signs.

ABORTION HOLOCAUST, the signs read. SINNERS REPENT! and SUFFER THE CHILDREN. Some of them were decorated with disgusting illustrations and photographs. Anna had been crying even before she saw the signs, and the tears incited her uncle to abuse.

"They're right, you know," he told her, as they walked past

the jeering crowd. He was wearing dark glasses and his collar was turned up so he wouldn't be recognized. Her father had forced him to take her, because he couldn't risk going himself in case someone recognized him. "Abortion is a terrible sin, Anna. God may never forgive you, and he may never forgive this family. If I burn in hellfire, it's for you, Anna, for you."

She knew what her uncle was saying was crazy, but at the same time it hurt her deeply. She thought about telling him the truth, because there was no reason not to, but then Mr. Spate would be sent to jail, Ryan would dump her, and inevitably her dad would find some way to make it all her fault. Or so she'd thought at the time.

It had been cold and bright in the exam room, Anna dressed only in a flimsy blue gown that tied at the back. The nurse was all business and she questioned Anna brusquely, as though Anna were a faceless nonentity, not even a person. In a way it was worse than the people outside holding signs.

Anna was made to lie down on a stretcher and hooked up to an IV. The nurse gave her something to relax and she didn't remember much beyond that moment. And thank God for that, she thought. Riding home in the car with her uncle, a yellow towel over her lap, he'd quoted Scripture to her as she'd thrown up.

What stuck with her afterward was the awful feeling of guilt, like she was falling down a bottomless well. She definitely hadn't wanted a baby, but she hadn't wanted an abortion, either.

"A necessary evil is still an evil," her dad had told her when she got back home, which made her feel even worse. Her guilt and despair became endless, as if there'd be no relief. It was after the abortion that her drinking increased, as did the sneaking out and getting high. Anything to blank out the pain.

"Listen," Stacey whispered, bringing Anna back to the present. The voices outside had suddenly become more excited, and there seemed to be a lot of them. Anna realized if all those men could get to the caves, there must be some kind of road or pathway nearby. If they got out of the caves alive, they could search for it and find a way out of the forest. But it was doubtful they'd get that chance.

Anna could hear Jume talking, and then a deeper voice, and then another. She couldn't tell if they were speaking Spanish or English. She heard Jume laugh. The men sounded like they were getting drunk or high out there. The echo complicated things, so when more than one person talked it became a big blur of noise. Still, Anna struggled to listen to the voices because her life depended on it. She wished it would all be over soon, whatever they were doing. The violence of men sickened her.

The sounds of their talking got dramatically louder, and Anna realized they were arguing. She heard a sharp slapping sound, and then a cry of pain. Then laughter.

"What's happening?" Kara whispered. No one replied, because Anna and Stacey were both too scared to talk, and Alice was still out of it.

A man was screaming now, a thin keening cry of pain that sounded like a wounded animal. It ceased when the gunshots began, one after another, popping off like firecrackers. The noises echoed through the caves so loudly that Anna went partially deaf. She grabbed onto Stacey next to her.

"Oh my God," she said out loud, involuntarily, but she couldn't hear her own words. Stacey clasped a hand over her mouth. Kara's eyes had gone wide with terror. The girls waited, frozen like statues.

As Anna's hearing gradually returned, she heard low voices, not Leod and Jume's, but those of the other men. What had happened? She thought she had a good idea. She wondered if the men would search the caves and knew that if they did, she'd most likely be killed. Tense moments passed, and for once Anna wished she believed in God so she could pray to him. It was an indisputable fact, however, that nothing she'd seen on Andros so far had encouraged her to develop any religious faith.

She could hear the men taking things out of the cave. Laughter. Then nothing. The girls waited a long time to make sure the men weren't coming back, hours and hours huddled together in the tiny, damp space.

"What do we do now?" Anna mouthed. Kara stared back blankly, in shock.

"We keep waiting," Stacey whispered.

Finally they had the courage to emerge from their hiding space, Anna staggering on cramped legs into the main cavern. A scene right out of *The Texas Chainsaw Massacre* awaited them, a brutal masterpiece of violence painted on the walls of the cave. Anna never imagined evil could be so abrupt. Candles were still burning in the room, so everything was illuminated, but Anna wished it weren't.

Leod was sitting in a plastic chair facing them, and most of his head was missing above the eyes. Anna averted her gaze immediately. A bullet must have caught him in the back of the head and blown out the front, she thought grimly. It was worse than what you saw in movies because of the smell, a mixture of burned rubber and grilled meat.

Even though Anna was trying hard not to look, she also saw Jume on the floor. It was impossible not to. He'd been shot a number of times in the chest and was lying face up, eyes open. His eyes looked no different than they did when he was alive, so Anna still felt afraid of him. He was in a pool of gore, and his blood was splattered all over the walls. It looked black in the yellow candlelight.

"They're dead," Anna said, over the ringing in her ears. "They got killed." She picked her way around the chair that held Leod's seated corpse, shaking.

Stacey knelt by Jume's body. "I have to make sure."

Anna didn't want to look at the corpses, but at the same time she was fascinated by them. She felt like something inside her had disconnected, and she was watching her actions as if in a dream. She thought if she had her camera, Leod's exploded head might make another pleasant picture. There was a nice symmetry Mr. Spate would have appreciated, between the jagged walls of the cavern and Leod's shattered skull. Anna wondered if she was going insane, and thought it was definitely possible. She certainly had a good enough excuse. She walked over to Stacey, who was rummaging through Jume's jacket and pants.

"There's nothing here," Stacey said. "The men must have taken everything. I was hoping he'd have a map or a compass."

Kara stumbled past them and through the short tunnel that led to the forest outside. Anna heard Alice moan, but she followed Kara anyway, suddenly desperate to be in the open air.

Let Stacey deal with Alice, Anna thought. Stacey was so rational about everything, she'd probably know what to do. If they had to leave Alice, they would. When they found help they could send someone back for her.

Anna saw Kara step through the tunnel in front of her and disappear into the daylight. She followed her out of the darkness, shielding her eyes from the glare.

Anna thought her eyes were broken at first because everything looked burning and white, like the surface of the sun. She'd lost all sense of time in the caves. It wasn't raining anymore and it seemed to be late afternoon. The air was hot and thick, wet with humidity, and the trees buzzed with insect life. There was no sign of anyone, no trail, not even any tire tracks to indicate how the men had gotten away. There was no sign of Erica, either. Kara sat on the ground, eyes vacant.

"We're safe," Anna said, wishing her ears would stop ringing. "We're okay."

"We're still lost."

Anna sat down next to Kara. Stacey wandered out of the cave and joined them, and they sat in the dirt together.

"Alice won't move," Stacey reported. "She says her head hurts too much. We could try to drag her out, but we'd probably hurt her more. I put some water and food down next to her in the cave."

"Forget about her," Kara said. She rubbed her neck. "I can't believe . . ." She didn't finish her sentence.

The forest didn't look any different than it had before, Anna thought. It was like nothing of consequence had occurred down in the caves, as if the corpses of Leod and Jume didn't exist.

"What about Erica?" Anna asked, concerned. "Do you think she got away?"

"Who cares," Kara muttered. "We're all going to die out here anyway."

"Kara, stop it," Stacey instructed. "Pull yourself together. We need to think. We need to stockpile food and water, and pack up our stuff."

Anna wondered idly why the expression was "food and water," when it really should be the other way around. It was water you needed most, much more than food.

"I feel so sick," Kara muttered.

Anna watched a squirrel climbing a tree. Her energy reserves were depleted and she felt like giving up. It made sense to Anna in a weird way that it should just be her, Stacey, and Kara left at the end. There had been seven of them, now there were three. "I don't know if I can hike any-more," Anna said. "I know we have to, but I'm so tired."

"We need to keep moving," Stacey insisted. "It's not safe here after what happened."

"Maybe someone heard the gunshots," Anna said hope-fully. "I mean, the police or something. Maybe they'll come and find us."

Kara scowled. "No one heard the gunshots because no one's out here. We're in the middle of fucking nowhere, or haven't you noticed?"

"I know, Kara."

"We need to walk," Stacey said. "We should rest for a while and then go back into the caves and help Alice. We can get our backpacks and gather some supplies for the trip."

Kara shuddered. "I'm not going back in there after what happened to me."

"Don't worry, I'll go," Stacey said.

"I'll come with you," Anna told her. She looked up at the green trees. Who knew such beauty could mask such horror? What looked like a tropical paradise on the surface was truly the worst place in the world. "I wish this was all over."

"I do, too, but it's not," Stacey said. "No one's going to help us. We have to help ourselves."

Anna nodded tiredly. God helped those who helped themselves. Her father would like Stacey.

"We went wrong at the start," Stacey continued. "We heard helicopters once, or thought we did, way back at the bluehole. If we'd just stayed put they would have found us. By now we could be completely out of their search area. This island is huge, and they can't search it all. It's like being lost in the middle of the ocean."

"Whatever," Kara said. "Too late now, Stacey."

Anna pressed her fists against her eyelids. "Did you see Leod's head?" she asked, without knowing why. She opened her eyes and Stacey was staring at her.

"Yes, I saw it. It's best not to think about that too much."

"It was like a nightmare, but much worse." Anna shut her eyes again. "You can wake up from a nightmare."

The girls sat in silence. After a while, Stacey got up and Anna helped her make several trips inside the cave to drag out food and water, as well as their gear. She avoided looking at the corpses. The two of them left more supplies next to Alice and reassured her they'd be back soon. Alice didn't hear them because now she was completely unconscious.

Stacey took out her notebook when they got back outside and marked down the position of the caves as best she could. Then the girls packed everything up and hoisted their backpacks over their shoulders. Anna felt so weak that just taking a single step was torture. Kara was a bitch not to have helped them with everything, she thought, but then Kara had been a bitch since day one.

Once again, they headed in the direction they thought was east. By now Anna had no idea if they were going the right way or not. For all she knew they were heading due west. Her feet throbbed and her head felt hot, and she was exhausted even though they rested frequently. When they came upon a thin running stream, they stopped and sat on tree stumps at the edge. The water was green and slightly brackish in places.

"I need to wash," Kara said. To Anna's surprise, she began taking off her clothes.

"Right here? Now?"

"Yes!" Her eyes blazed.

"But the water's dirty," Stacey pointed out. "You'll get sick."

"I don't care. I need to wash down there, where he touched me."

"He didn't—" Anna began.

"No! You saw. But he tried. Something was wrong with him and he couldn't get it inside me. I still feel unclean."

Anna nodded and understood.

Kara took off all her clothes and squatted in the slow moving stream, bathing herself, splashing water up her legs. She wore a serious look of determination. Anna glanced away. She remembered her envy of Kara's body just a few days before and felt guilty.

They could be a hundred yards from the coast, or a hundred miles, Anna thought. What a crazy decision it had been to leave the bluehole. If only they'd stayed there, then none of this would have happened. Anna hated the forest, hated the trees that were so maddeningly green and repetitive. She longed to be back in Atlanta, safe in the comfort of the city.

Her anger at her parents had been somewhat displaced, she was now starting to realize. Her dad was inflexible and cold, and a religious fanatic, but what Mr. Spate had done was far worse. He'd seduced her and violated her trust. She wished she'd told everyone what had happened between them, just opened the floodgates and let it all spill out. Maybe her dad wouldn't have taken his side, after all.

Anna remembered she'd actually threatened to do exactly that before losing her nerve. Mr. Spate had nearly started crying when she told him she was going to tell her dad that he was the one who'd gotten her pregnant.

"Please," he begged. "It'd ruin my life, Anna. They'd say it was rape, and you know it wasn't. I'd get fired and sent to jail, and they'd make me register as a sex offender, for God's sake. A sex offender! I could kiss good-bye to my teaching career. They'd make it seem like what we did wasn't mutual, like I molested you or something." His eyes were all watery. "They'd ruin your life, too, you know. What a mess."

She should have told anyway. He'd dumped her right after the abortion, informing her they couldn't go on sleeping together, although he was willing to still be her friend. Anna knew that was bullshit because she'd used the same line on ex-boyfriends herself. After that, she'd seen Mr. Spate talking closely with Meredith Ellis at school, another girl from her class. He was acting just how he'd used to act with Anna, his arm draped casually over Meredith's shoulders. Anna had been forgotten.

Why had she covered for him? She still didn't know for sure. Had it been because she nursed some stupid hope they might get back together again? Or maybe it had been the fear that if she told, no one would believe her. Everyone loved Mr. Spate because he wasn't old, and he was cool for a teacher. And he had a way with words, too. She wished she could get him out of her head for good, but even in the forest he continued to haunt her.

When Kara was done washing, she dried herself with her tank top before putting it back on, and the girls continued their trek through the woods. They didn't squabble as they had during the first few days, or even talk that much. Anna thought that for better or worse, a lot of Kara's bitchiness had been gobbled up by the evil of the caves.

The exertion was making Anna dizzy and several times she lost her footing and slipped. I can't end up like Amelia, she thought. She knew that getting hurt, even just twisting an ankle, could mean death. She craved protein now, and daydreamed of fried chicken and biscuits, and those greasy corn dogs they sold at the mall for a dollar.

The girls stopped to eat from cans, and as they'd forgotten to bring the can opener, they just smashed them open on rocks. Anna ate a can of mixed fruit, and guzzled bottled water and root beer. She wished they'd brought more cans with them, but supplies were heavy, and they'd thought it was more important to have fluids. All the candy bars were already gone.

They had matches and candles, and a flashlight, but when it got dark those didn't provide enough light to keep moving. The forest was too wet for them to make a signal fire, either, or light a fire to cook, so it was clear they'd have to spend yet another night outside. They sat in a clearing at the base of a jagged stump, flat enough for them to unroll their sleeping bags next to one another.

"I can't take much more of this," Kara said.

"If we've made it this far, we can make it all the way," Stacey replied. Anna and Kara just looked at her.

"I want to go home," Anna said.

"Me too."

"We'll get there, right?"

"I hope so."

That night the girls slept to the sounds of the island. None of them kept watch, because they were all too tired. Besides, what could they even do if whoever killed Leod and Jume came after them? Anna fell asleep and awoke with tears on her cheeks, but she couldn't remember any of her dreams.

This place has seriously fucked with my mind, she thought, wondering if she'd ever be the same again.

In the morning they headed toward the sun. Pain pulsed behind both of Anna's eyes, like she had a monster hangover. They only had a few more cans left from the cave and then it would be back to coconuts and berries. She felt like she'd lost twenty pounds already.

The more Anna walked, the more disoriented she began to feel. She stumbled for miles through the trees with Stacey and Kara. Sometimes they talked and sometimes they didn't. The only thing that mattered was maintaining a constant forward motion. Just when Anna thought they couldn't go any farther, and would have to stop for the night, she saw the first signs of human civilization since the caves.

"Look!" Anna yelled, her mouth dry and cracking. "Look at that!" She pointed, and Stacey and Kara followed her gaze.

"I can't believe it!"

"It's a house."

Up ahead, nearly obscured by the trees, was a clearing in which there stood a dilapidated wooden structure, little more than a shack overgrown with vines, with a flower garden behind it. The place was a total slum, but the garden looked too well tended for it to be abandoned.

"We did it! We're saved!"

Anna felt a surge of elation at Kara's words. They were finally going to get help, and get off the island. Anna and the girls ran toward the building as if it were a palace, with the urgency of beggars to a feast.

## Chapter Ten

## Cici

As she got closer, Anna saw that the house had partially fallen down on one side and the thin green vines were intertwined with the badly scarred wood. There were two old truck tires lying in the dirt, and squashed metal tins littered the ragged lawn. Above the house, white plastic bags hung from tree branches like a virulent new species of toxic flower.

Except for the garden, the whole place looked like it had been abandoned years ago, and Anna was stupefied to see a large, brown mutt with a collar sitting under a tree, black flies circling its snout. Dazed by the heat, its fur mangy and matted, the dog gazed at her. Anna felt hopeful it might have an owner nearby, but she was also afraid of it.

Move slowly, Anna told herself. She'd always heard dogs could sense fear, and would only attack if a person acted scared. Anna hoped this idea was bullshit, or she was about to get mauled.

"Disgusting," Kara muttered as she scanned the filthy yard. She hadn't noticed the dog yet.

"Be careful," Stacey cautioned.

"Fuck!" Kara gasped when she saw it. "That dog looks sick!"

"There's another one over there," Stacey pointed out. Anna looked and saw a second dog with patchy yellow fur lying in the dirt next to a bent bicycle frame. The dog was emaciated, its ribs showing like support struts, and it eyed the newcomers sadly.

"What if they have rabies?" Kara hissed. "I don't want to get rabies from some fucking Cujo. Stacey, do dogs have rabies on Andros?"

She shook her head. "I don't know."

This news didn't set Anna's mind at ease. After all the horrors she'd witnessed back in the caves, she didn't think anything could scare her again, but she hadn't expected to come across any sick dogs. Fortunately, they seemed too tired and malnourished to show much interest in her.

Anna assumed no one would build a shack and keep dogs in the middle of nowhere, so they had to be getting closer to the coast and to the towns. She felt a burst of renewed energy, long-dormant optimism returning in a flood. She was still going to make it off Andros okay.

"Hear that?" Stacey asked. "That humming sound?"

"Yeah," Kara replied. "What is it?"

Anna heard it, too, barely audible over the omnipresent buzzing of the island's insects. The noise sounded like a person humming softly, a woman maybe, although there was no visible source. Anna and her companions moved closer to the shack. When they got to one edge of it, Anna stepped forward to see who or what was making the gentle sound.

"Anna, wait—" Stacey whispered, but Anna ignored her. She felt like she'd been through way too much to be frightened off by a sound. At least this was what she told herself as she gritted her teeth and stepped around the corner.

She saw who was making the sound right away, an old, fat, dark-skinned woman who sat in front of the shack on a green plastic lawn chair. She was humming a melody to herself under her breath. There was a stack of rainbow-colored baskets next to her on the ground, and a pile of colored straw on the other side of her chair.

Initially Anna felt a moment of horror, because it looked like the woman had a second head growing out of her neck, just below her jaw. Then she realized it was a goiter. She'd learned about those in biology class. Not enough salt, or potassium, she remembered. Or something. The goiter made the woman look like an alien, although Anna had learned to expect anything on Andros.

The old woman's eyes were shut and deep crevasses cut through the dark leather of her face. She was swaying slightly in her chair, not doing anything particular, just swaying and humming, her hands folded in her lap. She was wearing a blue dress with white floral patterns on it and the fabric was stained yellow under the arms and along the hem. Her gray hair had receded and what remained of it was done in cornrows with little colored beads.

Anna stood there waiting, unsure of what to do. The woman seemed absorbed in her own world and she was afraid to disturb her. Stacey and Kara had stepped out behind Anna and were watching the woman, too.

"Hello?" Anna said after a moment's pause. She swallowed hard, and her mouth felt dry again. The woman didn't acknowledge her in any way, although Anna was just a few feet away. "Hey," she tried again, louder. "Can you hear me?"

The woman's eyes jumped open. "Who's there?" She stared wildly around. She had a thick island accent that made her sound Jamaican. "Marion? Is that you?"

The old woman was blind, Anna saw with surprise. Both of her eyes were covered with a milky white film, like those of a corpse. They reminded Anna of Jume, so she looked away.

"Hi," Stacey said, followed by Kara. The old woman looked in the direction of their voices. "My name's Stacey. We're lost."

"Is Marion with you?" the woman asked hopefully.

"Who?"

"Marion Jeffers, that's who."

"No, we're from America. We've been lost in the forest for days and we need help getting back. Do you have a phone?" Anna had daydreamed about the moment they'd find someone who could help them, and now it was finally happening, it seemed like an anticlimax. With just one phone call, it would all be over.

"Come here," the woman commanded and the three girls obeyed. "Kneel down. I want to know what you look like."

They knelt in front of her and she reached out a wrinkled hand. It found Anna's face first and began feeling her cheeks, her nose, and her lips.

"Ah, yes," the old woman said to herself. Her fingertips were crinkled and soft on Anna's face, like the surface of a decaying peach or a deflated balloon. It felt weird letting the strange woman touch her like this.

"Good nose," the woman muttered. "Full lips." Anna didn't know whether to pull away or not, because it was kind of creepy, but the woman's hand soon moved around to Stacey's face, and then to Kara's. Then she put her hands back in her lap. "Marion was supposed to come here yesterday. She brings me my pain pills once a month, and tends to my garden, and she's never late. You sure you haven't seen her?" Her blind eyes stared out blankly.

"Marion's not here," Stacey said. "We don't know where she is, or even who she is. But you need to let us use your phone so we can call for help."

The woman began to laugh.

"Don't you have a phone?" Kara asked, and her tone was too harsh, because the woman stopped laughing right away.

"Hell no," she said, irritated. "This ain't Nassau. There aren't any phone lines out here."

No phones? Anna thought with dismay. Unbelievable. "We're looking for a town," she said. "Can you help us?"

"There's just the three of you?"

"There were more, but they got lost, or shot. We met men in the forest who had guns, and they tried to kill us."

"Ah, yes," the woman said again. She didn't sound very surprised. She scratched the fold in her neck where the goiter met her chin. "Men and their guns." The woman shook her head. "My Jesus. I hope Marion's okay. She drives in from Nicholl's Town."

Stacey looked surprised. "Are we close to Nicholl's Town?"

"By the by."

Anna wondered what the hell the old woman meant by that, but Kara spoke up before she could ask.

"How long does it take to get there? I bet you don't have a car, do you?"

"No, no," the woman said. "No car. And I haven't been to Nicholl's Town in seven years. Marion comes and brings me my pain pills and my food, and straw for me to make my baskets. My boy Darryl came before that. He's dead now and his soul is in heaven with the angels, watching over me." She looked up at the sky as though she were trying to locate her son.

"Which way is Nicholl's Town?" Stacey asked. "We've been trying to head east, but we got lost somehow. Can you tell us where to go?"

For some reason the old woman got annoyed again. "I don't know! It's up the coast some twenty miles." She staggered out of her chair and grabbed a stripped tree branch that served as her cane. "Shoot. All these questions. I live out here to get me some peace. Why don't you all take a hike and leave me the hell alone." She started toward her dilapidated shack, using her cane as a guide.

Jesus, Anna thought. We finally find someone who doesn't want to rape us or shoot us, and they can't be bothered to help. Anna stood up and followed the old woman because there was no way she was going to let their one chance to get home slip through her fingers. They would just wait here with the goiter lady and refuse to leave until Marion showed up and drove them into town.

"Crazy old bag lady!" Kara called out. Anna was pretty sure the woman heard, because she started muttering curses of her own as she opened the door to her shack. It only had two rooms and was dark and filthy inside, a complete dump. Light poked into the dusty interior through cracked windowpanes.

"Please," Anna said. "Don't get angry with us. We don't want to be here, either, believe me."

"That's not my problem!" The old woman stumbled inside, leaving the door open, and Anna followed her in. Using the cane to navigate, the woman slumped in a splintered wicker chair. Anna noticed the shack was crammed with towers of multicolored baskets and piles of chopped firewood. There was a bizarre mixture of religious relics scattered around the room: African wood carvings, statues of Jesus, and even a menorah rested together in peace. It would have been funny anywhere else. "I'm tired," the old woman said. "Go away and let me rest."

"I'm tired, too," Anna replied. "More tired than you are."

"How'd you get all the way out here, anyway? No one ever comes around here. I haven't had a guest in years, except for Marion." Her voice sounded suspicious.

"We were at camp. We were taking a field trip and we got lost." How could Anna get the old woman to understand their predicament?

"What kind of camp?"

Anna was about to tell the woman a lie, but was struck by the ultimate futility of it all. "It's called Camp Archstone," she confessed, not caring what the woman thought of her. "It's a wilderness program for teenage girls, a reform school basically—"

The woman's white eyes burst open. "I know it! I know it!" she shrieked, sitting upright in her wicker chair. "Sammy Thomas worked there three summers ago, building a new cabin! That place is like a prison, child." She laughed throatily. "So that's where you're from! That's an awful long ways from here. Heh, you all are bad girls."

Anna was surprised, but relieved that the woman wasn't angry. If anything, she seemed to derive amusement from what Anna had told her.

"I shoulda known it," the woman cackled. "That's why you're running around out here in the forest. The old bitch who runs Archstone fired Sammy for stealing oranges and pudding from the pantry, and he was innocent! He's my second cousin, you know." The woman reached out her hand as if searching for Anna, so Anna took hold of it. The woman squeezed it, delighted, as Anna marveled at her change of attitude. Who knew that being from Camp Archstone would actually help them? "Bad girls. I understand you. You do one thing wrong in this world and they call you crazy. Or worse!"

Kara and Stacey had been watching silently from outside the door, afraid to disturb the conversation once it started going well. Anna felt proud that she was the one to sway the old woman, even if she'd done it accidentally.

"So you'll help us?" Anna asked, not wanting to lose the opportunity.

"I sure will, bad girl. You can stay here till Marion comes, all of you. She's got a four-door Plymouth sedan with air-conditioning. She takes my baskets to town and sells them at market."

If there were a car, Anna realized, there must be a road.

Even if Nicholl's Town were twenty miles away, they were so much closer to getting out of the forest than at any point during their journey. Anna looked back at Stacey and Kara. So this was it. They were going to be rescued.

"When's Marion going to get here?" Kara called out from the doorway, still sounding petulant. Anna was annoyed Kara would speak so rudely to the one person who was helping them, but the old woman didn't appear to mind anymore.

"Bad girl number two!" she cackled. "Come in, all three of you. We'll make a fire." Stacey and Kara complied. Even Stacey looked surprised at their good fortune. "Marion was supposed to be here yesterday. She's never been late like this before and I need those pain pills, so she better come soon."

"Do you think she'll get here today?" Stacey asked.

"I don't know, child. Sit down now, sit down. I can feel you all standing there. Make room on the floor to sit. It's messy and I don't give a shit."

Anna found a stained yellow cushion to rest on, and Kara and Stacey sat down next to her. One of the dogs wandered past the open front door and peered at the girls with rheumy eyes. It whined.

"That you, Lola?"

The dog whined again and took a tentative step forward, like it wanted to come inside.

Kara shuddered. "I don't want rabies," she said.

The old woman snorted. "Lola don't have rabies. She can't even bite 'cause all her teeth fell out. Now tell me your names again? When you get to my age, you don't remember things so good."

The girls reintroduced themselves and the old woman nodded. "My name's Felicia, but they call me Cici."

"I need some water," Kara said. "And do you have anything to eat? I'm starving."

"Sure, bad girl, sure. I got some Spam and I got tinned peas and corn, my favorite foods in the world. And there's a well out back for drinking water. I got diabetes so I gotta eat right unless I want to lose my feet." She cackled. "That's what they tell me! Anyway, girls, eat up. I'm not moving from this chair, so you can go get the stuff yourselves. The cans are in a storage shed on the left side of the house, and the well's right next to it. Bring me a can of peas while you're at it."

The girls got up and headed to the side of the house. Anna was still afraid of the dogs, but they seemed half-dead and stayed out of her way. Outside the dimness of the shack, the sun was impossibly bright and it burned her eyes. They found the shed, which was filled with stacked boxes of cans of various shapes and sizes.

"They're all fucked-up," Kara said despondently, sifting through the cans. "Look."

She was right, Anna noticed. A lot of the cans were either dented or bulging at the sides, and some were leaking.

"I'm surprised she can live out here like this," Stacey observed. "These cans will probably make us sick."

"She's insane," Kara replied, "like everyone else on this island. Why would anyone choose to live in a hovel like this?" She inspected a can of peas and then threw it on the ground in frustration. "I can't eat any of this shit! I don't want to die from food poisoning."

"You're being an asshole," Anna said, incapable of understanding Kara's attitude and unable to hold back her thoughts. "Cici's trying to help us, don't you get that?"

Kara scowled at her. "Fuck you. You eat this crap and die, then."

"If you don't eat, then I guess you'll go hungry," Stacey said. She was busy sorting the cans into piles, extracting the ones without dents. "We just have to be careful. None that look like they're going to explode."

"I'm not going to eat from any of them," Kara fumed. Anna knew that she'd pissed Kara off, and she actually felt glad.

"You realize it's possible we might have to walk all twenty miles into town?" Stacey asked Kara. "You heard what she said. Marion's never been late before. We need to eat to get strength for the journey. The food from the caves is running out."

"Marion will come soon," Kara insisted.

Anna picked out a can for the old woman, and then they headed back inside.

"You got any cigarettes?" Cici asked when they returned.

"No," Anna said. She placed the can in the old woman's hands.

"Thank you, bad girl." Her hands felt all around the can, making sure it wasn't too badly dented. "Now go and get me my can opener. It should be on the shelf right there." She waved her hand aimlessly, like a deranged orchestra conductor, but Anna spotted it on the mantel above the blackened fireplace. Anna brought it over to the woman, wondering how she functioned without anyone around to help her.

"Do you have electricity here?"

"Of course not, and I don't need it."

"Isn't it hard to live out in the forest?" Stacey asked.

The woman laughed. "No." She started rambling about why she left Nicholl's Town and moved into the wilderness years ago, but Anna couldn't stay focused. The story was too long and convoluted and she was feeling too tired. Besides, she was lost in a daydream of what her return to civilization would be like, and thinking about all the things she'd do when she got back home. She vowed never to take anything about her life for granted again.

The girls spent the long night waiting for Marion to return. They made a fire of old wood in the woman's brick fireplace and sat around it on moldy cushions. Cici seemed glad to have company, regaling them with stories about her son who'd been killed in a bar fight on South Bimini Island. Anna barely paid attention, her mind drifting, lingering over the details of her imagined rescue and dreaming of food.

When the old woman finally fell asleep, still in her chair, Stacey whispered something to Anna that shattered the comfort of her thoughts.

"I don't think Marion's ever coming back."

"What?" Anna asked. Kara wore a similar look of disbelief. Anna didn't want to think about the alternative if Marion didn't show, which was twenty more miles of hiking.

"You're such a pessimist," Kara told Stacey angrily. "What the fuck are you talking about?"

"Yeah, why wouldn't she come?" Anna asked.

"I just mean that we can't count on her," Stacey replied. "Marion hasn't been late in years, supposedly, and now she's gone missing? Doesn't that make you a bit suspicious? Cici said Marion was due yesterday. Maybe she ran into Jume or

Leod out there before we did, or whoever shot them. There could be a million possibilities."

"I hope not," Anna said, refusing to believe Cici was stuck just like they were. Surely Marion would come.

"I'm not saying I have it all figured out. I just think we shouldn't rely on anyone but ourselves. We can wait here as long as we like. We have food and water now, so we could live here for a month. But if we want to get back to America and to our families sooner, we might have to start walking."

"No way," Kara said. "Marion's coming, and I'm going to stay right here with this old bitch until she does." The pseudosophisticated tone she'd employed at the start of their journey was decaying into the voice of a scared child. "Even if it's not Marion, someone'll come and check on Cici eventually and then they'll find us. I don't want to hear any more stupid ideas from you, Stacey. You either, Anna." By the light of the fire, Anna could see the muscles of her jaw were rippling with tension.

"Whatever," Stacey said tonelessly. "I just think we need to plan and think about all our possibilities. I'm happy to stay here for a while, too."

"At least we're safe here," Anna said, thinking to herself, Safe: now there was a funny word. There was no way she'd ever truly feel safe again until she was off the island, and maybe not even then. Seeing three dead bodies changed one's perspective on life in a major way.

The old woman snorted in her sleep and her head fell forward, resting on her goiter.

"Disgusting," Kara muttered. "This island is full of monsters."

*"Isla del Espiritu,"* Stacey said wistfully. "The Island of the

Spirits. That's what they call Andros, according to the guide-books."

"Fuck you and your stupid guidebooks, too. You think you know everything, don't you?"

"I know a lot more than you."

"You don't know shit," Kara said, sneering, but Stacey didn't respond. Anna was glad because she was too tired for fighting.

The girls camped in the house that night, curled up in their sleeping bags. There were no beds, and even the old woman slept sitting upright in her chair. Anna thought of Erica, Alice, and Laura as she drifted off to sleep. They probably had it much worse than she did, if they were even still alive.

When the morning light came, the girls sat despondently, waiting for Marion to arrive. Cici was still snoring and snort-ing in her sleep. Anna stared at Kara and Stacey. She couldn't believe they hadn't been rescued yet.

Kara was showing her fatigue, with purple circles under her eyes. "Maybe Marion's not coming after all," she said dully. "I guess it's back to the waiting game."

"I told you. We can't rely on anyone but ourselves."

Kara got angry at Stacey, turning vicious in her frustration again. "Shut up, bitch. You're such an irritating midget, don't you ever get sick of yourself?"

Stacey rolled her eyes. "Save your drama for Sweet Valley High, or wherever you're from, Kara. I'm not interested."

"Please," Anna broke in. "No arguing. I'm too tired to listen to any bitching, and I'm too tired to take sides. We can bicker forever, but it won't solve any of our problems. I say we wait here another day and then if Marion doesn't show, we walk to Nicholl's Town ourselves. There's a road, so we're not really lost anymore. Cici said the town's just twenty miles from here. We could do that in two days if we really push ourselves."

"Cici's crazy and blind," Kara said.

Stacey shook her head. "There's no one else to help us, is there? I think Anna's right. If Marion doesn't turn up today, then tomorrow we should head out."

"So you've agreed on it?" Kara asked. "We're leaving tomorrow?" She looked at Stacey and Anna. "Taking sides against me, as usual. I know how it goes."

"Calm down, Kara," Anna said. "No one's taking sides. Anyway, we're a democracy, remember? The majority vote wins. It's not worth getting mad over."

"I'm not mad," she retorted. "You're mad and Stacey's mad. Look what happened last time, when we left the bluehole."

Anna couldn't believe it. "Come on, Kara. You were the one who wanted us to leave!"

Kara grew irrational. "Leod put his dick between my legs, not yours! What do you know about anything, Anna? Just shut the fuck up!"

"You can always stay here by yourself." Stacey's voice was cool and collected. "We can come back and get you, like Alice."

"Fuck you," Kara said. "Fuck you both." She stalked off to sulk on a slab of granite underneath a half-dead pine tree.

"What a bitch," Anna muttered.

"I guess it's the stress," Stacey said.

Although Anna knew there was no need for anyone to make excuses for Kara, it was true that stress and fear mingled and infused the air of the island like a virus. Anna was beginning to think it didn't much matter what they did, that their fates were already determined, like in *The Odyssey.*

Perhaps all the events on the island were some sort of karmic retribution for her abortion and her bad behavior, or a punishment from God. That would certainly be how Anna's dad would see it. But Anna knew that wasn't the way life worked at all, even if it seemed like it sometimes, or else Mr. Spate would be right there on the island next to her. The more torture she went through on Andros, the more she saw how unfair it was for her to suffer alone.

The morning stretched on, and when Cici woke up she was grumpy. "Don't eat all my cans, now," she cautioned, the goodwill of the previous day waning. Anna spent her time sitting next to Stacey while the girl wrote copiously in her notebook. Stacey was no longer making a map, and Anna wondered what she was up to.

"What are you writing about?" she asked. Her nerves were so frazzled that the sound of Stacey's pen on the paper irritated her.

"I'm making notes so I won't forget."

"Forget what?"

"The island. What's happened to us here."

Anna was totally stunned. "How could you ever forget?" Anna knew her experiences on Andros would be seared into her consciousness forever, whether she wanted them there or not.

"Details tend to fade. One week from now we might not be able to remember the exact shade of those palm trees, or how the caves smelled. Or what Leod and Jume did to us, especially to Alice and Kara. I'm writing everything down so I have an account of it for when we get back. Maybe I can even sell our story, you know. To *20/20,* or *Dateline NBC.*"

Anna wasn't sure if Stacey was joking. "Are you for real?"

"Maybe." Stacey shut her notepad. "How's Kara doing? Still sulking?"

"Yeah." Kara hadn't said much to either of them since their argument earlier.

"Marion!" Anna heard Cici moan loudly. "My pain pills!" Anna and Stacey ignored her, because Cici had been moaning for the past half hour. When Anna had approached her earlier to help, the old lady had cursed and snapped at her like one of the dogs. She was going through withdrawal symptoms from the pills, and the muscles in her arms and legs were twitching uncontrollably. There was nothing Anna or Stacey could do for her, and Kara didn't seem to care, so poor old Cici was out of luck.

When their food from the caves ran out, they turned to Cici's cans. Stacey picked out a can of corn and they heated it in a dirty pan over the fire. The corn tasted fine, but Anna noticed that true to her word, Kara didn't eat any of it.

Day turned to night, and again the girls sat on cushions in front of the fire in the old woman's house. They'd set up a signal fire outside in a metal drum, but they knew no one would see it. Anna watched it burning through the window. They would have been rescued by now if anyone was still looking for them.

Whimpers and moans reached Anna's ears over the crackling of the fire. Cici had stumbled off into the shack's crumbling second room and lay there unseen, emitting strange cries. "Marion!" she wept over and over, until Anna wanted to strangle her.

"Fucking bitch, I hope she dies," Kara said, and coughed. Anna assumed she was talking about Cici, though maybe she was referring to Marion. It was hard to know with Kara.

"Cici's sick," Stacey said. "She was nice to us before she ran out of her pills."

"She's probably just a crack addict. Probably just needs her fix."

Anna ignored Kara and looked through the window at the stars hanging above the trees. She thought she could see the Big Dipper. It was hard to believe this was the same constellation she'd seen from her backyard outside Atlanta for so many years. Of course, the stars seemed much brighter on Andros without the glow of electricity to detract from them. If she ever got off the island she vowed to learn more about the stars, and about the universe itself. It was far larger than she'd ever thought. Images of Leod's exploded head rushed to her mind, superimposing themselves on the night sky, and she looked away.

By the light of the fireplace, the girls looked like ghouls themselves, pale and willowy. Stacey, who'd been so thin at the start, was now totally emaciated, her arms and legs like sticks, and her eyes sunken. Kara didn't look much better. Anna knew they were her mirrors, and that she was just as malnourished and fatigued. She sometimes caught whiffs of her own body odor, even though she was mostly inured to the smell, and realized that she stank. What would Mr. Spate think of her now? She realized it didn't matter.

Kara fell asleep first, and Anna and Stacey stayed up talking for a few more minutes.

"Do you really think we're going to make it?" Anna asked. She knew what Stacey would say and just wanted the comfort of hearing it.

Stacey nodded. "I do."

"This place . . ." Her words trailed off. "I feel different now from when I first came here. Home doesn't seem as bad, you know?"

"No kidding." Stacey sighed. "You know you're screwed when toilet paper and soap seem like luxuries."

"True."

When morning finally came, thin rays of yellow sun darting through the windowpanes, Anna woke up with a headache and a feeling of discomfort in her gut. When she sat up, she felt dizzy, like she was getting the flu or a stomach bug.

I can't afford to get sick, she thought desperately. Not here, not now. Anna looked around and saw that Kara and Stacey were both still asleep. She got up and stumbled out of the shack.

Cici looked much better in the morning light and was sitting back up in her chair outside, weaving a basket from straw. Anna didn't know how she managed to do it, considering she was blind and that she'd been so ill the night before.

Anna's stomach gurgled and she wished for a nice, clean toilet instead of a hole in the dirt and leaves. Cici's shack didn't have any plumbing. She walked across the yard to find a place to relieve herself and Cici looked in her direction.

"Is that you, bad girl?" she asked. "You all still here?"

"It's me, it's Anna." She walked over to the old woman. She didn't want the others to wake up because she couldn't stand it if they started bickering again. "Marion never came."

"Don't I know it! I had a pain in my legs so bad yesterday I thought the devil himself was inside me. I prayed for the Lord to just take my soul, but today I feel like a whole new woman." She cackled. "I feel like dancing!"

"That's great," Anna said, "but do you think Marion's still coming?"

"She better. I'll have some words with her when she does."

Anna felt the pain in her belly getting worse. It felt like a cramp. She sat down on the ground and burped.

Cici laughed. "You feeling gassy?"

"No," Anna said, and Cici laughed again. "Can you tell us how to get to Nicholl's Town? I think we're just going to walk there. We talked about it yesterday, and I don't think we can wait for Marion anymore."

Cici's hands moved like snakes over the straw. The basket she'd started on just a few minutes ago was nearly half done. "So you're leaving me, bad girl?"

"Yeah."

"You don't want to stay with old Cici?" Obviously no answer was required because Cici just laughed softly to herself. "You find Marion for me when you get to town. Marion Jeffers, that's her full name. You tell her how I suffered."

"Okay." Anna rubbed her belly. The pain wasn't getting any better. This fucking sucks, she thought.

When Stacey and Kara woke up, they packed their belongings and with Cici's blessing took some cans with them from the stockpile. They filled their canteens from Cici's well, along with the water bottles they'd taken from the cave. Cici told them where the trail was and said there was a river six miles away where they could refill their bottles if they needed. There was a bridge over the river that connected to a trail on the other side, and if they stuck to that trail, always keeping right, then they'd get to Nicholl's Town in a few days. It sounded easy, maybe too good to be true, Anna thought.

Anna didn't tell Stacey or Kara how sick she felt because she was afraid any sign of weakness would mean they'd leave her behind. Kara definitely wouldn't think twice about it, and Stacey probably wouldn't have much choice.

Look at what happened to Alice, she thought. And Laura, too. She couldn't afford to be weak. The island chewed weak people up and spat them out. Anna decided she'd just have to tough out her stomach pain and nausea. If they made good time and didn't get lost, they'd reach Nicholl's Town soon and she could get medicine there.

Twenty miles, though, Anna thought. Shit, that's almost as long as a marathon.

The girls left Cici sitting in her chair weaving. Anna and Stacey said good-bye to the old woman, but Kara didn't even bother. Her repertoire of arrogant and contemptuous stares had been augmented by a glazed expression of despair, suggesting that life itself was futile. Anna sensed something even darker lurking behind her eyes, and hoped Kara wasn't going to flip out on them completely or something.

"Good luck, bad girls," Cici called out as they left. "If Marion ever shows up, I'll tell her all about you. Maybe you'll meet her on the way!"

"Bye-bye, Cici," Anna murmured. She felt sad to be leaving the blind old woman, even though Cici was moody and eccentric. Now it was just the three of them again, alone in the forest. She hoped they could survive the long walk ahead and weren't making a big mistake by leaving Cici's shack too soon.

## Chapter Eleven

# The Crossing

Even with her pack full, it was much easier for Anna to walk down a clear trail than to stumble blindly through the trees and the underbrush. Her stomach was still upset, but she was managing to deal with it. The best thing about having an angry stomach was that hunger no longer tortured her. The downside was that she continually had the urge to go to the bathroom. Her belly felt swollen, fat around the hips, but her clothes told a different story. Her pants and tank top hung off her frame, and she estimated they were four sizes too large, at least.

Anna walked next to Stacey, with Kara a few paces ahead of them. They stopped frequently to rest because they were all exhausted, but kept plowing ahead.

"They're going to be surprised to see us," Anna said. "Everyone probably thinks we're dead."

"I know."

Kara heard them and glanced back. "I bet my mom's suing the camp already," she said. She turned forward again.

"What's the first thing you're going to do when you get out of here?" Anna asked Stacey.

"Read," she said, and Anna shook her head. That sounded like Stacey all right.

"Are you serious? What about taking a shower? Eating a meal?"

"I'm looking forward to all that, too, but I'm halfway through a good book. *The Lovely Bones.* I tried to bring it with me, but they confiscated it at the camp. It's in a locker somewhere. How about you?"

"Wash my hair. I'm dying to take a shower and clean up."

"I don't know if I'll ever feel clean again." Kara kicked at a stone in the path as she spoke. Anna knew she was talking about more than just sweat and dirt.

A fat, gray bird with a blue triangle on its back waddled incongruously across the path in front of them, and the three girls stopped walking.

"What the hell is that?" Kara asked.

"Some kind of duck?" Anna speculated. "Stacey?"

"I don't know."

"I wonder if we can eat it. Cook it and eat it." The bird seemed to sense Kara's thoughts because it swiftly trotted past them and disappeared under a knot of branches. Kara strode after it a second too late and kicked, sending twigs and leaves flying into the air. She cursed and stomped her foot. "I almost had it," she said. "I could have killed it for us! Fuck!" Anna realized with dismay Kara wasn't joking around. "Then we could have eaten it." She sounded like she was about to cry.

"Kara, don't crack up," Anna implored. She wanted to go up and put her arms around her, but decided not to. Despite all they'd been through, she didn't really consider Kara a friend. Kara was frankly too much of a bitch, but that still didn't stop Anna from sympathizing with her. They were all in the same boat.

The girls started walking again, and after a while Kara recovered. "I'm sorry," she said. "It's pretty stupid to get upset over a bird. This place is really doing my head in." Her voice was thin and tight, so unlike how she used to sound.

"Hey Anna, are you okay?" Stacey suddenly asked. Anna was confused, because she thought she'd been doing fine, or at least better than Kara. Then she realized she'd been unconsciously massaging the painful spot on her stomach.

"I'm fine. Just a little cramp." Anna took her hand away from her waist. She refused to feel sick, or let the others know about her condition.

The three girls heard the river before they saw it, a rushing pulsing sound that echoed down the trail toward them. Anna was relieved because it meant they weren't lost, and Cici had told them the right way to go. Only fourteen more miles, Anna told herself. If you can walk six, you can walk fourteen. She tried to summon up all the inner strength she had.

The river was the first of three landmarks that Cici had told them about. The second was when the trail split into three, at which point they were to take the right-hand branch. The third landmark was very close to the town, a huge, granite stone called Highsea Rock that would inform them that they were only three miles away.

As the girls quickened their pace to get to the river, Anna

thought about how amazing it would be when they got out of the forest and back to America. Food no longer sounded so good because of her stomach, but a shower, clean clothes, and a soft bed seemed heavenly.

Yet when they got to the river, Anna's heart sank lower than she thought it could go. The river was much wider and rougher than Cici had led them to believe, at least twenty feet across. The water was moving fast over rocks, and it rushed past the muddy banks, carving a path through the island. Worst of all, where there was supposed to be a bridge, there was nothing. Anna saw only splintered wood pylons on either side of the riverbank, the merest traces of where a bridge had once existed.

"Oh no," Stacey murmured, as Anna tried hard not to collapse.

"Where's the bridge?" Kara asked, sounding angry and confused. "Stacey, you know everything, right? So where's the fucking bridge?"

"Calm down, calm down. Look, the storms must have washed it away."

Anna squatted in the mud and grass at the edge of the water, fighting nausea. How could the bridge be gone?

"At least this explains what happened to Marion," Stacey said. "She probably couldn't make it across."

"Well, I'm glad that little mystery has been solved, but what the fuck are we going to do now?"

"Yeah, what the fuck," Anna echoed Kara. She whispered the words to the water, to the island itself. After all that had happened in the caves with the men, the island owed her something. It couldn't betray her now.

"We might have to wade across, you realize that," Stacey was saying. Even she didn't sound too sure of that plan. Considering their emaciated states and the size of the river, it seemed nearly suicidal to Anna. "Can both of you swim?"

"Of course I can swim," Kara affirmed. "But look at how fast it's going."

Anna nodded tiredly. "I can swim, too."

Stacey rubbed the sweat from her brow. "It's too wide to cross here. We need to walk along the bank and see if it gets narrower. Maybe we can find another bridge."

If Stacey wanted her to walk, then she would walk. Anna felt feverish and there was no longer any denying she was getting really sick. She dabbed some water on her forehead, hoping it would cool her down, and then stood up.

"Maybe we should wait here," Kara said to her. "Someone'll come along and fix the bridge, right?"

"Are you kidding? That could take forever."

"We could go back to Cici's place."

No one liked that option because it meant retreat, turning around and losing valuable hours of progress. Besides, Anna thought, what could Cici do to help that she hadn't already done?

So they sat at the edge of the river, listening to its hypnotic roar, mesmerized and fatigued. The sun sparkled on the rippling water. Normally Anna would have found the scene one of tranquil beauty, but now it only made her feel despair. Beauty was meaningless when its price was so high.

The blisters on Anna's feet had started to heal during the time spent at Cici's shack, but now they were breaking open again, making her toes and heels sting. Coupled with her stomach problems, she felt like a cripple.

After half an hour the girls got up and began exploring the riverbank, walking north along it, looking for another way to cross over. The river didn't get any narrower the farther they walked, and there was no indication of any kind of bridge. Anna headed back to the trail behind Stacey and Kara, dejected. She knew if they wanted to get across, they'd need to get in the water and wade to the other side.

Stacey got a stick and probed the depths. The stick only went in a foot and a half, but it was impossible to tell if the river remained that shallow in the center. She tossed the stick into the river and Anna watched it get swept rapidly downstream. Anna could tell Stacey was nervous about going into the river, because Stacey probably didn't weigh more than ninety pounds, and the river was huge.

"I don't want to drown," Anna said. She hadn't really meant to say it out loud, but she had, and there it was.

"We won't drown," Kara insisted. "As long as no one falls, we'll be fine."

Stacey nodded. "We should take off our shoes and put them in our backpacks. That way they won't get wet. We can carry our packs over our heads."

"Okay."

The girls began to prepare for the crossing and Anna struggled to keep up. It was hard to bend because her stomach hurt so much, but she managed to get her boots unlaced and stowed in her backpack. She took off her socks, which were black from the inside of the boots, and revealed raw, red skin underneath.

"Your feet are fucked up," Kara declared when she saw them.

"Yours are just as bad," Anna replied.

Anna and the girls lifted their packs, clutching them in their arms, and prepared to cross the thundering river.

"I'll go first," Kara volunteered.

No argument there, Anna thought nervously. "Go for it," she said.

Kara walked down through the mud and right into the edge of the river. Her ankle disappeared, and she gasped, "Shit! It's cold!" She pulled her foot back and then put it in again. Stacey and Anna stood right behind her, watching apprehensively. The water stopped at Kara's knee, but it looked like the river might get a lot deeper. "Well, come on! I'm not going to do it alone."

The rushing water made Anna feel terrified, but the promise of rescue that waited fourteen miles away on the other side gave her strength and motivation. She took a deep breath and followed Kara in. Soon they were all standing there in the cold river, next to the edge. The water was moving so fast it was disorienting, like the earth was shifting under Anna's feet. The current sucked at her legs creating large eddies around her thighs, and it was hard to keep her backpack above the foaming water. She couldn't believe how strong the current was.

"Come on!" Kara yelled, and she set off for the other bank, which looked even farther away now that they were in the river.

Anna scrutinized Kara's progress before she followed. Each step looked like it took a lot of effort. There were rocks in the water, and sometimes Kara was standing up high and sometimes down low. Kara was crossing it only with great difficulty, and she was the tallest of them. Anna knew it would be even worse for her and Stacey.

Stacey followed after Kara, and Anna realized she had to do the same. She stared at the other bank and found a strip of purple orchids in the green backdrop. She fixed her eyes on them.

I have to make it to those flowers, she told herself. If I can get there, I'll be okay. Then I can walk out of here, right down the trail and into town.

Step by step, Anna followed Kara and Stacey across, clutching her pack to her face and chest. The river bottom was slippery, and jagged rocks lacerated her ravaged feet as she walked. The water got deeper, up to her thighs, and then up to her waist. Anna didn't look down at the rushing water because it made her feel sick. Instead she kept her eyes on those orchids. Kara was almost at the other bank, less than five feet away from it, and Stacey wasn't far behind when it happened.

Stacey's backpack slipped from her grasp and splashed into the river. She reached a hand out to snatch it without thinking, almost snagged it by one strap, and then suddenly, horrifyingly, tumbled all the way into the water. The river cascaded around her tiny body in sheets of white foam. She struggled to stand up, but the force was too great, and she fell back down, swept away by the current.

"Stacey!" Anna screamed.

Kara saw what had happened and, instead of trying to help, took a few more steps of her own and made it up to the other bank where she sprawled in the mud.

Anna tried to wade toward Stacey, but almost fell herself

and had to stop. She was transfixed by the sight of the girl tumbling in the water, scrabbling to find a foothold and stand up. It had only been a few seconds since Stacey had fallen, but she was already a ways downstream.

"Anna, come on!" Kara called out, taking her attention away from Stacey for a moment. "Don't think about it! Keep heading this way!"

Anna realized she had to get to the other side before she could help Stacey, or she was going to get swept away, too. The purple flowers, she told herself, get to those fucking flowers. She was scared to take each step now and her fingers clutched her backpack like talons. She took one step, then another, and before she knew it, she'd made it all the way to the other bank. She flung her backpack onto the ground and collapsed in a tangle of limbs next to Kara's heaving body.

She could barely speak. "Stacey fell!"

"I know."

"Oh God! Kara, we have to help her." Anna forced herself to sit up and scan the rushing river. There was no sign of Stacey. "She's going to drown if we don't do something. We have to go downstream and see if we can find her."

Kara just remained lying in the mud, so Anna struggled to her feet, alone and unsteady. "We can't just leave her."

"We left Laura," Kara said. "And Alice." She sounded exhausted.

"That's different."

"'Cause Stacey's your friend?"

It had been at least a minute or two since Stacey had been swallowed by the river and precious time was being wasted. "We can't argue now, we have to go look for her."

273

"Sure." Kara strained to sit up. "You need your friend, don't you? Someone to whisper to. You two have been tight this whole trip."

"This is insane!" Anna nearly wept. "Don't have this argument with me now!" She stared desperately at the river, hoping to see any indication that Stacey had survived. "She's probably drowning!"

"Run after her, then," Kara said, and Anna realized that Kara didn't have the energy or desire to try to help Stacey.

"I will." How could Kara not care at all? If it weren't for Stacey, they probably wouldn't have made it this far.

"I'll be waiting when you get back," Kara said. "Right by the trail." Then she fell backward, stretching her arms out in the mud.

Anna ran down the length of the river, in the direction which Stacey had disappeared. She refused to believe that Stacey had drowned. Her stomach churned and ached as she searched the pounding water. Stacey had too much determination and brains to drown, and Anna refused to bear witness to another death.

Her heart leapt when she saw a tattered bundle of clothes on the opposite side of the river, about two hundred yards downstream from where they'd crossed.

"Stacey!" she yelled, breaking into an approximation of a sprint, much closer to an old woman's hobble.

The bundle of clothes was moving and Anna knew Stacey had survived.

"Are you okay?" she called out over the noise of the river as she ran closer. She finally reached a place on the bank opposite Stacey. "Can you hear me? Are you hurt?"

Stacey's voice came back faintly. "I ran into a rock. I pulled myself out."

"You have to get back over here!"

"I can't. I hurt my leg." She pointed at it. "It's broken."

They were screaming back and forth. Had Anna heard her right? "Stacey, are you sure? What are we going to do?" She felt rising panic. "Stay there, I'll come back over to you."

"No!" This response was louder. Stacey waved her arms. "Don't! Too dangerous."

"But I have to."

"Listen! Stop! My leg's messed up. I can see the bone."

Anna was already wading into the water.

"Please! It's useless! Don't get hurt for no reason. I can't walk anymore. I lost my pack. I don't even have my boots."

Anna paused, partly because of what Stacey was yelling, but also because the water was even deeper than before and she knew she didn't have the strength to fight the current again. She stood there, water up to her thighs already, only a few feet in.

"It's okay," Stacey yelled. "You and Kara go on. You're so close now. You can send people back for me. I'll stay put."

"Stacey!"

"I'll be right here. I'm not scared. I know you'll find help." There was a pause. "I lost my notebook."

"I'm sorry."

Was Stacey crying? Not Stacey, Anna thought, not Stacey. She decided it was hard to tell over the noise of the water. Anna climbed back up onto the bank, soaking wet, her stomach throbbing.

"What about food?" she called out to Stacey when she was on dry land. "Maybe I can throw something over?"

"I'm not hungry. Save the food for yourselves. At least I've got plenty of fresh water."

Her words were getting drowned out by the pounding of the river.

"We'll come back, I promise."

"I know you will."

"You'll be out of here by tomorrow."

"Get moving!"

"See you soon, Stacey."

Anna walked back up the river, her battered feet stinging, to where Kara was waiting on the bank. The accident had happened so quickly she couldn't believe it. She'd thought if anyone would get out of this okay, it would be Stacey. She'd had even more faith in Stacey than in herself. Now it was down to just two of them, her and Kara.

A voice came unbidden into her head. *What comes after two, Anna?* the voice asked cruelly.

Shut up, Anna thought. Screw you. I'm not going to listen to any negative thoughts.

The voice was oblivious. *After two comes one, and after that comes zero. You're all going to die out here, Anna, like you deserve, and no one's going to care.*

"No!" Anna said out loud. "It's not true! Fuck you!" She became conscious that she was talking to herself like a crazy person, but she didn't care. She started humming so she wouldn't hear the voice, but she couldn't quell the feeling that something else bad was about to happen to her.

Kara was squatting in the mud, coughing, when Anna got back to the place where the river met the trail. It sounded like she was getting sick, too. She stopped when Anna got there. "Did you find Stacey?"

"Like you care. She's on the other side, and she's got a broken leg."

"She should have been more careful." Kara's words echoed what Adler had said about Amelia, all those days ago.

"She told us to go on without her."

"Good call." Kara seemed relatively untroubled by what had happened. "Now that it's just you and me, we'll move a lot faster. I told you it should have been us from the start. I bet we'd be there already."

"Kara, I don't know if Stacey's going to be okay. I don't know if I can leave her."

"She's a smart girl. She can take care of herself. Besides, we're not even fourteen miles from Nicholl's Town. We can walk it in no time."

"I told her we'd send help back."

"Then good. It's settled." Kara stood up. Anna noticed Kara's arms were covered with tiny sores. She hadn't noticed them before, but the river had washed away some of their grime.

"We better get going," Anna said, and although her bones ached and her stomach hurt, there was a new urgency in her desire to reach the town. "We have to start before it gets dark, maybe even walk all night."

Kara nodded. After a time of rest, she and Anna shouldered their packs and began heading down the trail. This trail was slightly wider than the one on the other side of the river, nearly the width of a two-lane road in places. If Cici were right, they'd reach the junction where the trail split in a few more miles, but at their slow pace they'd be lucky to get there before sunset.

The path was fairly clear, but still littered with twigs and leaves. Anna could see tire tracks in the mud, faint signs of the civilized world, and she wondered if the tracks belonged to Marion's sedan.

"I hate this place," Kara said. "Have I mentioned that?"

Anna nodded. She was too tired for Kara.

"I'm so hungry I'd cut off both my arms for a piece of chocolate," Kara said. Her words made Anna's sick stomach lurch with nausea, and she grunted in response.

"You know, you never told me why you got sent here," Kara said after they'd been walking for a while. "I've been wondering about you this whole trip, Anna. You and Stacey act like such good girls, like you don't fit in. Everyone knows what Stacey did, but what about you?"

"I don't know what you did," Anna pointed out.

"True." Kara looked like she hadn't considered this. She kicked a coconut down the path, and it skittered across the leaves and into the underbrush. She seemed giddy to Anna since Stacey's accident, but maybe it was just the promise of rescue. Still, it made Anna wary. She thought about Stacey with her broken leg on the riverbank and felt worried for her.

Kara smiled. "You really want to know?"

"Why not."

"I'll tell you if you tell me."

It didn't matter much anymore, Anna understood. She'd probably never see Kara again after they got rescued, so what did she care if Kara knew her secrets? She was too sick and tired to hide anything.

"I got pregnant," Anna said, and the words hung in the humid air. "I ended up having an abortion."

"You got sent here just for that?" Kara sounded surprised, but amused. "What's wrong with that? Three girls I know had abortions last year. It's no big deal."

"And I broke curfew, went to parties, came home drunk. I got high a bunch, too. My dad thought I was still hanging out with the guy who'd gotten me pregnant."

"Were you?"

Too worn out to lie, she said, "No. He thought it was my boyfriend, but it was a teacher at school."

Kara laughed. "No way. So maybe you aren't a good girl after all."

"Maybe. So what did you do, Kara? Why are you here?"

"Now I feel bad saying." Kara sounded coy and Anna wondered if she'd renege on her promise. "It's so bad. Much worse than what you did." Kara laughed nervously, as though telling her misdeeds gave her an electrical charge.

Before she knew what was coming, Anna leaned over the edge of the trail and threw up. Burning bile scorched her throat, making her choke. Where the fuck had that come from?

"You're sick." It didn't sound sympathetic at all, but more like an accusation.

"I'm okay," Anna managed. All of the girls had thrown up at least once during the journey.

"Okay for shit."

Anna wiped her mouth on her still-damp tank top. "I'm telling you, I'm fine."

"Do you have a fever?" Kara felt Anna's forehead before

279

Anna could stop her. "You're burning up! Anna, we've got miles to go. How are you going to make it if you're sick?"

"Don't worry about me." She knew Kara wasn't voicing any real concern for her, just worrying that Anna's illness would slow them down.

"You should have said you weren't feeling well. We could have rested more."

"I'm fine."

The two girls began walking again. Anna felt better after having thrown up. "You're not off the hook," she said to Kara at last. "Why'd you get sent to Camp Archstone?"

"It's such a long story, I don't know if I feel like telling it anymore."

Anna stared at Kara. "You'd better."

Kara laughed again. "Sure. This girl I teased at school freaked out and ended up going crazy, okay? And then they blamed it on me."

"Huh." Was that it?

"I mean, I never really teased her too much, you know? No more than any of my friends. They said we were a clique, but we weren't." Kara coughed. "Any bunch of popular girls who hang out together gets called a clique. You probably understand."

"I do."

"Anyway, this one girl in my class was a real joke. She had braces, not the invisible kind, but big, metal, square ones, and thick glasses, and a bad perm. I mean, everything was wrong with her. All her clothes came from Kmart and WalMart, even her shoes. Everyone made fun of her, not just me."

Anna nodded. She could picture the kind of girl Kara was

describing; every high school had a generous helping of them. Stacey probably fell into a similar category at her school.

"So we drew up this petition called WHORE," Kara continued, "or We Hate On Rebecca Everyday. That was her name, Rebecca. I thought of what to say and another girl typed it. It said we all hated her and each of us had to do one mean thing to her every single day. It was incredibly childish, but we all thought it was really funny. We got most of the girls in our class to sign it, and some of the boys, too, and we put a copy in her locker. It was typical dumb stuff, just for a laugh, you know? Who would have guessed?"

Anna looked at Kara and she was smiling, but it didn't look like a real smile. "So what happened?"

"The stupid bitch went crazy and slit her wrists, vertically, like you're supposed to. Everyone said I made her do it and suddenly I was the devil. The school shrink and Rebecca's parents and my mom got together and talked about it. They said I needed counseling, and my mom said she was going to make me live with my dad in Tempe. I just went nuts. I kicked her and she fell down some stairs and landed right on her face. I didn't even know you could break your eye sockets!"

Anna listened numbly.

"Then she pressed charges on me and got me arrested. I almost got tried as an adult, but in the end it was juvie or Archstone, just like Stacey, if you can believe that. Archstone sounded better at the time." She paused. "So what are you thinking? Are you horrified?"

"No."

"That old bitch back there was right. I'm a bad girl, Anna."

"I guess so." Was the story meant to shock her? If so, she didn't care. It wasn't much worse than Erica's story and she'd known Kara was mean and screwed-up from the start.

They walked in silence for a minute. "Don't you feel bitter that you got sent here?" Kara asked.

"I did at first," Anna answered truthfully, "but now I just want to get back home. I don't care about anything else."

Kara's brow furrowed. "You're lucky. You're going to go home and even though you slept with your teacher, you haven't really done anything that bad. Your parents will probably welcome you back with open arms after what's happened. It'll be different in my case. I bet my mom's going to get me sent to some other program, or juvie. I just know it."

Anna's stomach cramped and she doubled up in pain. It felt like there was a skewer going in under the ribs on her left-hand side, and she stopped walking.

"I need to rest," she managed to gasp as she knelt at the side of the path.

"Okay." Kara coughed once, hard, and spat in the dirt. "I feel like a break, too."

They sat in the shade at the edge of the trail and Kara ate from a tin of canned Spam. The pain in Anna's stomach wasn't getting any better, but eventually they got up and pressed onward until the sun began to set. When it got dark, they hadn't yet reached the fork in the road and Anna was disappointed with their progress. They built a small fire together, unable to find enough dry wood to make a large one, and set out their sleeping bags beneath the sheltering branches of a huge oak tree. Anna was too sick to move by this point, and it was hard for her to sleep knowing they were so close to safety, but still so far. She thought of Stacey and hoped she was doing okay all alone out there in the dark.

Anna didn't sleep that night for more than a few minutes at a time. She kept waking up dizzy and sick, drenched with sweat, throwing up on her sleeping bag. What a fucking mess, she thought in a lucid moment. She knew she had food poisoning or something worse, and needed medicine badly.

When the morning arrived, Anna was groggy and felt like she couldn't wake up. The light, as dim as it was, filtered through the trees lining the trail and hurt her eyes.

I'm really sick, Anna thought with true dread. Ultrasick. What am I going to do?

Vomit and saliva were caked all over her sleeping bag. She didn't want to stand up, but felt a desperate urge to go to the bathroom. She struggled out of her bag and over Kara's slumbering body to reach the brush, yanking down her pants and underwear just in time.

She felt as monstrous as Leod had looked. She wiped herself with leaves and staggered back to her sleeping bag. She didn't think she'd be able to do any more walking for a while. She'd given it her all, but her body had finally had enough. She supposed she was a little surprised it hadn't happened sooner. Kara would have to continue alone to Nicholl's Town. It would be better that way, and faster.

I can just rest here until help comes, Anna told herself, and the thought gave her solace. She didn't know her greatest challenge still lay ahead.

## Chapter Twelve

## The Gift

When Kara woke her up an hour later, Anna was almost delirious. She could tell Kara was stunned at how much her condition had deteriorated during the night. "God, you look like shit! What's wrong?"

Anna just moaned. She started crying, even though she'd promised herself she wouldn't. "It's my stomach. I can't take another step." The hope of a shower and a soft bed had receded into the distance. "You'll have to go on without me."

Kara sat on her backpack. "Fuck. I'm sorry, Anna."

"I'm sorry, too," Anna replied, wiping her eyes. Then she felt dumb for saying "sorry," because she couldn't help getting sick any more than Stacey could help breaking her leg.

"I'll keep going until I get to Nicholl's Town and find help. You'll be out of here by tonight, I bet. It's going to be okay."

The words Kara said sounded right, but even through the haze of her illness, Anna could detect a strange look in

Kara's eyes, as though she weren't telling the truth. For a sickening instant Anna thought perhaps Kara wouldn't bother to tell anyone where she was. But surely no one could be that evil? And what possible motive would Kara have to act that way? She wouldn't gain anything from it. Still, Anna couldn't shake her sense of unease, just like the moment before Adler got shot.

"Kara, you'll tell them, won't you? About me and the others?"

Kara frowned. "Yeah, of course I will. How could I not?"

"You know I'll die out here if you don't get help. You have to tell them where I am, and about Stacey and Alice, too."

"I know, I know." Kara stood up. "What's got into you? Why wouldn't I tell? You really must be sick because you're acting crazy." But there was that strange, cold look in her eyes again that was hard for Anna to ignore.

Anna shook her head. "Stacey and I need you."

"I know."

Anna rubbed her forehead. Maybe I'm just losing it, she thought. Reading something into Kara's expression that wasn't there. Anna was about to dismiss her feelings as nervousness at trusting a girl like Kara with her life, but then Kara began to speak.

"You and Stacey," she suddenly muttered. "Like a couple of lovers." She grinned viciously, showing her teeth. "And I thought Erica was the only lesbo out here."

"Kara, please. I'm sick."

"Well, I'm sick, too! Sick of this island and sick of you!"

Her words rang through the trees and Anna flinched. So she'd been right. There was something weird going on with Kara.

Kara turned away from her and threw her hands up in the air. "I told you I'd get help, didn't I? Why don't you believe me? Have I ever done anything bad to you, Anna?"

"Don't get mad," Anna implored. Now she was really worried. If Kara refused to get help for some inexplicable reason, then Anna would die. She felt like throwing up again. She had to placate Kara, as she was now at the mercy of the girl's whims. "Please, Kara. Calm down." How had they gone from being civil one second ago to having an argument? "It's okay."

"I tried to be your friend. I tried to be nice to you, but you still didn't trust me."

"Kara, I'm sorry. Please—"

Kara crouched at Anna's side, anger visible in the narrowed pupils of her electric blue eyes. "You know something? I'm glad you're sick. I couldn't take another second of you. You're just a boring little whore who sleeps with her teachers." She scrunched up her nose like a pig. "And you stink, too. Don't you have any self-respect?"

Anna sat up. "Kara—"

"You and Stacey didn't want to listen to me from the start. I had to fight you every step of the way, and then you tried to boss me around when it was just the three of us. Now you're sick, and you want me to walk all those miles by myself, all alone, and you don't care about me. You just want me to run along and bring back help for you and that midget."

"It's not like that!"

Kara smiled meanly. "Sure it is." She coughed. "You know, I wasn't going to tell you, but since you've insisted on making it so hard on yourself, here's the truth about everything." She stood up again, walking around Anna like a shark circling its prey. "I'm never going back home. If you knew what it was like living with my mother, you'd understand. I'd rather slit my wrists than go back to that place. And I'm not going to turn myself in so I can get sent to Tempe or juvenile hall. When I get to Nicholl's Town I'm going to run away, understand? I'm going to sneak into town, get on a boat to Nassau, and lose myself. I'll be free. I've got it all figured out. While you and Stacey and that freak Erica were yammering away like babies, just trying to stay alive, I was busy making plans. This whole thing, this whole accident, is one huge opportunity for me to escape and start my own fucking life, without being controlled by everyone. I'm the only one left who's not sick or lost, because I'm the only smart one." She paused to cough again.

Anna was so astonished she thought it was possible she was still asleep and dreaming. "What?"

"You were right about me not telling anyone," Kara continued. "I don't know how you figured it out, but you knew somehow. I'm not going to tell them where you are, or where Stacey is, either. I'm just going to disappear."

Anna comprehended that she was looking into the face of someone without any morals or a conscience. A psycho, basically, and she was scared beyond belief. "Kara, listen to me. It's not too late to change your mind."

"No way."

Anna's mind raced. "What about an anonymous note? When you get to town you could leave a letter at the police station."

"I won't take that chance."

287

Urgency gave Anna a burst of energy. "But your plan makes no sense! They'll be looking for you. As soon as you turn up in Nicholl's Town, they'll know who you are. We'll be in the newspapers and on TV. You'll get caught right away! You don't have any money. How are you going to live?"

"There are lots of things a girl can sell," Kara replied. Her words gave Anna a chill. "I'll do anything to avoid being caught, and I mean it."

"You won't really," Anna said. "You won't let me die out here."

"Look on the bright side. Maybe someone will find you. Marion, perhaps."

She was enjoying herself, Anna thought. Oh my God. Another wave of nausea passed through her and she clenched her hands. If she weren't so weak, she'd attack, even though Kara was taller and bigger than her. Anna knew whatever she said was useless because Kara had lost her mind, and you couldn't reason with a crazy person.

"Well, so long, babe," Kara said. She stood up and put her backpack on. "It was nice knowing you, I guess."

Anna choked back bile. "I hope you die."

"Oh, Anna. So bitter. Well, survival of the fittest, just like they say."

"You're not the fittest, just the most evil."

"I never said I wasn't."

"You're worse than Leod and Jume."

"I don't think so, Anna."

"The police are going to find you and send you straight to juvie, or a real prison. You just wait. You'll never get away with this."

"Let me worry about that. Maybe I'll cut my hair and get fake glasses, so I can look nerdy like Stacey. Maybe I'll think up a new name for myself." Her eyes sparkled with the madness of hunger and fatigue. "I'll start a whole new life."

Anna didn't answer.

"Well, good-bye, then." With a wave of her hand, Kara turned away and began walking down the trail with her backpack. Anna couldn't believe she was really leaving. "So long!" Kara called out behind her. And then, "Good luck!"

"You fucking bitch," Anna muttered to herself. She wanted to say more, so much more, but instead she just leaned over and threw up. Bright yellow bile came out and she sank back onto her sleeping bag. At least she had some water and food with her. If Kara were really smart she would have taken everything, but Kara had been in a deranged frenzy. Anna knew that Kara had attempted to murder her just as surely as if she'd shot her in the head.

The rest of Anna's morning was spent on her hands and knees throwing up the last possible contents of her stomach in the underbrush. Despite her increasingly frail physical condition, something was happening in her mind, as if she grew mentally stronger while her body failed. Kara's actions had given her a new clarity, and the desire to keep forging ahead.

Anna made up her mind to survive, despite her overwhelming physical suffering. It wasn't an easy decision, especially sitting there in her own vomit, shaking and crying, but she was determined not to die in the forest, a random victim of another person's cruelty.

The only way to survive was to get up and walk down the

trail into town, she thought. She was done hoping for rescue, done hoping for someone else to help her. She'd been a victim of Mr. Spate, her father, and the island itself, but she refused to be a victim anymore.

"I'm going to get out of here," she said, and it made her feel better to hear the words spoken out loud. "I'm not giving up, do you hear?" She was speaking both to Kara's shadow and to the forest, neither of which gave a shit if she lived or died.

During an interval between bouts of nausea, when her chest stopped heaving long enough to move, Anna checked her supplies carefully. She only had one can of food left, but as she wasn't eating, it didn't matter. The water was more important, and she was distressed to see she only had half a bottle, not enough to get very far. She wished they'd been able to carry more supplies back from Cici's well, or the river, but water was so heavy. She'd have to find some on the way.

Anna didn't think she had the strength to lug her backpack anymore, as the weight of its frame was too much for her. But she needed her sleeping bag and her water, so she decided to improvise. She scrounged around in the dirt and found a jagged rock, and with a lot of effort she used it to sever the straps where they were sewn into the fabric of the backpack. Then she managed to roll the sleeping bag up tightly and tie the backpack straps to the cords of the bag. That way she could wear the sleeping bag on her back, and slip the water bottles inside it. By discarding the backpack and its heavy frame, the weight of her load was cut in half.

The stomach cramps returned and Anna waited a while before she got moving. With her illness and blistered feet, she knew she'd be lucky to manage five miles a day. Maybe only four, she thought. That meant she probably had two or three more days of walking ahead of her, unless someone came down the trail and picked her up. Of course, so far she hadn't seen a single vehicle.

I'm going to do it, Anna told herself. Kara's not going to win.

Anna had heard about people who summoned great strength from within during times of crisis, like mothers who lifted cars when their kids got trapped underneath. She'd need to conjure up that kind of strength in order to survive. Could she do it? She thought about praying to God again, but she still associated him with her father's religious dogma. She'd get out of this mess herself and then worry about God later. If she was ever going to find her own sense of spirituality, it would be long after she was off Andros.

When her spasm of illness subsided, she took three sips of water and stood up slowly to avoid the rush of blood to her head. From the position of the sun, she guessed it was early afternoon, but it was hard to tell. Her altered backpack wasn't entirely comfortable, but it felt much lighter. Anna decided to take it slowly, a few steps at a time if she needed to. She could only manage a slow pace anyway.

She started down the trail, painfully taking small steps toward freedom. Her progress was slow but steady. There was no indication that Kara had been there before her, but somehow Anna knew that she had.

Anna walked the rest of the day, and when she was too tired to move, she made camp by the side of the trail. Other than the tire tracks in the mud, there was still no sign of human civilization. Her water was all gone and she'd have to leave the trail in the morning to go in search of fresh. So far she'd been lucky when it came to finding water, and she hoped her winning streak would continue.

*What if it doesn't?* the voice in her head asked, but she pushed it away.

That night she thought about all the ghosts in her mind that refused to leave, from her father and Mr. Spate to Stacey and Kara. Shockingly, she thought she was feeling better than she had for most of the day. Her stomach still hurt like someone had kicked her, but it felt like her fever was down. She hadn't been sick in three or four hours, either, which was also a good sign. She knew at some point she'd have to start eating again in order to maintain her strength, but she didn't want to risk food yet. She promised herself she'd eat in the morning, even if it was just a bite of coconut.

With the sun gone, Anna was surrounded by darkness and the noises of the island. The sounds of crickets and frogs, along with other creatures, no longer scared her, even though it was her first night sleeping alone since Adler was shot.

Better alone than with Kara, she told herself.

Anna had made a strange peace with the island. As she'd walked during the day, the forest seemed less menacing than it had at any point so far. It was almost like she was starting to get used to it. She fell asleep that night and didn't have bad dreams. In the morning, she ate a small piece of dried coconut meat she'd splintered on a sharp rock and thought about water. If only she could get at the coconuts still hanging high in the trees, she could drink their liquid. She wished she knew more about the plants surrounding her, because she imagined some of them were probably safe, and she could suck the juice out of their stems. If only Stacey were here, she thought.

Anna wasted valuable time stumbling off the trail, afraid to venture far, but desperate for something to drink. She finally found a depression in the ground filled with water, covered at one edge by green scum. She knelt down and scooped some up with a bottle. She brought it to her lips and could smell its foulness. Not knowing what else to do, she choked the putrid water down. Just swallow, she told herself. It couldn't be worse than what people drank on *Fear Factor.*

If I get sick again, so be it, Anna thought. She needed water and this was the best she could do. Maybe by now she'd become immune to the germs on the island.

Anna filled her two bottles with the slimy water. It was light green with little white floating particles, and she tried not to think about what was in it. Now her makeshift backpack was heavier again. She found the trail and continued walking.

If only I had a car, she reflected. I could be there in less than half an hour. The thought made her want to laugh and weep at the same time.

I can do it, I can do it, she repeated, like some dumb self-help mantra. I don't need a fucking car to get down this road. She forced her body to walk. It was now a test of willpower and endurance, of mind over matter. Despite her appearance, Anna had found her well of previously untapped power. Barring any unforeseen event or a recurrence of her illness, she was confident she could make it to Nicholl's Town. She wondered why she hadn't found such inner strength while dealing with her father and Mr. Spate. It had been a terrible choice not to reveal the truth about her teacher, no matter what the consequences were. Somehow the island had made her see this clearly for the first time in her life. She expected things would be very different when she got back home.

What Anna wasn't expecting was that she'd encounter her nemesis again, sprawled in the middle of the trail like a deer hit by a car. Anna knew it was Kara the instant she saw her, and she froze.

Oh shit, she thought, as she ran through all the options in her mind. She wanted to just sneak off the trail and circle around Kara. That was the smart thing to do, to pretend she never saw her at all. Then Anna contemplated the situation further and worried maybe it was a trap, that Kara was waiting to hurt her and would spring up to attack.

Yet that didn't make any sense. Kara had left her for dead miles down the road, so the girl was probably hurt or sick for real. She remembered how Kara had been coughing on and off for the last few days. Although Anna was filled with rage at the thought of what Kara had done, she refused to let her emotions get the better of her. She decided to stay focused on the task at hand and not waste any energy on Kara. For all Anna knew, Kara might even be dead. Anna's task was simply to survive, and Kara was just another obstacle in her path.

She walked directly down the center of the trail, right past Kara's body, and stood a few paces away. Kara sensed her presence and squirmed sideways on the ground to face her, eyes wide and staring.

"Anna?"

Anna looked down at her.

"Anna, I've been so sick, I can't believe it. My chest hurts like crazy."

Anna would have definitely suspected this was a trap, were it not for the fact that Kara's face was ghostly white and her bottom lip was daubed with blood.

"I've been coughing a ton, and I can't breathe. Do you think I've got pneumonia?"

Anna stared at Kara silently. She didn't know what the hell was wrong with her.

"I didn't think this would happen," Kara continued. "I've been coughing my lungs up since last night. Blood's coming up, from the inside." She struggled to sit up. "Maybe I've got some tropical disease."

The irony of the situation didn't escape Anna, but it didn't bring her much satisfaction, either. Kara was merely a delay she didn't have time for if she was going to save herself and the others.

"Didn't you hear me?" Kara moaned. "I'm sick!"

"I heard you. What do you want me to do about it?"

"I need some water. Please, I couldn't find any. I should have—"

"Should have taken mine?" Anna shook her head. "You left me to die."

"That's not what happened," Kara pleaded. "I was just playing. I was mad at you for making me go on alone. I was always planning to tell them where to find you, and Stacey, too."

Anna said nothing, but knelt down and took out one of her

water bottles. She knew very well that Kara was lying, so she took a long drink from the bottle in front of Kara's eyes. It was mean, but Kara deserved it. When she was done, she licked her lips, even though the water was awful and green, and tasted like vinegar.

"Anna, please," Kara begged, coughing.

Anna took another sip, and then tossed the bottle at Kara in a gesture of contempt. "Drink. I want you to live. I want everyone to know you tried to abandon us. They'll send you somewhere worse than Tempe or juvenile hall."

Kara grabbed the bottle and drank the disgusting water gratefully. "It's not like that."

"Sure it is."

"I'll deny it." Kara looked up at her. "Whatever you say, I'll deny it."

"I'm sure you will." Anna stood up. "I better get going, Kara. We're not far from town, so I'll send someone back to find you. Unlike you, I'm not going to run anymore." She paused. "You can keep that water bottle." The bottle was empty.

Kara's cheeks suddenly flushed so it looked like she was wearing rouge. "You can't leave me here!" she fumed. "You won't tell them about me, I know it. You'll punish me like the rest of them."

"No I won't, I promise. Don't you trust me?"

"Anna—"

"I have to go now, Kara."

Kara struggled to her feet, coughing, and Anna backed away. Kara looked like a walking skeleton, like something out of a monster movie, or a story by Edgar Allan Poe. Anna was surprised and a little scared that Kara had the strength to stand up. Kara took ragged breaths, like an old man with a broken oxygen tank, as she advanced.

"You're not leaving me, Anna. You're going to stay right here. You got better, so I'll get better, too. We can camp here for the next few days and you'll nurse me back to health." Kara coughed noisily and there was a wheezing sound in her chest that Anna could hear from a distance of several feet. "You can bring me food and water." Snot hung down from one of Kara's nostrils and then got sucked back up. The circles under her eyes were deep, black pits.

Anna kept moving backward as Kara walked toward her, arms outstretched. Anyone who'd seen Kara when she first arrived at Camp Archstone would have failed to recognize this stumbling creature in filthy clothes. Kara was emaciated, and looked far older than her years, her cheekbones threatening to punch through the skin of her face.

"I'm leaving now," Anna exclaimed, feeling nervous. "I'll send help, I promise I will." She had to keep walking backward, afraid to turn around in case Kara jumped on her.

"How dare you try to leave me!" Kara ranted deliriously. "I'm the prettiest, I'm the smartest, and I'm the leader of this group. I'm the one who counts. Me! You're going to die out there on your own, Anna. You can't make it without me."

"I can make it just fine," Anna murmured, so mesmerized that she didn't react quickly enough when Kara lunged forward. Kara was surprisingly fast for someone so sick and thin. She smacked Anna in the face with a hand that felt like a claw, and when Anna stumbled, she threw herself on top of her and both girls fell to the ground. It took a second for Anna to understand the fight was real, and this crazy girl was actually trying to hurt her. Kara was screaming and cursing as she thrashed away at Anna's face.

Anna realized with horror that Kara was trying to gouge her eyes out with her fingernails. If she didn't do something soon, she was going to get hurt. Even though Kara was bigger than her, Anna managed to get up on her hands and knees and force Kara underneath her body. Anna had never physically fought anyone in her life. Only once had she ever shoved another girl, in fifth grade, and all the boys had crowded around, yelling "catfight!" like assholes.

Kara was still writhing and flailing, and Anna felt a pain in her earlobe as Kara sunk her teeth into Anna's flesh like a wild animal. Anna had seen enough movies to know what to do next. She pulled back her arm and plunged her fist right into Kara's nose. She was stunned by how much it hurt her hand, and also by how much blood gushed out of Kara's face. Anna rolled to the side and got up on her feet, clutching her throbbing hand, breathing hard.

Kara was still on the ground, rolled up in a fetal position with her hands over her nose. Bright blood spilled through her fingers and onto the leaves.

It's not like the movies at all, Anna thought. At least not when guys punched each other. Her fight with Kara was over in less than thirty seconds. Anna glanced down at her hand and tried to move her fingers. They hurt, but they moved, and she knew her hand would be okay.

"You broke my nose, bitch!" Kara sobbed. She rolled onto her back, hands still over her face.

"You made me do it." Anna stepped away from Kara, in the

direction of Nicholl's Town, making sure there was a large distance between them. She wouldn't make the same mistake twice.

"I hate you!" Kara's voice sounded funny because of her chest infection and because her nose was already swelling. When she took her hands away from it, it looked lumpy and misshapen. "Oh my God! I'm going to kill you!" She sat up, coughing blood. Her shirt had turned crimson.

Anna took a few more steps backward, but Kara didn't make any attempt to stand up again. "You did this to yourself," Anna told her. "Because you're evil."

Kara couldn't meet her gaze anymore. "Go on then. Leave me here. You've done enough damage. Don't tell them where I am, I don't care."

"Oh, I'll tell them."

"Why bother? I don't need your help. I don't need anyone."

"Sure, Kara. Whatever you say."

Kara hacked up mucus. "Why do you hate me, Anna? Why?"

"I don't hate you. Honestly, now I just feel sorry for you."

"You're jealous of me," Kara said tiredly. "Everyone is. They always have been. That's why I got sent to Archstone."

It was pathetic. "I don't think so." Didn't Kara realize what she'd done?

It was Anna's turn to leave Kara weeping and coughing in the dirt. She backed away from her until it was safe to turn around, and she walked as fast as she could for the next several minutes. She heard Kara yelling after her, the words turning into an anguished cry of pain, as if Kara's facility for language had broken down.

Anna forced herself to ignore the pitiful sounds. Now there were just a few more days of hiking ahead of her, and she hoped to reach Highsea Rock before sunset tomorrow. There was no room in her mind for anything except the desire to survive.

When night came, Anna slept off the trail in a small clearing. She hid herself well in case Kara rallied and came looking for her, which was doubtful. It wasn't the best place to sleep because tiny stinging ants gravitated to her wounds, but she was too tired to move. It felt like there wasn't an inch of her skin that didn't contain an insect bite, a bruise, or a cut.

Anna only managed a few hours of sleep, and she staggered up in the green morning glow of the forest. The repetitive nature of her journey made it hard to find the will to keep going. Her knees were so stiff it took her a couple minutes before she could even bend them. Her hand was swollen and hurting from where she'd punched Kara in the face, but she didn't regret it.

Just a few more days, she told herself. She could handle that. She had no idea how far she was from the town, except she knew she was heading in the right direction. That thought alone was enough motivation to make her pack her sleeping bag and water bottle and start moving again.

I'm going to make it, she thought, and no one can stop me.

When Anna emerged from the trail and into the clearing three days later, she was no longer walking. Instead, she was crawling on her hands and knees. Unable to find water the previous day, her fever and stomach pain had returned with a vengeance. Often she was aware she was babbling to herself, like a preacher speaking in tongues. The blisters on her feet were infected and her toes had swollen to double their size. She couldn't put any weight on them without crying out in agony. Her knees were rubbed raw and bloody from crawling on the trail, and she'd torn apart her dirty tank top to use as bandages. She'd had to discard her sleeping bag because she no longer had the strength to carry anything but herself.

Anna began to sob when she saw the trail end in a cluster of white, wooden houses and red-brick buildings. She saw two goats in a pen outside one of them, and an enclosure with three chickens inside it.

I made it, she thought. This is Nicholl's Town, and I'm really here.

It felt completely unreal. She slumped in the brown dirt at the edge of the clearing and wept. She just couldn't help it. Over the roar of disease in her head, she suddenly heard the patter of little feet.

"Hey missus," said a voice.

Anna looked up from the dirt and saw three tiny, dark-skinned boys staring at her curiously. They were wearing shorts and T-shirts and all had the same intense look in their eyes.

"Water," Anna tried to say, but her tongue was so swollen it came out as a mangled whisper. She knew she had to make them understand her, but all she wanted to do was sleep.

"Hey missus," said the boy again. It was the tallest of the three who spoke. The other two hung back, afraid. "Your booby is hanging out."

One of the smaller boys laughed gently.

"Help me," Anna mouthed. "Please." Each word was impossible, and her head sank back onto the ground.

"Are you okay?" asked the tallest boy.

"No," she said into the dirt. She didn't think they could hear her.

"You look real sick."

Anna tried to push herself up and explain that they needed to go and get a grown-up, but her attempt at movement scared the two littlest ones and they ran away. The other boy stayed, however, and continued to scrutinize her.

"I'll find my papa," he said at last, to Anna's relief. "He'll make you better." The boy trotted off after the others.

Anna shut her eyes and listened to the thrum of the island that came from all directions and even permeated the soil. It felt like the sound had gotten inside her body, and she knew it would never leave.

She wondered if the little boy would return. She'd understand if he didn't. To him she was probably a monstrosity, some damaged creature fallen to earth. But the boy came back anyway.

"I told my papa," he informed her. "He's coming straight away."

"Thank you," she mouthed. Her vision sparkled with black dots.

"Here, drink this."

Anna felt something cold being pressed into her hand and realized it was a can of soda. The boy had opened it for her. She brought it to her mouth and drank deeply, cold liquid running down her lips and onto the dirt. It was delicious.

"Not too fast," the boy cautioned, but she didn't listen because her thirst was so intense.

"John!" a man's voice yelled, and Anna heard footsteps.

"Papa!"

Anna felt strong hands on her, rolling her over. She stared into a concerned black face, lines furrowing the brow.

"Oh Lord!" the man said. "I've seen you! On Channel Seven, and on satellite!" He sounded impressed. He was wearing a white T-shirt that said MIAMI DOLPHINS on it, and ripped denim shorts. "You're one of the lost girls!"

Anna nodded. She stared up at the man and at the blue sky beyond.

"But so far north," he marveled. He had the same island accent as Cici. "The whole world is looking for you, girl. How did you get here?"

"I walked."

He gave her a look of pity. "You're safe now. I have a truck, a four-wheel drive. I can drive you to the hospital in Nicholl's Town."

Anna was confused. "I thought . . ." The fever was compressing the sides of her skull like a vise, and it was hard to pay attention to what the man was saying. "I thought this was Nicholl's Town."

"No, no." He shook his head and looked over at his son. This woman is crazy, is what his look said. "You really are lost. This is Shaygill's Point. Nicholl's Town is thirty miles from here."

"But Cici—" Anna managed.

"Cici?"

"The old woman. In the forest."

The man shook his head and smiled. His son smiled, too. Then the man put a hand over his mouth to hide his grin

303

because Anna could tell he was embarrassed to be smiling when she was clearly so sick.

"Felicia," he mused. He rocked back and forth. "That crazy old fool. She gets mixed up. You can't trust a word she says. This is Shaygill's Point, named after my grandfather." The man pointed at one of the shacks, a fresh coat of white paint sparkling in the sun. "That's my house, right there."

The boy whispered something in his father's ear.

"Yes," he answered. "You're right." He turned back to Anna. "We need to get you out of the sun. Can you stand up?"

She shook her head. There was just no way.

"I'll carry you, then. John, go prepare a bed. Tell your mother we found a lost girl."

Anna felt him lifting her into his arms as though she were a baby. He was strong and didn't seem bothered by her weight. He took her down a gravel pathway and into his house, where he set her down on a narrow mattress in the back room.

"I'll bring you a pillow."

The bed was incredibly soft, and Anna couldn't believe how good it felt. She lay still, feeling the mattress support her aching limbs. Through the window in the room she could see a wall of trees beyond the clearing. The bright sun made everything look washed out, like she was staring at a color photocopy instead of reality.

The man's wife appeared in the doorway, a big woman in denim overalls who revealed a gap in her teeth when she smiled. Anna could tell she was shocked at her sickly appearance, but pretended not to be.

"What's your name, girl?"

"Anna Wheeler."

"Yes," the woman said. "You're who I thought you were. We've seen your photo on the television. My name is Deb."

The man returned clutching a pillow and a blanket. He lifted Anna's head and put the pillow underneath and covered her with the blanket. Then he left. His son peeped through the door at her. When he saw Anna notice him, he disappeared, but then he came back and sat down inside the doorway. Anna tried to smile at him, and he smiled back.

"I'll make you some tea," Deb told Anna. "John, go boil a pot."

The boy didn't want to leave the room, but he did as he was instructed.

"Are you hungry?" Deb asked. "I'm making pork chops and lemon salad."

Anna shook her head. She wasn't ready for food yet. She turned her head to the window and gazed out at the forest beyond. "There are others," she managed to say. "Still out there. You have to help them."

"Yes, we know." The woman patted her leg again. "Don't talk. Save your strength."

Anna nodded, grateful.

"My husband's gone for his truck. We park it behind the garden shed next door. When you're feeling better he'll take you to Nicholl's Town."

The little boy appeared in the doorway. "I put the water on, Mama."

"Good boy."

Anna shut her eyes.

She was safe.

# Epilogue

Looking down at the island from her seat in the helicopter to Miami, Anna could see why the multiple rescue teams had failed to find her. Nothing was visible but an endless expanse of green treetops, and there was no way to see beneath them.

Since she'd crawled into Shaygill's Point two days before, so much had happened. The man, whose name was John like his son, had driven her to the hospital and she'd spent the night and the next day there, in cool, white, air-conditioned rooms.

Of the thirteen girls who'd been lost, twelve had been found, and some of them just a day or two after Adler got shot. Anna and her traveling companions had wandered out of the range of the initial search. They'd then been missed by a larger air sweep a few days later, enacted while they were down in the caves. The plight of the missing girls had been picked up by the Associated Press and carried on CNN for the nation's entertainment. Anna smiled when she remembered Stacey's talk about selling their story. In a way, Stacey's comments had been prophetic.

Anna told the police and hospital staff what had happened in the caves, and gave them Stacey's position. She also told them about the rest of the girls, even Kara.

Alice had been found wandering in a daze near the caves, and Stacey had been discovered near death by the side of the river. She'd been flown directly to a hospital on the mainland because of her serious condition, although it was expected she'd make a full recovery. Anna longed to talk to her, just to confirm that her friend had really survived and was doing okay.

Ironically, Maria had been found by a search party the day after she'd wandered away from the group at the bluehole. She was already back home with her family in Jacksonville.

Laura and Erica had also been found. Anna had hoped they'd managed to escape death, but they hadn't been so lucky. Both of their bodies had been located not far from the caves. Anna felt weird and somehow guilty that she'd made it and they hadn't. Erica's death was hard to take, and she cried whenever she thought about it.

Kara was still out there somewhere, the only one unaccounted for. Anna was surprised she hadn't been found already, as she'd been so close to Shaygill's Point. Anna wondered if Kara had somehow recovered and executed her plan to escape into a town, but she doubted it. Kara was either dead or still trapped in the forest. If she were still alive out there, Anna hoped that she'd be rescued. Anna understood Kara was evil and Stacey was mostly kind, but she'd needed both of them to make it back safely, and she didn't want the island to have them.

Anna didn't feel nervous at all about seeing her parents,

who were waiting for her in Miami. Many of the parents, including hers, had come to the island immediately upon being notified of the situation, but after a week the search had been called off and the parents sent home. This decision, she later found out, was due to a misguided attempt by the Bahamian authorities to quell fears that the incident would hurt tourism.

The police had interrogated Anna about Leod and Jume and she'd told them everything she knew. Although the authorities were reluctant to reveal anything to her about the two men, Anna learned they were wanted for drug trafficking in the United States. They'd apparently come to Andros to execute a drug deal, one that had gone horribly wrong. The police were now searching for the men responsible for their deaths, but as Anna had never seen their faces, she couldn't be much help.

The helicopter was suddenly flying over white beaches and then blue-green water. Anna was surprised to feel a weird ambivalence at leaving the island. She realized that on Andros her thoughts had grown clear.

It had been a strange kind of freedom, she mused. There'd been no school, no boys, no parents, and no distractions, just the struggle to stay alive. She'd passed the test, and although the only reward was self-knowledge, it mattered more to her than anything.

Anna thought maybe one day she'd return to Andros when she was better, to visit the place that had forged her spirit. She shut her eyes and listened to the comforting drone of the helicopter, bearing her home.

# Acknowledgments

First and foremost, thanks to my brilliant agent, David Dunton at Harvey Klinger, for all his help and support (and his fantastic music recommendations). Dave made this entire process easy and fun, and I can't thank him enough. Huge thanks also to my great editor at MTV Books/Pocket Books, Lauren McKenna, for her insightful comments and suggestions. Big thanks also to Shari Smiley at CAA, Susan Lewis at MTV Films, and Matt O'Keefe (whose generosity helped this book a great deal).

In addition, thanks go to: Leah Stewart, Nikki Van De Car, Larry Venuti, Bobby and Sarah McCain, Manish Kalvakota, Pam Cooper, William Sleator, Kimball King, Julius Raper, Linda Wagner-Martin, Maria DeGuzman, Dale Bieber, Chris Nosal, Martha Kessler, Keith Gumery, John Paul Jones, Bill Van Wert, Joey Santiago, Perry Serpa, Stefanie Shapira, Megan McKeever, William Keach, Glenn Dicker, Greg Broom, Wharton Tiers, Eurydice, Tim Taylor, and David and Sherry Wright.

Love to Lisa AKA Elizabeth Wright (who also helped shape this novel), our cat Ishmael, and of course lots of love to my mom, Carol-Julia, and my dad, Alastair.

As many as 1 in 3 Americans
have HIV and don't know it.

# TAKE CONTROL.
# KNOW YOUR STATUS.
# GET TESTED.

To learn more about HIV testing,
or get a free guide to HIV and
other sexually transmitted diseases.

**www.knowhivaids.org
1-866-344-KNOW**